Dancing with Temptation

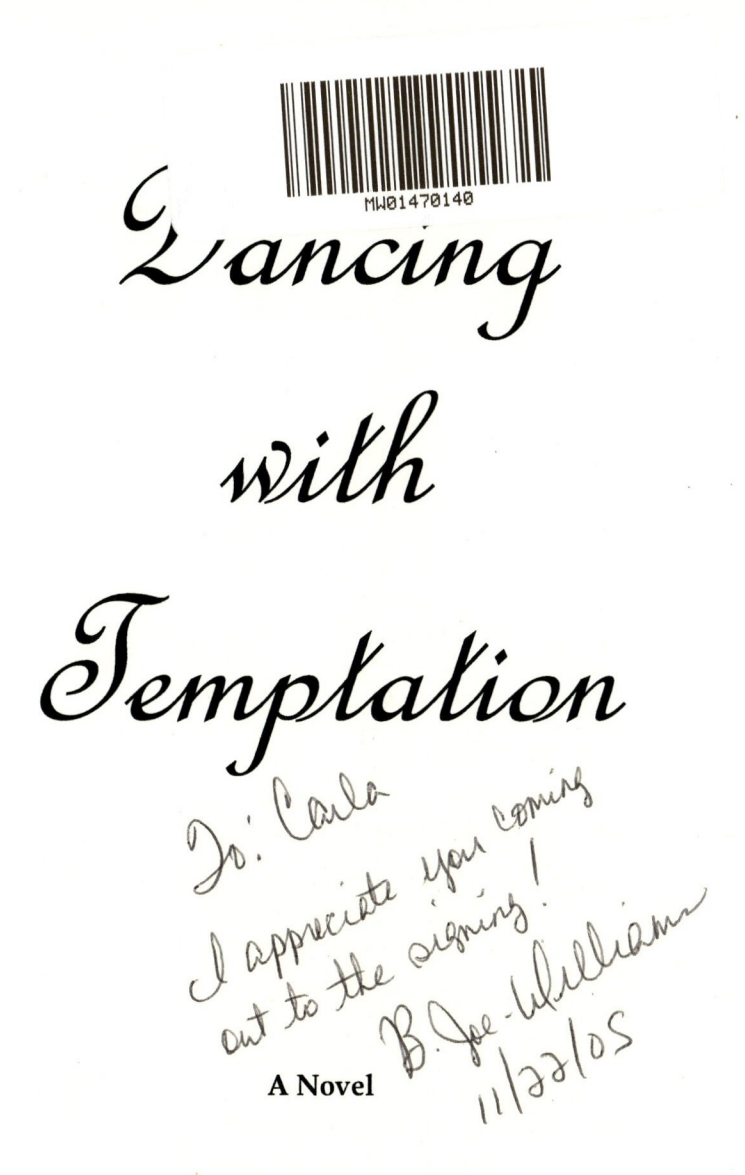

A Novel

BARBARA JOE-WILLIAMS

[AP]

This book is a work of fiction. Names, characters, places, and incidents are the product of the author's imagination or are used fictitiously. Any resemblance to actual events, locales, or persons, living or dead, is coincidental.

All Scripture references are from the New King James Version of the Holy Bible.

Copyright © 2005 Barbara Joe-Williams

Published by:

[AP]
Amani Publishing
P. O. Box 12045
Tallahassee, FL 32317-2045

A publishing company based on faith, hope, and love

Visit our website at: **www.Barbarajoewilliams.com**

E-mail us at: **Amanipublishing@aol.com**

Printed in USA
First printing in November 2005

ISBN: 0975285122

Library of Congress Control Number: 2005906027

Cover photograph courtesy of: Istockphoto.com

Dedication

This book is dedicated to my husband, Wilbert L. Williams, a man who has been strong enough to live with me for the past twenty-four years without complaining too much. I love my life because of you.

When I needed someone to love,
You were there,
When I needed someone to touch,
You were there,
When I needed someone to love me,
You were there,
Throughout our marriage,
You have been here,
In my heart,
Where you will always be dear,
Until death do us part!

3-23-05

And do not lead us into temptation,
But deliver us from the evil one.
For Yours is the kingdom
And the power
And the glory forever. Amen.

Matthew 6:13

Prologue

Tina was almost ready to slice her birthday cake in front of the hundred or so guests that were gathered in the great room to celebrate her forty-first birthday. Just as the crimson sun was setting, she welcomed the final guests into her home. It had been a magnificent May Day for a party that extended from the six-bedroom house out into the well-maintained back yard. Ethnically dressed in a beige and gold trimmed pants suit with a matching hat, she appeared to be a happily married woman.

Skimming the room, admiring all of the guests that were likewise wearing their African attire in accordance with the cultural theme of the party, she was astonished at what a magnificent job the professional party decorator had done with her immaculate home for this special occasion. From the colorful printed banner hanging over the entrance way to the table donned with African violets, Tina was amazed.

Suddenly Tina felt her flip-style cellular phone vibrating against her waist. Noticing the loud music thumping along with her heartbeat to the sound of Mary J. Blige singing, "It's a Wrap," she reached down to check her phone. She reviewed the second text message that she'd received this evening: "Baby, please meet me outside for your birthday present."

Gasping for air, she quickly erased the message from her cell phone. Tina looked up, trying to conceal the panic on her face, and scanned the room for her husband. There he was in the corner, having a lively conversation with his friends Michael, Ralph, and Terrance. *I could sneak out the front door for just a few minutes since everyone is inside and waiting for me to cut the cake. This man is probably not going to leave unless I meet him outside soon.*

With her heart pounding and the blood racing through her veins, she took another look at the extra large birthday cake on the far end of the table. It was decorated with one of her most recent portraits recreated in the center of the cake. She was wearing a striped sundress in her favorite colors of orange and green. There were many small orange flowers with green leaves along the perimeter of the frosted cake surrounding her smiling face. It had one layer of chocolate cake and one layer of yellow cake with extra buttercream icing, just the way she liked it. Tina hadn't eaten any sweets in months so she decided to splurge on the cake. Right now, she wished that she could go back to the day that she had taken that picture over two months ago before she started this affair with "Mr. Smooth," Debonair Jenkins.

Tina and Martin had been planning this elaborate bash since the beginning of the New Year, and she wanted it to be a stone cold blast. However, this was not exactly the type of blast that she had anticipated having today. This was her first time having a birthday party in all of her adult life. She had wanted to have one for her fortieth birthday, but Martin and she were just too busy with their friends, Alese and Michael Wayne, who were separated at the time. Anyway, that was over with now and all of her friends and neighbors were there to congratulate her on reaching this milestone in her successful life.

"Tina, girl, are you all right? You're not looking too good. Is something wrong?" Shenedra was touching Tina's arm and searching her best friend's eyes for an answer. She sensed that something wasn't right.

"Shenedra, Debonair is outside. He just sent me a text message on my cell phone that he's waiting for me. Girl, what am I going to do?" Tina stretched her panic filled eyes in horror.

"Girl, I know what you better not do. You better not even think about going out there to see that young man. I thought you said that you told him it was over," Shenedra stated, eyeing Tina suspiciously.

"I did tell him that, but he's been calling me and sending me text messages every day for the last seven days straight."

At that very moment, Tina felt her phone vibrating against her waist again. She knew who it was but still reached down to read his third message for the evening: "Baby, please meet me—I'm waiting outside."

Shenedra arched her thin eyebrows and stretched her gray catlike eyes as she spoke to Tina. "Please don't tell me that was him contacting you again."

"Yes, it's him. This is his third time sending me a message in thirty minutes, and I don't think he's going to stop unless I go outside to see him. He claims that he has a present for me."

"Well, I know somebody else that's going to have a present for you if you get busted tonight. Now you stay right here and let me go talk to him." Shenedra turned to walk away but Tina grabbed her by the left forearm.

"No, Shenedra. I can't let you do that. Besides, I want to see what he got me for my birthday. Keep your eyes on Martin while I slip outside for just a minute, okay?"

"Tina, don't even try..." Before she could finish her statement, Tina had already checked to make sure that Martin was still preoccupied with his friends as she walked towards the door heading outside.

When Shenedra looked towards the corner where she had seen Martin engaged in conversation a few seconds ago, he was gone. Before she could block his bath, she caught a glimpse of the back of his head as he walked toward the master bedroom. *Oh, my God! The master bedroom is adjacent to the front door!*

Chapter 1

It was pouring down rain on a cool February morning. The kind of day that made lovers determined to stay in bed, snuggle up together, and make love all day long. It was the type of day where couples were tempted to call in sick, telling their bosses or supervisors that they weren't able to make it into work this morning. One of those days that you could lock lips with the one that you loved, squeeze them, and rock gently against each other's warm body until the rain stopped beating against your window pane.

With the heavy raindrops drumming against the skylight in the far corner of their master bedroom, Tina rose from slumber, gently rolled over in their cherrywood king sized high poster canopy bed, and laid her head on Martin's strong shoulder. Easing back the green satin sheets, she slowly slid her hand down the length of his heated cocoa brown muscular body in search of his manhood. She slightly raised her head to check out the time on the digital alarm clock by their bedside. *Good, we have almost an hour before we have to start getting ready for work. Maybe we'll be able to have sex if he has a morning erection. I could sure use some hard peter today. Shoot! My body is craving this. He has always enjoyed making love in the early morning hours during romantically cool rainy days like this. It's time for love, and I'm ready.*

Once her roaming hands touched his male organ, Tina was sorely disappointed to feel that it was just as limp as it had been last night when she tried to arouse him. Releasing a small sigh, she remembered rushing home from work the previous evening to start preparing a special meal for their Valentine's Day celebration. Since she didn't get to come home early very often, she thought that it would be a surprise treat for Martin to have a homemade dinner with his favorites: grilled pepper steak, Italian roasted potatoes, and sweet corn pudding. Being southern bred, he was a meat and potatoes man. So after stopping at the Publix supermarket on her way home from work, she took her time preparing the best meal that she had made in months.

First, Tina made sure that their two sons were away for the majority of the evening, and then proceeded with her plan of action which included seducing her husband into having a heated sexual exchange. Setting the mood for romance, Tina went all out with the expensive Cristal champagne chilling in a sterling silver bucket of ice in the center of the dining room table. She loaded the compact disc player with several slow jazz numbers, setting the adjustments where the sound would flow through every built-in speaker throughout the spectacular house.

Tina soaked in the extra deep whirlpool tub for almost an hour before emerging to wrap herself in a heavyweight white cotton bathrobe. Then, after lighting jasmine scented candles all over the bedroom and spraying herself in all the right places with Attraction, the sexiest perfume available, she chose a delicate piece of crimson lingerie to complete the seductive evening.

Easing into a satin and lace teddy with a sheer matching kimono and a pair of red feathery high-heeled shoes, Tina smiled inwardly. *Oh, yeah, we should be making love all night long. Martin loves this red outfit. He's never been able to resist this.* Even though it had been months since they'd been intimate, she smeared creamy glittering lotion all over her redbone skin in anticipation of his touch.

Martin was late getting home, as usual, and barely ate any of his dinner, which had gotten cold by that time. He simply peeled off his clothes, left them in the middle of the bedroom floor, and climbed into bed wearing his Calvin Klein boxers. He never even commented about the lovingly prepared food or the sensual atmosphere she had set up for them in their oversized master bedroom. What a waste of time and money for an evening which had started out with so much promise for the once overly romantic and head over heels in love pair.

Tina could tell right away that Martin had been drinking and was trying his best not to face her. That would explain why he was in such a hurry to jump into bed, pretending to immediately fall into slumber. Normally, he drank vodka so that she wouldn't be able to smell liquor on his breath, but she could always tell when he had been drinking from the disoriented dazed look in his chestnut brown eyes, his slight slurring of simple words, and the careful way he stepped. The fake snoring was definitely a dead give away that he was trying to avoid any and all contact with a wife that was ready for mating season.

Now, while she lovingly caressed his soft member in her heated hands, Martin raised both arms in the air, hunched his torso upward, stretched his body, and yawned before turning away from Tina. Not being one to give up easily, Tina started lightly kissing his back, moving her tongue in an arousing circular motion, and massaging his midsection, to no avail. Normally this was all that she had to do to get his engine revving for morning love.

Finally, after several minutes of this alluring maneuver, she gave up in frustration and decided to at least try to tactfully approach the annoying subject with her husband. "Martin, are you awake?" she asked, lightly nudging him. When he didn't respond, she tried again. "Martin, I need to talk to you," she spoke a little louder that time using a stern voice.

"What, Red? Can't you see that I'm trying to get some sleep?" he replied, sounding irritated as he referred to Tina by her affectionate nickname. He'd often teased her during the course of their marriage regarding her light skin and even joked about being married to a "white" sister.

"Martin, how can *you* sleep when we're in so much trouble?"

He rolled over towards Tina with an aggravated look on his face as he asked, "How are we in trouble, Red?"

"Well, for one thing, we haven't made love since Christmas; you're coming home later and later every night; and I know that you're drinking heavily."

"Look, I don't know what you're talking about, and I need to get this last hour of sleep, if *you* don't mind."

"So you mean to tell me that it's not bothering you that we haven't had sex in months?" she asked, slightly raising her voice. "You're working too many hours, and you're drinking too much," she added, showing the irritation in her high-pitched voice.

"What I mean to tell you is that I need some more sleep right now. Tina, I've got a lot on my mind, okay. I've got some issues that I'm dealing with, and I just can't talk to you about them right now. I need some time to sort through some things on my own. And, of course, it bothers me that we haven't made love in awhile, but it's just a passing phase. I mean every man has this problem every now and then."

"What about the other two issues, the working late and heavy drinking?"

"I've always had to work late when we're working on a deadline for an important project. You know that this McGregor account is the biggest thing that our firm has ever handled. Everyone is working extra long hours trying to complete this deal. And as far as my drinking goes, that's the only way for me to unwind after a long day at work."

"Well, I know another way you used to like to unwind after a long day at work," she sniped.

"Red, I told you, that's a temporary problem."

"You keep saying that, Marty, but you won't tell me what's going on. I think that your impotence is related to your drinking, but you're not willing to face either one. You know I am your wife; you should be able to tell me anything. That should tell you that we have a problem right there," she stated, rising up on one elbow in the bed to get a better look at Marty's face. She could barely believe the words that were coming out of his mouth and needed to look directly at him to verify her thinking.

"Well, whatever problems we have are not going to be resolved this morning. So can we just go back to sleep, please? You know that I get my best sleep when it's raining like this," he stated sharply, turning away from Tina again, dangling his arm over the side of the bed.

Tina flung herself back against the warm sheets, swinging her arms out in frustration. She knew that she would not be able to get back to sleep after that unpleasant exchange with her spouse and decided to get up, take a cool shower, and start her busy day. As she rose from the comforts of her bed, wishing that she could stay inside today and do what lovers like to do, she silently cursed Martin for his irregular behavior.

Standing in the shower with the cool water hitting her directly in the face, Tina recalled how the early morning hours used to be their favorite time to get busy, especially if there was just a hint of moisture in the air. Rainy mornings were the best for the romantic, satisfying, baby-making love that they had once enjoyed so much. Whenever they came home from work too tired to please each other, they would go straight to bed and set the alarm clock to awaken them an hour earlier than usual just so they could make out. They would have so much fun in bed, using most of the hour engaged in extensive foreplay before the actual sex even took place. Those were the days when coupling was a lightweight pleasure to be enjoyed with ease. These days, he treated her like it was a burden to even hold her hand or embrace her in his arms, let alone have sexual foreplay for a whole hour before intercourse.

He's had this problem before but it's never lasted this long. More than likely, it's the drinking that's causing his sexual dysfunction. I read a Harvard report on the Internet the other day about how alcohol can seriously affect a man's sexual drive and performance. They also reported that stress could be a major factor in cases like this, too. Since Marty has been working a lot of extra hours, he's probably stressed out, too. That's certainly not helping us either, but he really needs to make an appointment for a complete physical examination; he hasn't had one of those in over a year now. But I also wonder if there could be another woman behind this sudden case of impotency after seventeen years of marriage. I know Martin is not bold enough to be cheating on me, not after what his best friend just went through with his wife. Turning off the shower, her mind continued wandering about this situation.

Martin's best friend, Michael Wayne, had slept with one of their employees last year. His wife, Alese, took their three-year-old daughter, Bianca, and left him after learning about the one night stand with a little help from Tina. She and Alese weren't the best of friends, but they enjoyed each other's company on special occasions considering their husband's were best friends, and Tina had been Alese's natural hairdresser for the last four years. She'd known Alese since she and Michael first started dating and liked her right away, although they didn't share a lot of common interests. They did spend time together when they could, called each other every now and then, and saw each other on a semi-regular basis outside of the hair salon. Alese normally tightened her own locks, but she would come in for a professional style session with Tina whenever she was in the mood for something different. She and Martin had both been there for their friends in their time of need. *He would never imitate Michael's mistake.*

Stepping out of the shower stall, she reached for her fluffy extra long peach towel to dry off her body. She wanted to press the issue with Marty again but just didn't feel up to it this morning. She had quite a busy day awaiting her at the hair salon, and it would be in her best interest to get there as early as possible today. The shop had been so busy lately that she hadn't had much time to do the major bookkeeping tasks. Besides, she couldn't wait to get to the coffee house to get a hot steaming cup of her favorite drink, mocha java express. The Insomnia Coffee House closed late and opened early so she never had a problem getting her fix no matter how late she worked or how early she managed to make it in. That hot creamy brew would have to be her sex again today. She was getting warm just from the thought of having the brown liquid slide down her throat and settle in the pit of her stomach, giving her the satisfying feeling that she dangerously craved this morning.

Tina took her time applying scented lotion to her red tone skin as she looked in the mirror at her expressive pure honey eyes and applied mascara to her long naturally curly eyelashes. She completed her make-up routine by applying Fashion Fair's cream to powder foundation and her favorite shade of red lipstick, Forever Red, to her full lips. She decided to wear something colorful today since she was feeling quite down. Figuring that might give her the pick me up that she needed to get through the long day ahead, Tina chose a radiant orange, red, and gold duster pants set with an opulent border print and a solid orange collar to wear. Of course, she had the matching silk fabric mules and purse to complete her lively outfit. She pulled her blonde streaked micro braids up into a topknot and secured it with a silky orange scrunchy band.

Just as Tina was about to exit the bedroom, romantic thoughts entered her mind once again while standing with her hand on the doorknob. Turning towards the direction where her husband was sleeping quietly, she stood there looking at him for several seconds before returning to the side of the bed and gently planting a kiss on his forehead. Things may not have turned out the way she had planned last night or this morning, but she still loved him beyond a shadow of a doubt. Being angry with him was certainly not going to solve the problem. It would be in her best interest to play the loving, understanding role until this undetermined time period was over. Hopefully that would be real soon. Anyway, Martin didn't stir, but he did mumble, "Good bye, and have a nice day. I love you."

"I love you, too, baby, but we need to talk about our situation because I don't want to live like this indefinitely, you know."

"I hear you, babe. We'll talk, I promise."

"I hope so, Martin. I need you like crazy."

"I need you, too. We'll talk soon."

Tina tipped through the bedroom doorway and quietly eased the door closed. Now that she was up and dressed, it was time to get her two sons, Malique and Jordan, up so that they could get dressed for school. Malique was the oldest at fifteen and in the tenth grade at Paxton High School. He was a sports fan just like his father and played in a starting position on the football team. Although Malique usually didn't make the honor roll, he kept his grades up enough to maintain his spot on the field. And being the good looking, well developed young man that he was, the girls had already started calling him all times of the day and night wanting to go steady with him or at least be seen on one date with the handsome rising star. Jordan, on the other hand, didn't care for sports at all. He had just turned eleven and was attending the sixth grade at Bayside Magnet Middle School. Being a typical nerdy guy, he consistently made the honor roll and excelled in math and science. When he wasn't working on school projects, he could be found in his room playing the latest video game. It was almost as if he had become addicted to playing on those machines. As soon as he had reached the top score for one, he was ready for another one, which usually didn't take very long at all. Jordan wasn't worried about being teased at school for being a smart guy and neither was he concerned with the girls for that matter. If he had his video games, he was happy.

They were both very handsome, attractive, and outgoing boys but neither one was above average height. Considering that Tina was barely five-foot-one and Martin was just shy of five-foot-six, they didn't expect their son's to be taller than their father. But since Tina's father was six-foot tall, there was a slim chance that they could be taller than either one of them expected.

Anyway, after Tina managed to get the boys up and out of the front door for school, she was ready to start her day at the Braids and Locks Hair Shop where she had been the sole proprietor for the last eleven years. She'd spent five years in the corporate world at IBM as a marketing consultant just to appease her parents after completing undergraduate business school at Jacksonville State University. Although Martin really wanted her to go into business with him and Michael, she decided to take on steady employment with a major company while he worked on building up M & M Incorporated. She never had any intentions of staying in the business world once Martin and Michael had their business up and running; it was time to do what her heart had always desired as a professional occupation.

Tina's heart and soul had always been in hairdressing from the time she was a little girl braiding her dolls' hair with colorful beads dangling from each braid. Later on as she became a teenager, she experimented with her own natural hair and all of her other friends' hair whenever the opportunity arose. Her mother would even let her braid up her hair on the weekends when they had their special mother and daughter times. Tina shared her dreams with her parents and while they encouraged her to pursue hairstyling as a hobby, they never spoke of her owning a hair salon. They were pleased when she announced that she was going to business school to secure a degree in business marketing and then work for a major corporation. Secretly, she chose this major because she had every intention of becoming a business owner and being able to help Martin with his marketing strategies as well as promote her upcoming hair facility. Taking a steady job would temporarily provide for her family and give her the experience necessary to promote their beginning businesses.

Her mother, the lovely petite-sized, Delilah Sloan, had been employed at Jacksonville Memorial Hospital as a nutritional specialist for over twenty years. When she first arrived in the city for a summer internship out of Chicago, she didn't intend on staying past the six-week program. However, after meeting her potential husband, Delilah decided to transfer to the Sunshine State and eventually settled down here. Tina's father, the rather tall and admirable pediatrician, Dr. Malachi Sloan, was born and bred in the south. He had been in private practice with four fellow doctors for the last nine years. After being the head of the pediatrics unit at Shands Jacksonville Medical Center, he wanted more flexibility and status that could only come from being a private healthcare provider with a group of his distinguished peers.

Both parents had urged her to remain with a practical career. Of course, they only wanted the best for their daughter and did not consider hairdressing a prestigious enough career considering her pedigree. They both came from a family of doctors and since Tina was their only child, their hopes were for her to attend medical school or at least something in the medical field where she could receive a doctoral degree. Tina decided early on that was not in the cards for her, but she would appease them by receiving an undergrad degree in the field that would most benefit her career aspirations.

Tina was the apple of her father's eye, and she could do no wrong as far as he was concerned. Her every wish was immediately his command. And while Delilah loved her only daughter, she didn't appreciate her husband spoiling their child rotten. So as Tina grew to become a teenager, she and her mother began to drift apart. Not to the point where she was ever disrespectful to Delilah, but she was keenly aware that she had to tread lightly to have her way with that parent. However, her relationship with her mother became stronger once Tina reached adulthood and started dating Martin on a regular basis while in college. She had come to rely on her mother's outspoken wisdom when it was needed.

When her parents were first introduced to Martin, Delilah took a strong liking to him right away, but Malachi openly disliked him and angrily dismissed him as a possible suitor for his princess. That's when Delilah stepped in with encouraging words for Tina, "Child, please follow your heart, let Malachi simmer in his own juices until he decide to come around. Your father will eventually accept the man that you love as his son-in-law." Well, Malachi had never accepted Martin as his son-in-law, but he was at least cordial to him on the special occasions that they shared as a family, especially after the birth of their two sons.

With the loving support of her husband, Tina had decided to leave the corporate world once Martin's business started to turn a profit, and he was financially able to support their family. She enrolled at the Unique Natural Hair School for one year to become trained and licensed in cosmetology. Then she worked at the Natural Essence Hair Salon for a year before starting her own business. She had always enjoyed doing braids and favored natural hair styles. Tina had prophesized that this growing trend would be the wave of the future; she wanted to be one of the first stylists in Jacksonville to be able to capitalize on it. In the last five years, natural styles were really becoming a hit with the urban crowds. Tina's hair designs had been featured in the major hair magazines, including *Braids & More*, *Braids & Beauty*, *Hype Hair*, and *Natural Hair Styles*. Winning several awards at hair conferences, she was proud of her many accomplishments and growing business. Becoming the Chamber of Commerce's Small Business Owner of the Year almost two years ago had been the highlight of her career.

All of their hard work as a couple was finally paying off now. They owned a beautiful champagne-colored, Tudor styled two-story, six-bedroom house in the primarily residential community of Jacksonville Beach, located east of the city between the Atlantic Ocean and the Coastal Waterway. This area is a solid business, resort, and residential community with over twenty-one thousand people where you'll find miles of un-crowded white sandy beaches.

Naturally, Tina and Marty were proud to own their dream home where they could take romantic walks along the beach at any time of the day or night. They had lived in the house for the last eight years and were elated to find a place with three-bedrooms downstairs as well as three-bedrooms upstairs. The house was a joy for even the richest landowner to behold with eye-catching windows all around its perimeter. Inside, high ceilings and large-scale living spaces prevailed, beginning with the foyer, which was crowned by a two-story ceiling. Martin and she shared the oversized master bedroom on the bottom floor which also included a stone fireplace. The lush master bedroom was tastefully decorated in vibrant shades of peach, ivory, and green. The cherrywood furniture looked spectacular from every angle in the room, showcasing its own vaulted ceiling and two walk-in closets. The sky-lighted master bath featured a spa tub, a separate shower, and a dual sink vanity.

They converted one of the downstairs bedrooms into an office for Martin; and the other one was converted into a fully equipped exercise room for Tina. Unfortunately, Martin was hardly ever home long enough to use his warmly decorated office, and she didn't have time to use any of the high tech exercise equipment after spending long days at the salon, but the extra space had inspired them to purchase the house. At least they had started out with good intentions.

In addition to the three-bedrooms downstairs, there was a great room for entertaining; a huge family room which offered a vaulted ceiling, a corner fireplace, and a big screen television; a game room with a professional-sized pool table; and a separate formal dining room from the kitchen and the breakfast nook. The main dining room table, made from solid maple wood, was large enough to accommodate up to eight people with a matching china cabinet displaying elaborate dishes and crystal. Even though she didn't spend a lot of time in the kitchen cooking, Tina adored the huge, all white facility with the oblong, smooth pebble island in the center for chopping and preparing foods. Right above the island was a custom made automatic rotating rack for hanging pots and pans. The S-curved arch over the kitchen window brought a sense of character to the all white room.

It had taken Tina almost two years of painstaking efforts to finally finish decorating the six thousand square foot house to suit her unique taste in furniture and decorations. Every piece had to be an original product that she had never seen anywhere else before or thought that no one else had. Some pieces had been flown from overseas retailers specifically for her eyes to inspect before making a permanent decision. She was especially drawn to the European designers and sometimes traveled overseas to do her own household shopping. Tina was also fascinated with a variety of African art stone carvings and Shona art sculptures. These pieces were individually hand carved and no two pieces were identical. Whatever piece she purchased was immediately removed from the catalog once it was shipped to her. Over the years, she had put together a large collection that was prominently displayed throughout their home. Some of the beautifully carved pieces weighed more than fifty pounds and were priceless.

Each of the boys had their own personally designed bedroom upstairs with a set of twin beds in each, including a state of the art computer center for their educational enrichment. Tina seldom bothered to climb the stairs to their rooms because she was content to let them have their own private domains. It was up to them to keep it clean and livable in between maid visits. Their work schedules made it impossible to maintain a properly cleaned house, so the Merry Maid Service was employed to send someone to their home at least twice a week. Last but not least, the lavishly decorated guest room, located to the right at the top of the stairs, was painted in a serene powder blue with a matching floral ensemble for the queen sized panel bed and window treatments.

Tina drove a new white convertible Chevrolet Corvette to work every day. Martin drove a black BMW X5 sports utility vehicle; they owned all the latest designer clothing, shoes, perfume, and jewelry that they wanted; they could travel whenever and wherever they desired while dining in the finest restaurants along the way. And Martin's commercial business, M & M Software Development, Incorporated, which he co-owned with his best friend, Michael Wayne, was doing exceedingly well. He and Michael had been like brothers since their freshman year in college. Shortly after they both graduated from business school, almost twenty years ago, they opened up their software business together with each concentrating on his area of expertise. They shared a huge one-story brick office downtown with Martin's office in one corner of the building and his partner's office in the other corner side of the complex. Michael secured software development projects while Martin planned them out. All of the other major duties they split between the two of them and their fifty plus employees. Martin was over the Omega Team and Michael spearheaded the Alpha Team. Each team was composed of four head program designers who supervised a staff of at least five people including competent administrative support.

Tina was living the lifestyle that many African-American women only dreamed about, and she was enjoying every minute of it. Now if she could just help her husband get his groove back, she would truly be living in paradise.

Chapter 2

"Good morning, Ms. Tina. Are you having your usual today?" Debonair Jenkins asked, admiring Tina's vividly colored outfit. He also admired her alluring eyes, luscious red lips, and contagious smile.

"Yes, I'll take an extra large this morning. I have a long day ahead of me," she stated, flashing a broad smile while handing him a five-dollar bill. Tina avoided the piercing stare from his dark rum eyes while admiring his short stature, tight athletic physique, enchanting smile, and the long adorable locks he wore pulled back into a ponytail. He had started coming to her shop once a month to get his locks washed and tightened.

"You must really have a lot of appointments today to be here this time of morning. Is that hair shop keeping you busy, my lady?" he asked, giving her change for the small bill.

"Yes, and that would be an understatement," she replied laughing. "I have clients lined up for just about every hour of the day, so I won't have much of a break or a decent lunch. But I did come early to catch up on some of my office work. I really hate bookkeeping, but somebody has to do it."

"I see. So you won't have time to squeeze me in today for a quick wash and touch up?"

"No, I'm sorry. But there's no way to fit you in for today. Why don't you come by tomorrow afternoon around three o'clock, and I can tighten them up for you then?"

"Okay, okay. That sounds like a date—I mean, thanks for working a brother in. You know that I appreciate it, with your *very* pretty self."

"Thank you, but you do know that I'm *very* married, don't you?"

"Yes, I know that, but what I want to know is, are you *very* happy?"

"Well, that's a *very* personal question, and I have to run. Thanks for the coffee."

"Oh, no problem. That's no problem at all. I look forward to seeing you tomorrow." He sexily eyed Tina as she turned from him and exited through the front door. He shook his head, smiling to himself as she disappeared from sight, and then returned to his work.

Tina smiled to herself as she left the small coffee shop with her favorite hot potion in her hand. She didn't know if she was attracted to Debonair because he was so charming or if it was just the fact that she hadn't had much companionship with the opposite sex lately. *Martin had better get his act together soon or I'm going to explode, and it won't be a pretty sight to behold. I don't know what his problem is but he'd better get it together. It's not even like him to keep secrets from me. But I guess I need to keep busy until I can get my husband into therapy. As a matter of fact, I need to check the business directory for a professional marriage counselor today. Maybe I should look for a male counselor. That way, Martin might feel comfortable enough to open up about his sexual problem.*

Tina took a second to enjoy the cool day, the after rain smell, and the stillness of her surroundings before taking out her keys to unlock the front door to the shop. She loved living in the warm Florida climate and hardly ever having to wear a heavy coat. Even though the unpredictable and ever changing weather kept her confused, she enjoyed the clear atmosphere the majority of the time, wearing a lightweight jacket during the two months of winter that they endured. Normally, the sun would come out during the day and warm up the city by the early afternoon.

Most of the stores surrounding the Beach Boulevard shopping center weren't even opened yet. Tina fondly remembered how lucky she had been to find this terrific location on the east side of the town that she loved. It was located just twenty minutes from her luxurious estate so it didn't take her long to get home no matter how late she had to work, which was beginning to be later and later.

Upon entering her spacious salon, she went straight to her office in the back area. Tina settled down for a minute in her comfortable armchair and then pulled out the accounting books that were locked away in the four-drawer steel filing cabinet. She was halfway finished drinking her extra large mocha java express before she started analyzing her records. Tina was mortified when she realized how far she had gotten behind with her bookkeeping as she turned to the page documenting her last recorded entry. *God, I have got to do a better job with this or hire someone that can at least help me to get caught up.* Tina could easily afford to hire an accountant, but she was hesitant to trust anyone with her growing business affairs. Previewing her bookkeeping tasks, she turned another page in the ledger.

Before she knew it almost two hours had passed. Tina heard Shenedra and Taneka, her only other hair stylists, bustling about in the main area before they came knocking at her office door. Shenedra Brown had worked with her for the last eight years and had become her best friend and confidante during that time. Tina loved her outgoing nature and keen ability to tell it like it is. Physically they were complete opposites, being that Shenedra was three years younger, five inches taller and two sizes smaller than Tina with a deep ebony complexion shining against gray catlike eyes. Still, both of them were very attractive workaholics and quickly became best girlfriends. Tina seldom left the shop before 8:00 p.m. and Shenedra was usually determined to stay just as long as she did whenever necessary.

Taneka Price joined them about three years ago after the business had grown to the point that they were weeks behind in meeting customer appointments. Taneka, a coffee brown twenty-four-year-old sister with round amber eyes, was hired when she came in looking for work as a single mother in desperate need of employment. She was casually dressed wearing a brown plaid skirt and a white lace blouse with the best looking Bantu knots hair style Tina had ever seen. Holding her four-year-old daughter, Ashia, by the hand as she strutted in, neither she nor Shenedra could resist the child's pleading smile as she clung to her mother's skirt. Tina hired the skilled hair designer on the spot and so far, she had not regretted her swift action.

Tammy Franklin, a young college student and the part-time receptionist, was hired over a year ago just to answer the telephones and set up appointments. Being a full-time business major, and an outgoing young lady, made her a valuable asset to the team. She normally came in around noontime which was usually the busiest time of the day and stayed until after five o'clock six days a week.

Eloise Hardy also joined them last year as the professional beauty specialist offering manicures, pedicures, and heated back massages in the mid-sized room towards the back of the salon adjoining Tina's office. Initially the room had been used for additional storage space but after befriending Eloise, Tina was eventually persuaded to rent the space out to her each month, especially since she would be one of the major recipients of her services. Eloise generally worked by scheduled appointments only and was not at the salon on a regular basis.

"Tina, you're here already?" Shenedra asked with an element of surprise in her voice.

"Yes, girl, come on in. I've been here for a couple of hours now working on these accounting books."

"Is everything okay? I don't know why you don't just hire someone to handle all of that."

"Yeah, everything is fine. The shop has been so busy lately that I haven't even had a chance to do much bookkeeping or paying the bills around here. I just decided to come in early and do it myself. I'm not ready to pay someone for something that I'm more than trained to do. However, I should probably consider investing in a simple computerized accounting program."

"That a good idea. Well, I see you've already downed a huge cup of coffee this morning from the shop next door. Was 'Mr. Suave and Debonair' in this morning with his fine self?" Shenedra asked, narrowing her eyes as she laughed lightly.

"Yeah, he was there bright and early all right. Would you believe that he's still trying to flirt with me? I had to tell him again that I was very married."

"Yes, I believe he's still trying to flirt with you, but what I can't believe is why he's not trying to flirt with a sexy dark chocolate single sister like myself," she stated, laughing with Tina, pointing both index fingers towards her face. "He must just be into the light skinned sisters since he can pass the paper bag test. Oh, well, his loss. Besides, I have a new man in my life."

"Then concentrate on your man and stop hating on Mr. Debonair."

"All right then. I'm going back out to get set up for my first appointment. I have about three appointments back to back today before I can take a break."

"I know what you mean. I don't have my first appointment for about thirty more minutes, and then it will be a non-stop day. I just can't believe how busy we are for a weekday. Now I'm not complaining, but we have been unusually busy lately."

"Have you considered hiring another hair stylist? You know several young ladies just out of training came by here last week."

"I may have to do that eventually, but right now I need to concentrate on this paperwork before taking on someone that we don't know and may not be able to depend on."

"That is important, but it was just a thought."

"Thanks for your suggestion, girl, and it is something that we can revisit in the future, especially if things keep going this way."

"It's all good. Enjoy your last few minutes of peace, and I'll see you in a little while."

"Okay, Shenedra, I'll see you in a few."

After an additional twenty minutes of balancing the ledger, Tina couldn't take looking at anymore numbers so she slammed the accounting books closed as she rubbed her droopy eyes. Even though she had gotten an early start, she wished that she had gotten that extra hour of sleep this morning instead of trying to stimulate Martin, for all the good it had done her. Anyway, she could sure use a good nap right about now, but it was almost time for her first client of the day to arrive, and she needed to get prepared.

After working non-stop for several hours, Tina took a late lunch break, made a few telephone calls, and returned to work. Before she realized it, three o'clock had passed, and she was doing tiny cornrows on her fourth client of the day. She liked to schedule her hair braiding appointments in the afternoon because that normally took longer than doing locks and twists. That way, she wouldn't have to worry about someone waiting for her if she ran over time braiding hair. She surveyed the room to see that each of the employees had a customer still waiting for service. Shenedra was busy putting in large box braids for a young teenage girl as she swung her long jet black micro braids with the curly ends away from her face. Taneka was finishing up with putting in reddish tone natural twists for a professionally dressed woman that was one of her regular customers. She wanted her hair to look similar to the style that Taneka wore.

Tina had her favorite CD entitled, *Maxwell's Urban Hang Suite*, playing in the background and she was moving to the song, "Sumthin' Sumthin'," as she braided her customer's hair. All she ever seriously listened to everyday and all day in the shop was Maxwell and somebody was tired of it.

"Tina, can we please listen to something today besides Maxwell? I want to try and win a cruise from 102.5 FM today," begged Taneka.

"Girl, what kind of cruise are you trying to win? I haven't heard about a cruise giveaway on the radio," Tina replied.

"That's because you don't listen to the radio during the day, girlfriend. Station 102.5 is having a contest where they are giving away tickets for a Carnival Cruise to the Caribbean. You have to be the ninth caller each day when they open the lines up to get registered for the drawing at the end of the week. Then on Friday, one of the lucky callers from during the week wins the cruise. They have the contest going on for the entire month of February."

"Yeah, that sounds great. But you know that you can never get through to the radio stations when they open the lines up like that."

"Well, I figure if I keep trying everyday that I might just get lucky and win. I could sure use a trip to the Barbados or any other island for that matter," Taneka said, laughing as she touched her client on the shoulder. Her client looked up from the magazine she was reading to smile at Taneka and share in her laughter.

"All right, you can go ahead and turn on the radio to that station. But if you win, you better bring me back a really nice souvenir,"

Tina said teasingly. "Even with all the traveling that Marty and I have done, we have never been on a cruise and that's one of my dreams, too."

Taneka dashed to the stereo and clicked off the Maxwell CD before Tina could change her mind. She hurriedly turned to the radio station that was having the promotional contest and ran back to the booth where her customer was waiting.

"Hey, everybody listen up. I'm planning to have a major party for my birthday this year and you all need to help me with the plans. Martin and I have been talking about this since New Year's Day and I think it's what I really want to do."

"Oooh! Tina that sounds great! How old will you be this year?" Taneka asked, sounding overly excited. She was always ready for a party, especially if it was at someone else's expense.

"I'll be forty-one, girl. I wanted to have a party last year for the big four-zero but we were both just too busy. But this year, I'm having a celebration no matter what."

"Yeah, it sounds like you've given this some thought. Where do you plan on having the party?"

"Well, I'm thinking about having it at my house because it's certainly big enough, and we never do any entertaining. I want it to be an all adult party, too. My parents are going to take the kids with them on a week long trip to Fort Lauderdale and stay in the time-share duplex that they own down there. So we can party all night long without any interruptions," she sang, clapping her hands and moving her hips in a dance.

"Yeah, I like the sound of that!" Taneka shouted out. "You should do one of those theme parties. You know like a seventies party or an eighties party, or maybe even an adult pajama party like they did in the movie, *How Stella Got Her Groove Back*. I've wanted to go to one of those ever since I saw that film with that fine Taye Diggs in his silk boxer shorts." Taneka started laughing, looking around the room for a reaction.

"Well, I think it should be an elegant black tie affair with evening gowns and everything. You know, something that we can invite all of the high society black folks to," Shenedra chimed in with her nose in the air.

"Please, please, please," Taneka fired back. "Who wants to be around a bunch of bourgeois colored people all night long? I say we have a costume party—you know—something different for a change."

"Girl, no, it is not Halloween. We will not be having a costume party for my best friend's birthday. We are not in elementary school, thank you very much. May we have the next suggestion please?"

Shenedra asked, clapping her hands together three quick times, eyeing the customers for support.

"Excuse me Miss Thang, but I believe its Tina's birthday and not yours. So that makes it her decision," Taneka came back.

"Yeah, whatever," Shenedra looked at her friend and quickly turned her head in the opposite direction.

"I don't know about any of those ideas, but I will give it some thought," Tina responded grinning at both of her employees trying to keep the peace. She loved the camaraderie that they shared every work day and enjoyed their lively commentary on every subject that came up in the shop, especially when it came to soap operas. "Well, I know for certain that I'm going to hire someone to do the decorations. My friend, Alese, recommended that I use Beverly Williams at *Creative Decorations and Designs*. She has a reputation for hosting the best theme parties in town."

"Oh, yeah, I've heard of her. I've seen her picture in the newspaper coordinating all these local celebrity events," Shenedra commented.

"That's right. I know who you're talking about now," Taneka chimed in. "You should definitely give her a call, but I bet she's going to cost a fortune, Tina."

"Yeah, I know, but if I'm going to have a birthday party, I want it to be the major event of the year."

"I know that's right. So you take your time and do whatever it is you want to do, Tina," Shenedra said, lightly patting Tina on the back.

"I have a few months to think about it before my birthday in May. On second thought, I better go ahead and call that Beverly Williams right now. She's probably already booked up months in advance," Tina commented as she finished up with her client and headed towards her office.

Minutes later, Tina returned with the good news that she had hired the professional party planner and would be meeting with her personally within the next two weeks.

"That's great. I'm really looking forward to this event. It's been a long time since I have been to a real birthday party," Shenedra commented.

"I know people just don't have parties like they used to. I can't even remember the last time that I went to a house party," Taneka pondered.

"Well, one thing about it, this will not be an ordinary house party, not if I know Tina the way that I think I know Tina. You better have your camera prepared and ready for the action is all that I can say," Shenedra warned Taneka.

"Tina, did you all discuss having a theme for your party?" Taneka asked.

"No, we didn't discuss it, but I did mention it to her. She said to write down all my ideas and we'll go over them when we meet in person," Tina replied, pulling out a notepad and pen. It was time to start planning the birthday party that she had less than three months to prepare for.

Chapter 3

It was exactly 8:46 p.m. by the time Tina pulled her Corvette into the three-car garage. She was hoping that Martin had made it home by now so that they could have that talk that he had promised her this morning. Entering the front door, she could hear the thumping of the hard rap music coming from Malique's room at the top of the staircase. She had told him to wear headphones when he wanted to play the music loud. But since she and Marty were hardly ever home; many of the family rules had become very lax. This was another issue that they needed to add to their list for discussion. *Jordan is probably in his room either doing his homework or playing one of those video games that we paid so much money for.* Tina exhaled a deep breath as she began climbing the stairs.

"Malique! Malique!" Tina called, knocking at his bedroom door. She waited several seconds for him to slowly open the door just enough to see his head. Her fifteen-year-old son looked down at her through the slight opening in the door. She couldn't believe that he was actually taller than she and Martin both as he stood there wearing his Pepe baggy jeans and Pepe orange T-shirt. "Malique, you need to turn that music down or either put on your headphones, okay. I can hear that noise all the way downstairs and that is too loud. Do you understand me?" she asked in her stern motherly tone.

"Yeah, yeah, ma, my bad."

"Have you done your homework? Where is your brother?"

"I've finished all my homework, and Jordan is in his room."

"What did you all eat for dinner tonight?"

"Ah, Dad called and told us to order pizza."

"Your father called? What time was that?"

"I don't know, ma. But we ate most of the pizza already."

"Well, I'm going to stand right here until you turn that music down, all right?"

Malique made a face as he strutted back into his room to lower the volume on the stereo. Then he came back to the door to see if his mother was still there waiting for him.

"I don't want to hear the music that loud again, Malique. Just because your father and I are not here does not mean that you have permission to do whatever you want to do."

"Okay, okay, I'm sorry, ma."

Tina turned on her heels and stomped over to Jordan's room and knocked on the door before entering. Just as she had imagined, his eleven-year-old body was sitting on the side of the bed playing the latest video game and talking to the television set about his skills. He glanced up at his mom as she stood over him waiting to be acknowledged.

"Hi, mom," he said quickly, returning to his game.

"Hey, Jordan. Did you finish doing your homework?"

"Of course I did. Remember mom, I'm the smart one," he replied with a sly smile.

"I don't know who told you that. Anyway, how was your day?"

"It was okay. I don't have anything exciting to report if that's what you mean."

"All right, then. I'll be downstairs if you guys need anything," she said, turning to leave the room.

"Sure mom. See you later," he replied while still looking at the television screen.

Tina took her time going down the stairs, thinking about her two sons. *Where have all the years gone? What happened to the times when they were happy to see me and greeted me with hugs and kisses?* She had a sinking feeling in her stomach that nobody in this house needed her anymore.

Upon entering the bedroom, Tina pulled off her long tunic top, and tossed it onto the bed. She heard the front door slam shut just as she finished reading the time on the bedside clock.

She remained immobile, waiting for her husband to enter the suite. Speaking to her as he passed the doorway, Martin went straight to his office carrying a black leather briefcase in one hand and a laptop computer bag in the other. Still wearing his brown suit coat and necktie, he was about to take a seat behind his oblong wooden desk when he heard Tina's voice. "Marty, I need to talk with you," Tina stated, entering his office space behind him showcasing a black lace brassier with a pair of orange pants.

"Not now, Tina. I've got some financial reports that I need to look at before it's too late," he replied, sounding tired without looking at her.

"It's already late. You promised that we would talk tonight," she retorted, placing one hand on her hips.

"I promised that we would talk, but I didn't say that it would be tonight," he replied, speaking sternly.

"I just want to tell you that I've made an appointment for you to see your regular doctor for a complete physical examination next month. I had a busy schedule today, but I took a few minutes during lunch to make some telephone calls because this is very important, Marty."

"Thank you. I'll write down the date and time on my calendar later," he stated, glancing in her direction. Martin popped the locks on his attaché case, waiting for her to leave.

"I've also found a male marriage counselor. Someone that I thought you might feel comfortable with us seeing together. His name is Dr. David Johnson, and he comes highly recommended."

Martin turned swiftly and walked towards Tina. He stopped within an inch of touching her stiffening body. "I've told you before that I'm not going to see any marriage counselor. Now please don't approach me about that again. We can work this out with time, Red."

"Look, I can't take this anymore!" she blurted out, clenching both fists.

"I can't take it anymore either!" he screamed back with a ferocious look on his face. "Now I'm out, bye!" Martin stormed past Tina, waving his right hand in her stunned face.

"Martin! Martin! Don't you dare walk out on me when I'm trying to talk to you, dammit!" she yelled, marching behind him as he strutted to the front door. Marty never turned around to acknowledge her ranting; he just slammed the door shut as he stepped outside into the cool night air.

Tina stood there fuming, her chest rising and falling rapidly as she struggled to breathe. She didn't believe that he had the nerve to just up and leave like that without even trying to have a decent conversation. She cursed to herself as she threw up her hands and stomped her feet extra hard. She ran to her bedroom and slammed the door behind her with all the force she had. Tina sat on the edge of her bed holding her head between two palms. *I need to talk to someone that's sane before I go crazy. I can't take this madness anymore. He's lost his mind, thinking he can do me like this.*

Reaching for the telephone, Tina was so enraged that it took her several seconds to remember Shenedra's home telephone number. She punched in the numbers as quickly as her narrow fingers would allow, paced the room, and waited for her friend to answer. After the fourth ring, Shenedra's voice mail picked up, "Hi, you have reached Sexy Chocolate; sorry, I'm not available to take your call right now. Please leave a message at…" Tina clicked the telephone off before she could finish and dialed her cellular phone number. Shenedra's voice mailed picked up on the third ring as the same message began to play, "Hi, you have reached Sexy Chocolate; sorry, I'm not available to take your call right now. Please leave a message after the beep, and I promise to call you back." This time Tina waited the few seconds for the beep to come.

"Shenedra, girl, this is Tina. I need you to call me back tonight as soon as you get this message, okay?" she requested, clicking off the phone and slamming it back into the receiver. Tina continued pacing the room for several more minutes before throwing herself across her king sized bed in disgust.

Pulling herself up, Tina decided to slip out of the pants that she had worn all day. Changing into a long, silky peachy-colored chemise with a matching striped robe, she felt feminine. Stretching herself out across the bed, Tina reminisced about the days when she had a man in her life that she could talk to about her heart's desire. She would have given anything to be able to have the Marty that used to have all the time in the world to listen to her talk about her dreams. That was one of the major reasons that she had fallen so deeply in love with him. She would ramble on and on for minutes thinking that he had fallen asleep on her, but whenever she took a breath between thoughts, he would make a comment to let her know that he had heard her and rapidly processed every word she had said. Even though he loved to talk as much as she did, he was a much better listener than she would ever be.

He had helped her to make all of those dreams come true and now he was suddenly turning away from her. She didn't miss the sex as much as she missed the long conversations, the cuddling, and the holding that they would do all night long. They would sleep so close together in the bed that it looked like one person underneath the covers. Neither one of them wanted to move away from the other because they were both content being nestled together and feeling the electricity that lovers feel when they embrace one another.

Oh, man, what am I going to do? I just wish I had a man to talk to. Tina glanced at the clock to see how late it was. The green digital numbers displayed 10:33 as she tried to think of someone to call that would be willing to listen to her this late in the evening. Instantly her thoughts drifted to Debonair and the way that he had smiled at her today. And just as quickly, she dismissed the thought of him. A few moments later, she found herself reaching for the local telephone directory looking under the last name Jenkins. There he was. It had to be him because there was only one listing with the distinctive name Debonair Jenkins. Tina felt her shaking hand reach for the beige cordless telephone and lift it from the base.

"Hello," Debonair answered after the second ring.

Tina just held the telephone, too numb to speak. Sure, it was easy to pick up the telephone and dial the number but actually talking to him was a different story. She held the telephone for a few more seconds and decided to ease it back down to the receiver rather than just click it off.

"Tina? Tina? Is that you?" she heard him asking through the telephone receiver.

"Ah, how did you know it was me?" she stammered.

"I have caller ID," he replied.

"Oh, yeah, I guess everybody has that now. I'm sorry for calling you. I—I really don't know why I called you."

"Well, I hope you called me because you wanted to talk. That is why you called me, isn't it?"

"Yes, but it's so late, I'm sorry. You're probably busy."

"No, no, don't worry about that. It's never too late, and I'm definitely not busy. I was still up watching television and listening to the radio. Why don't you tell me what's on your mind?"

Tina gently breathed in and then lightly exhaled before answering. "I was just upset earlier, and I just wanted someone to talk to."

"Well, I'm listening. Speak, my lady."

"It's not that simple. You see, I'm going through a hard time right now with my husband, and we just had a huge fight. He walked out on me."

"I see. I'm sure he'll be back at any minute. I know he's not going to leave a pretty woman like you alone for long. I mean—I wouldn't."

"That's sweet of you to say something like that. I just don't think that he'll be home anytime soon." Tina held the telephone to her ear as she walked to the bedroom window and peeped through the open curtains, searching the driveway for Marty's black SUV. "He's been staying out really late most evenings whether we fight or not."

"Oh, well, I don't know what to say except, he's a real fool."

"Look, I shouldn't be talking to you about this. I better go; thanks for listening."

"Tina—please, wait! I don't want you to hang up on me. I have to tell you something," he said, pausing slightly. "I'm sorry about your marriage. I want you to know that I find you very attractive. I think you already know that, but I wanted to say it."

"I think that you're very attractive, too, but I just need a friend right now."

"I'll be whatever you need me to be. If I can be your friend, I'm happy with that. If I can be more than a friend, I'll be even happier. I'm not pressuring you for anything. I just want to get to know you better. I want to know your heart."

"I appreciate what you're saying, but all I have to offer is friendship."

"I understand, and I will respect that."

"Thank you, Debonair. I really needed to hear a calm voice before I fell asleep tonight."

"You can call me anytime, Tina. I mean that. It doesn't matter about the time, all right? Remember that, will you?"

"Yes, I will. Good night," she said slowly.

"Good night, my lady. Sweet dreams," he softly replied.

Tina clicked the off button on the cordless telephone and slowly placed it back on the base. She knew that if and when she fell asleep tonight, she would most certainly be having sweet dreams about Mr. Debonair Jenkins. She imagined his thin lips smiling at her as she sat on her bed and leaned back against the smooth satin comforter. Tina remembered the melodic sound of his voice as he had patiently spoken to her. At least she had a willing male voice to console her in a desperate time of need. At this point, she would have to settle for that and keep her growing attraction to him in check. There was no harm in having a male friend to talk to as long as she knew where to draw the line with him.

Tina had a mind to go out and find her husband. It's not like she didn't know where he spent most of his time when he wasn't home. More than likely, he was at that Chauffeur's Bar and Lounge that he had taken her to once a long time ago to have a drink with some of his employees. He mentioned that he would stop by there sometimes after work to shoot the breeze with some of his friends. The night he had taken Tina there, one of his employees was relocating to another city and they chose the bar as the location for his going away party. She didn't remember much about the place except that it had been dark and pretty crowded on that Friday night. Tina wasn't sure what street it was on, but she had a good idea about the area and believed that she could find it by herself. *Oh, forget that. He'll only get angrier if he looks up and see me coming into a bar alone at this time of the night. But this is not over, not by a long shot.*

Shortly after slipping off her silky robe and placing it over the sage-colored wing chair in the corner, she pulled back the covers on her bed and slid between the light green satin sheets. Picking up the remote control to the Bose stereo system, Tina tuned in to an easy listening oldies radio station that she enjoyed unwinding to at night, particularly after a long stressful day at work. Lying back against puffy satin pillows, the mellow sound of LTD featuring Jeffrey Osborne singing, "We Both Deserve Each Other's Love," filtered through the speakers causing her to reflect on how she'd met Martin Anthony Carlisle.

She had seen him several times sitting in the very front of her Business Economics class. Tina always sat in the last row of the room because she wasn't exactly interested in the subject and didn't want to be called on to answer questions. She noticed that the professor usually called on the willing students in the front of the class or either they volunteered to answer the questions that were raised. On this particular day, she followed Martin to the department library after class and waited about ten or fifteen minutes for him to get situated with his studies before she quietly took a seat in the cubicle right next to him. Noticing that he seemed to be rather old fashioned and mannerable, she didn't want to make the first move, and decided to use the shy innocent girl approach. So when it was almost time to leave the facility, she purposely dropped her pen and a book, hoping to gain his attention. When he did the gentlemanly thing by bending down to retrieve her items and handing them to her, she quickly seized the moment. "Thank you so much. My name is Antina Sloan, but my friends call me Tina," she said, extending her right hand towards Marty while he placed her pen and book on the desk beside her.

"You're welcome, and my name is Martin Carlisle, but my friends call me Marty."

"I like that name. It sounds so masculine."

"Well, thank you, I like your name, too. I don't think that I've ever met anyone named Antina before; it's really nice."

"Thank you, Marty. I was on my way to the coffee house in the student union building. Would you like to join me for a cup of hot brew?"

"Ah, yes, it would be my pleasure. Just let me wrap this up, make a few notes in my tablet, and I'll be right with you, okay?"

"No problem. I admire a man with good study habits," she stated, smiling broadly at him.

A few minutes later, Marty was pulling out a seat for her in the crowded coffee shop. They talked for what seemed like an eternity until they noticed that the establishment was almost empty. The workers were beginning to stack the chairs up on the tables preparing to mop the floor before closing time.

"I think they're trying to tell us something," Marty stated, looking around at the dispersing crowd.

"Yeah, I guess they are."

"Listen, why don't I walk you over to your dorm, and we can say good night properly?" he asked, smiling at Tina with twinkling eyes.

"That sounds like a great idea. I live on the other side of campus. It's scary walking around alone at night."

"Well, you don't have to worry about that tonight," he said, standing over her, signaling that he was ready to leave.

Marty walked with Tina across campus to her dormitory as they took the longest route, walking slower than a snail's pace, savoring every minute that they had together. When they arrived at the dorm's entrance, Marty took her hand into his and told her what a marvelous time he'd had sharing stories with her. That was something that he didn't do with many people that he came into contact with on campus. While Martin was a very outspoken individual, he never shared much about his personal life except to say that he was an only child with no family living in the area, and that he was on a full academic scholarship.

Tina hadn't meant to let Martin kiss her on that very first night, but she'd felt so comfortable with him for the last five hours that it felt like the natural thing to do. His lips were so sweet and inviting that they held and kissed for almost five minutes straight before coming up for a deep breath of fresh air. Tina knew then that she and Marty were destined to be lovers for life because there was an unexplainable connection that she felt to him. She had developed more feelings for him in five hours than she had felt for all of the arrogant obnoxious wealthy guys that she'd dated in the past five years. It didn't matter to her that he was a scholarship recipient, working part-time at a pizza shop, living in campus housing with no means of transportation; they both deserved each other's love.

As the station DJ changed to a more upbeat song, Tina glanced around her luxurious bedroom thinking of how far they had come together and how much their lives had changed over the course of seventeen years. Remembering the marriage prayer that they would recite together each night after saying the Lord's Prayer, Tina whispered the words she hadn't spoken in over a year:

Lord, help us to remember when we first met and the strong love that grew between us. To work that love into practical things so nothing can divide us. We ask for words both kind and loving and hearts always ready to ask forgiveness as well as forgive.

Dear Lord, we put our marriage into your hands.

Amen.

Reaching up and turning off the Victorian style lamp beside the bed, Tina pulled the black night mask over her eyes, covering her mouth as she yawned silently. She was determined to get some rest this evening without thinking anymore about Martin Carlisle or Debonair Jenkins.

Chapter 4

"Bartender, may I have another drink, please?" Martin was sitting in the center of the bar at the Chauffeur's Bar and Lounge, waiting for his fifth drink of the evening to arrive. He needed one more drink to help him relax after the heated verbal exchange he'd just had with his wife. When Martin had first arrived home, he had every intention of talking with Tina tonight regarding their dilapidating sex life, but after only a few seconds of seeing her sensuous body in that sexy sheer lace bra and silky long pants clinging to her round bottom, he'd quickly lost his courage. Knowing that he wouldn't be able to satisfy the woman that he loved tonight, he looked for a way out of the situation.

Her mentioning the idea of going to see a male counselor had dramatically changed his mood, giving him the escape he needed. This wasn't the type of thing that he could easily share with an unfamiliar male, but there was no way for her to understand that. Tina thought that she was being considerate of his feelings by securing a male relationship specialist although she would have preferred seeing a female counselor. The truth of the matter was that Marty wasn't ready to talk to anyone about his personal problems; he was planning on solving them himself.

"Marty, man, what's bothering you tonight?" Lucius Adams, the middle-aged, balding bartender asked as he eyed Martin. His six-foot-two, heavy set body towered over everybody sitting at the bar.

"I just came out to have a good time. What makes you think that something is bothering me?"

"First thing, you don't look like you're having a good time. And second thing is, you been hanging out here a lot recently, you're drinking more than you normally do, and you're staying later each night you come in."

"Look, can I just get another drink without the questions or any commentary, please? You sound more like a nagging wife than you do a bartender."

"Yeah, yeah, my brother, whatever you say."

"Well, I say give me another drink and keep your thoughts to yourself."

"Marty, I've known you a long time. I'm just trying to look out for you."

"I don't need you to look out for me. I'm a grown ass man, I can look out for myself," Marty replied sharply.

"Hey, I know that, but I've been married a long time, I have three teenage kids, and I know when a man is having woman problems."

"Oh, yeah, and how would you know that?"

"Man, please. You got the down home woman blues written all over your face," Lucius replied, laughing at his friend.

"Now that's the truth," Billy stated, easing into the conversation at the bar. "Marty, I've known you longer than Lucius. I've been drinking with you for over five years now. I know you, brother. And I agree with Lucius here. You're having some female problems, my friend." Billy Watson and Marty were long term social drinking buddies. Marty occasionally swung by the bar on Friday nights for a quick drink before heading home to start his weekend. Billy was always there, sitting at the center of the bar counter, engaged in a lively conversation with some young guy. Being that he was an older fella, he was always giving advice to the younger crew that stopped in.

"Here's your drink, Marty," Lucius said, placing his double shot glass of vodka on the bar.

"Thanks, man," Mary replied, downing the drink in a couple of big gulps.

"Man, I believe you're going to need our chauffeur services tonight. You want me to page Calvin to come give you a ride to the crib?"

"Hell no! I don't need a chauffeur to drive me home tonight or any other night, okay. I know how to hold my liquor."

"Marty, you know I live just a couple of blocks from here if you need a place to crash for tonight," Billy intervened.

"I don't need to crash at your pad tonight, man. I got a six-bedroom house."

"Yeah, but if you go home tonight, you'll be sleeping alone on the couch." Billy shot back, laughing with Lucius as Marty shrugged them off.

"That's a good lie. I'm sleeping in my own bed tonight," Martin proclaimed, stressing his words.

"Take it from me, alright. I've had three wives, and I've got a grown child from each one of them. You can take all the marriage vows you want, but love don't last always."

"Billy, man, you're drunk. What are you talking about—love don't last always? What the hell kind of advice is that?" Marty chuckled at his friend's statement.

"I'm trying to tell you something, youngblood. I've been down the aisle three times, and I'm here to tell you that it's not easy being married to a beautiful woman. Now my first wife, Joyce, and I parted ways because we were both too young to know what the hell we were doing. She got pregnant our senior year in high school, and I tried to do the honorable thing. You know, be responsible for my child, but that marriage only lasted about three years. She worked the day shift and I worked the evening shift. I was trying to attend community college part-time so we hardly ever saw each other. Finally, we realized that the only thing we had in common was the baby. The next think that I know, I'm a twenty-year-old man with an ex-wife and a two-year-old son to take care of."

"I'm listening, keep going," Marty encouraged him, downing another drink.

"Well, I was twenty-five when I met my second wife, Regine, and we got married after dating for only a year. My mother hated her right off the bat and begged me not to marry her, but I was still too young and too dumb to listen to motherly advice when it came to pretty women. Now she was something else," Billy paused at the memory of her, closing his eyes, shaking his head, and creating an upward curve across his lips. "She's still the finest woman that I ever met in my life to this day, but she was too expensive for my bank account. I'm not kidding with you. She went through money like it was a bucket of rain water waiting to be poured on the ground. Her thing was name brand shoes. This woman didn't even want to try on a pair of shoes if they didn't cost at least eighty dollars, and this was in nineteen seventy-four."

Martin and Lucius were both holding their sides laughing at that one. Billy even laughed while he was telling the story about this ex-wife. "Yeah, I still miss her, but I had to let her walk out in a pair of two hundred dollar shoes. I was working three jobs trying to keep her in high-heeled pumps. Anyway, that leads me to my third and final wife, Lucille."

"Wait a minute, Billy," Martin butted in while still chuckling, "I want to know how long your second marriage lasted."

"We managed to live together about three years, then it took us about another two years or more of going back and forth before we finally got divorced. So all together, we were married for about five or six years. I was trying to give her time to change her ways, but she wasn't going for that. Now she did give me a beautiful baby girl, though.

And she's remarried to some banker guy, living in a big house, and probably owns about five hundred pair of designer shoes. I guess I'll never understand about women and shoes."

"Right, right," Marty commented.

"Anyway, as I was saying, when I married my third wife at thirty-five, I thought I knew what I was doing and that I was ready for real married life. But as it turned out, she wasn't ready for marriage at all. I thought that because she was almost thirty-years-old and had her career going well—that she was ready to settle down to be a caring mother and a loving wife. Man, I couldn't have been more wrong. As soon as she popped out my son, she was ready to go back to the night life, talking about how she missed her freedom. Well, needless to say, that union didn't make it very long either. In fact, that was probably the shortest marriage that I had because she was already three months pregnant when we married. And my son had just had his first birthday when we divorced."

"Wow, Billy, that's some story right there. I can't imagine myself getting divorced even one time. I don't see how you made it through three divorces," Martin stated, looking bewildered.

"Hey, I've had some hard knocks to deal with, but I'm still here today, looking for love. Right now, I'm fifty-six-years-old, and I don't care how long love lasts or don't last; I'm going to keep trying."

"I know what you mean, man. There's just nothing like being loved and being in love. When Tina and I started out, it was all good. I swear we were happy living in that one-bedroom apartment eating pizza on the floor every night because we didn't have a dining room set. We were a very loving, romantic couple and did everything together. Now we have two dining tables and can't even share one of them without arguing or…"

"Marty, I'm sorry to interrupt you," Lucius said, leaning over the counter. "I forgot to tell you something earlier. This old dude, looked to be at least sixty-years-old, has been by a couple of times this week looking for you, man. He wouldn't tell me his name or nothing; he seemed like he could have been a drifter just passing through. Anyway, he said that somebody told him that you hang out here a lot, and he needed to see you," Lucius leaned over the counter, trying to whisper to Marty.

"Really, Lucius, man? What did he look like?"

"Well, honestly, he looked like an older version of you without a suit and tie," Lucius watched Marty carefully for his reaction to that statement. Marty was looking into a blank space in his mind, trying not to show any emotions or let on that he knew who this stranger might be.

Of course, Lucius' one statement had said it all. He knew that the mature man looking for him had to be his long lost father who had abandoned his family over thirty years ago.

"Thanks for letting me know that, Lucius. I appreciate that. Good looking out, man," Marty said, reaching up to shake his friend's hand in appreciation.

"No problem. You know I got your back. Uh, what do you want me to tell him if he comes in again?"

Martin didn't know what to say as he stared straight through Lucius in a mesmerizing daze. Now he knew why this recurring nightmare had been haunting him for the last two or three months. It was the primary source of his excessive drinking and his unresponsiveness to having sex with Tina. Now it was a reality that was staring him directly in the face.

"Just tell him that I'll be around, if he really wants to see me, I'll be around," Marty said slowly. "All right, fellas. That's it for me tonight. I'll see you guys later."

The few men left at the bar turned to bid Marty good night. Lucius offered him the chauffeur's service again, but Mary turned it down. He felt like he hadn't had anything to drink all night after hearing that his father, Ezekiel Harrison, was in town searching for his youngest son.

Driving home on the almost bare late night streets, Martin realized that he was losing control of his life, and he didn't know how to get back in the driver's seat. *What could my daddy want with me after all these years? He must have some type of disease and need a body part or something from me. Well, I'm not giving him anything, and that's the truth, right there. He probably wants to apologize for leaving my mother with two young sons to raise by herself. Or better yet, he probably wants to milk some money out of his millionaire son that he abandoned to travel the world and become a drunken bum. I bet that's it, this little trip is all about the Benjamin's, baby. I was wondering how long it would take for him to find out that one of his sons had become successful. I'm truly surprised that I haven't heard from him or someone in the family long before now. But it really doesn't matter what he wants. If he wants to see me, then I'll see him, and then maybe — just maybe, I can put these nightmares to rest for good after I've shared a good piece of my mind with him.*

Marty couldn't face the real pain that was eating up his interior organs, causing his whole life to be in disarray. He had never told Tina the truth about his immediate family. She thought that he was an only child just like she was and that both of his parents were deceased. But in truth — the truth that he would have to face sooner or later — his father had abandoned his mother, Cora Lee, along with him and his older brother, Walter, exactly thirty-three years ago. His mother was a bronzed skin, full sized woman with pretty brown eyes that smiled at you just as bright as her lips did. She loved to wear fancy colorful dresses and attended the Ebenezer Baptist Church, whenever she didn't have to go to work at the nursing home, which wasn't too often. Martin could remember fantasizing about the day that he would be able to buy his mother a designer dress with a matching hat, shoes, and purse for Mother's Day. She would laugh heartily at just the idea of her precious son wanting to provide for her in such a grand fashion someday. Cora Lee's eyes would brighten when she spoke to him in that loving motherly voice saying, "Son, one day you're going to make us all very proud. I know that you're going to be somebody!"

Martin's heart saddened at the thought of how Cora Lee lost so much weight in the months following Ezekiel's departure. She went from being a plump happy woman to a thin fragile brokenhearted person. Feeling her pain, as well as Walter's, Martin tried to be the family savior by coming up with activities and encouraging them to do things together. He would plan a family night for them to stay home and watch an old movie on television, but as luck would have it, Cora would get called into work at the last minute. He could still hear her voice speaking into the telephone, "Yes sir, Mr. Simon, I can fill in for Ms. Percy tonight. I'll be there in the next thirty minutes." Then she would turn to him and Walter and say, "All right, boys. You know, your mother needs this overtime money for us to make it next month. So, I need you both to stay inside and go to bed at a decent hour." Then, she would be out of the door in a matter of minutes.

Walter would come up with somewhere to go with his friends the second she closed the door behind her and started up the old cranky piece of an automobile that they owned. Going to bed at a decent hour for him was around 11:00 p.m., but a decent hour for Walter was a few minutes before whatever time their mother was supposed to be home. He would tip in the house around the time for Cora's shift to end and wrap up in the covers like he had been there all night long, right with Martin.

Martin was nine-years-old, and Walter had just turned eleven when they woke up, and their daddy was gone. He slipped away like a thief in the night and never returned to see them. It took their mother almost three months to actually sit them down and tell them that she didn't think that Ezekiel Harrison was coming back to his family. Somehow, Marty had already sensed that his father wasn't returning home, but he hadn't mentioned it to his mother or his brother. Anyway,

Walter broke down and cried like a baby for three whole days. He couldn't believe that what mama had said could possibly be the truth.

About a year later, after Walter was all cried out, he became a different person; he started hustling and running in the streets. Their mother had tried to reel him in but due to the pressures of trying to work two jobs to make ends meet, it was a losing battle. Nonetheless, Cora Lee tried to keep a close eye on two budding young men by soliciting the help of her friends and neighbors. After a while, Walter stopped caring about anything except for what he wanted. All he ever had on his mind was hanging in the streets with his buddies, smoking and drinking or sneaking some young unsuspecting female into the house every chance he got. Marty could remember many nights lying in the dark listening to Walter in the twin bed beside him making out with a girl while he covered his eyes and ears. Sometimes the girls would stop once they realized that another person was in the room, but the majority of the time they didn't care. Some even seemed to take it as more of a turn-on, knowing that Walter's little brother was listening to them get it on.

Cora Lee had her suspicions about Walter and the girls being in her house when she wasn't there. Whenever she asked Marty about it, though, he always covered for his brother. Marty felt like he at least owed Walter that much even though he was never thanked personally for his discretion with their mother.

Marty watched Cora Lee struggle for the next nine years after their father left, trying to support their family. She managed to keep a roof over their heads, second hand clothes on their backs, and food on the table, but that was about it. They didn't have money to spare for any co-incidentals that might have come up. The only reason Martin had been able to go to college was because he had listened to his mother and heeded her words by doing well in school. He never worried about meeting people that he knew in a city the size of Jacksonville, especially after changing his last name to Carlisle shortly after finishing high school and moving to the college campus. Most of the students on this side of town seldom ventured out to other parts of the huge urban city.

Luckily, he'd saved every cent from his weekend job at the local grocery store with the goal of someday changing his last name. Wanting to distance himself from the Harrison title, he selected Carlisle to be his new calling. A name that would not easily be associated with a poor struggling black kid from the ghetto.

Graduating in the top five percent of his senior class, he received a full scholarship to several colleges but opted to remain in town. He was determined to make it in the same place where he had started.

Marty was about to turn eighteen-years-old when Cora Lee was killed in a car accident early one morning on her way home from the overnight job at the nursing home across town. It appeared that she had fallen asleep behind the wheel and was killed instantly when she crashed into a semi-truck. At that point, Marty severed all ties with his other family members and concentrated on his education. Once he met Michael Wayne in college, they quickly became best friends and decided to go into business together after graduation. Then when he met Tina in college, he knew that he wanted her for always. However, he was afraid to share his real life with her after learning about her wealthy and sophisticated background. Even knowing that he and Michael shared similar humble beginnings, this was one part of his life that he hadn't considered sharing with his closest friend. He figured that Michael would probably be very understanding of his painful past, but it was easier to not even open up that wound. Besides, if no one knew about his secret, he would never have to worry about it being revealed at a most inopportune time in his life once he reached the pinnacle of success.

By the time Martin entered college on a full academic ride, Walter was so far gone to the streets that they parted ways as brothers and hadn't seen each other once in the last twenty years. From what Marty had heard over five years ago, his brother was a big time drug dealer until he started using the stuff himself, now he was a drug addicted junkie living in shelters or on the streets. He was notoriously known for robbing and stealing from people to support his habit.

Marty also later learned that his father was living the life of an alcoholic drifter, moving from one city to the next. Just staying in one place long enough to make enough money to get a drink and some pocket change before moving on. *Well, well, I guess Malcolm X was right. The chickens have finally come home to roost,* Martin thought, pulling into his circular driveway, clicking the remote control button to open the garage door. *Time will tell. Oh, yes, only time alone will tell what's on Ezekiel's mind after a thirty year absence.*

Chapter 5

"Shenedra, girl, where were you last night? I tried to call you around 10:30 p.m. and you didn't answer the telephone. You didn't even answer your cellular phone, so give me the details," Tina demanded, entering the hair shop at the same time as Shenedra. Before her best friend could respond, Taneka spoke as she rushed past them, headed straight to her station, and started setting up for her first client.

"Tina, I was out on a date last night with this new guy that I met at a party two weekends ago, and he is super fine. I'm talking dark delicious chocolate with nuts inside," Shenedra smiled, licking her fingers one at a time for effect. They had entered the shop and were speaking to each other across stations while preparing for another day of business.

"Yeah, and what is the name of this specimen, and what does he do for a living?"

"Well, his name is Carson Forde, he's thirty-five-years-old, and he works at the local airport in the baggage claim department. The only drawback to his job is that he has to work all different shifts, so I can't see him every evening. He's a little on the shy side, but I can work with him on that. At least he has his own place and his own ride. I don't want another man that's staying at home with his mama and looking for me to drive him around everyday. I have been there and done that; hell, I even bought the T-shirt," she said, laughing at herself.

"I'm with you on that," Taneka responded, laughing along with her. "I'm happy not to have a man with drama in my life right now. When I kicked Romeo to the curb six months ago, I said that was it for me for awhile."

"Well, where did you all go? Did he wine you and dine you?" Tina asked, giving Shenedra an inquisitive look.

"He sure did. Let me tell you, we had the most romantic dinner at Sorrento Italian Restaurant on St. Augustine Road. They have delicious food served in a warm and friendly Mediterranean-style atmosphere. They have several small cozy rooms and gentle music playing in the background. Oh, it was great, and then we went to see a movie. Now don't ask me which movie because by that time I was so gone on the man, I didn't pay it much attention," Shenedra was about to continue bragging about her date but then she thought of something, "Why were you calling me so late, anyway?"

"Oh, it was nothing. Don't worry about it, okay," Tina responded, trying to sound casual.

"Hey, Tina, I'm surprised you haven't gotten your morning java yet. Are you going to the coffee shop anytime soon since your first appointment hasn't arrived yet?" Shenedra asked, turning to welcome in her first client of the day.

"Yeah, I think I will go ahead and get my morning fix before my customer gets here. Do you want something this morning?"

"Thank you for asking. I just want a huge cheese Danish; I didn't eat breakfast this morning," she stated, digging in her purse for coins as soon as her client was seated.

"And I just want an extra large French vanilla café," stated Taneka, handing Tina a five dollar bill.

"All right, you two, I'll be back in a quick beat," Tina said, walking out the front door of the hair salon.

Once she was outside and past the front window of her hair shop, Tina stopped to gather her composure before entering the Insomnia Coffee House next door. The cool morning air felt good against her anxious face and helped to calm her nerves down quite a bit. She knew that in all likelihood, Debonair was probably at work by now, and she would have to confront him about their short conversation last night. *Why did I call him? I must be losing my mind. I cannot play games with this young man. I better nip this in the bud right now. I made a mistake calling him, and I just have to own up to it,* she thought, reaching for the entrance door handles.

Tina casually walked in the store wearing her Hilfiger jeans with a red, white and blue striped top with long loose sleeves. She felt like she was floating through time and space as she strolled to the back of the store to place her order. Debonair had his back to her as she cautiously approached the counter. "Good morning, Debonair, how are you today?" she asked.

"Good morning, beautiful, I'm doing fine and how are you?" he asked, turning around to greet her wearing navy twill pants with a Ralph Lauren signature white shirt.

"Hey, I'm doing great. I just wanted to say thank you for listening to me last night. I was wrong to call you like that, and I do apologize, it won't happen again," she said, forcing a smile.

"Well, I accept your apology, but I hope that you will call me again," he stated, placing both elbows on the counter and leaning in closer to her. "I enjoyed hearing the soft tone of your voice; it was better than smooth jazz music playing low in my ears," he replied, flashing his teeth at her.

Tina couldn't keep herself from smiling at his gorgeous light tan face, intoxicating dark rum eyes, and even, pearly white teeth. But she quickly coughed and shook her head, trying to remember the other reason that she was there. She placed her order and waited patiently for Debonair to put it together in a carrying box. She received her change, picked up the box, quickly turning away from the counter and Debonair. Tina was about to place one foot in front of the other when she heard him softly calling her name. Suddenly she stopped in her tracks.

"Tina, don't forget that I have a three o'clock hair appointment with you today, all right?"

"I didn't forget, I'll see you at three," she said, stepping towards the front entrance, thankful that she was able to maintain some sense of composure in his presence.

As soon as Tina entered her shop with the goods in hand, Shenedra started questioning her about Debonair. "So did Mr. Handsome flirt with you today, girl?" she asked, teasing her best friend.

"No, ah, he just reminded me that he has a three o'clock appointment for today," Tina responded, handing them their change while deliberately avoiding eye contact. Shenedra gave Tina a suspicious look but decided to keep her mouth shut this time.

The morning passed by quite fast and before any of them realized it, it was after two in the afternoon and no one had eaten lunch. Tina agreed to cover the shop while her three employees slipped out for a quick bite. They had about thirty minutes before their next customers were due and Tina was almost done with her client, Lauren Jeffries. Just as they strolled out the shop laughing and talking, Debonair walked through the front door and slowly approached her. "Tina, I'm a little early, I hope that you don't mind if I wait for you."

"No, why don't you take a seat. I'm almost done here, and I'll be right with you." She clipped the ends of Lauren's braids, wrapped them in a topknot at the center of her head, and placed a few cowry shells around the bun. Lauren admired Tina's handiwork in the mirror, paid her bill, and left the shop happy. Tina then turned her attention to Debonair since they were the only two people left in the shop. They eyed each other amorously as he stepped closer to her still body without uttering a word. Feeling slightly faint, Tina couldn't command her body to move as she felt his warm presence getting closer to her. She stared up at him as he stopped within an inch of her face. Tina could intuitively tell that he wanted to place his full lips over hers. Slowly lifting her hand to touch his face, Tina felt engulfed in a hypnotic trance gazing into his dark colored eyes. Holding their stare, Debonair begin lowering his face to hers.

"Hey, Tina, we're back," Shenedra called, opening the main door and stopping abruptly. "Hey, Debonair."

"Hello ladies," he said, snapping up his head as he turned towards them.

"Hi, Debonair," Taneka replied. "You're looking fine today."

"Well, thank you."

"Tina, would you like some of my salad since you didn't order any lunch today?" Shenedra offered. "We decided to get take-out orders instead of eating at the restaurant."

"No thanks. I'll pick up something after I'm done with Debonair." Tina stated, escorting Debonair to the back of the salon to wash his long locks. Neither one of them spoke the entire fifteen minutes that it took her to shampoo his hair. He laid his head all the way back in the sink with his eyes closed, concentrating on the enticing fragrance that she was wearing. He wanted to ask her the name of the scent, but he was too busy remembering how close he had come to tasting the moist lips of his dream lover. Tina wrapped a clean towel around his hair before leading him back to her booth.

"Tina, did you ever decide on a theme for you birthday party?" Taneka asked, smiling over at her.

"Not yet, but I did call that professional party planner to confirm the date and location."

"So you have a birthday coming up soon, I guess," Debonair inquired.

"No, it's not until May first, but I'm planning ahead because I want it to be a major event," she said, sounding excited. "Right now, I'm trying to get ready for the World Natural Hair Expo that we have coming up next month in Atlanta. You know, March is just right around the corner."

"Yes it is, girlfriend. Have you made our reservations at the Crowne Plaza full service hotel yet?" Shenedra asked, eyeing Tina for a response. She was looking forward to this trip as well as staying at the fabulous establishment.

"You know I have. I need to give you both the details so you can stop asking me questions everyday. I guess I also need to make a hotel reservation for that shop owners' conference coming up in July that I have to attend in Fort Lauderdale. But I might be able to stay at my folks time-share duplex while I'm there for that one though," she sighed.

"Well, I just can't wait for the Atlanta trip myself. I'm looking forward to that four-day weekend in HOTlanta," Taneka bragged. "It's going to be so much fun since we're closing the shop down for four days plus we're already closed on Monday's. So that will give us a day to get back and rest."

"Yes goodness. That was a good idea to close the shop down a day ahead of time so we can get an extra day in for shopping before the convention starts," Shenedra added.

"Well, who's driving? Since I have a two-seater, I know it won't be me," Tina looked at her friends and smiled.

"Shenedra, you have a gorgeous new Mitsubishi Eclipse, can we ride with you?" Taneka asked.

"Yeah, I don't mind driving. You two are welcome to ride with me as long as you don't complain about my music because there will be absolutely no Maxwell playing in my car," she stated, rolling her grayish eyes at Tina. Shenedra was an all the way hip-hop fan with her old self.

"Whatever, you're not hurting my feelings," Tina laughed, waving her right hand through the air.

It didn't take long for Tina to finish up twisting Debonair's locks and place him under the hood dryer for twenty-five minutes. By the time she removed all the clips from his hair and had him ready to go, she was truly starving.

"Tina, do you have anymore appointments for today?" Debonair asked.

"Yes, I do, but my next customer is not due in for about forty minutes," Tina replied, looking at the gold and diamond Bulova watch on her small wrist.

"I see. Well then, why don't you let me treat you to a late lunch at the Chinese restaurant across the street?" Debonair asked with a hopeful look in his eyes.

"Hey, I am hungry, and I appreciate the offer."

"So that means that you'll take me up on it, right?" he interjected quickly.

"Yes, I believe that I will since you're being so generous today."

"Good, are you ready?"

"Just a minute," she said, holding up one finger, turning towards her co-workers engrossed in work. She walked over to the receptionist desk in the center of the room, "Tammy, I'm going to lunch, and I'll be back before my next client arrives in about forty minutes."

"All right, Tina," she replied, watching them until they exited the shop.

Debonair was a complete gentleman. He helped her cross the busy street, opened the door for her to enter the China King restaurant, and pulled her chair out for her to sit down at their table for two. After they had both placed their orders for sweet and sour chicken with shrimp fried rice, vegetable egg rolls, and sweet iced tea, Tina tried to avoid looking at Debonair. Feeling his deep penetrating eyes on her, she pretended to be enamored with the authentic culture scenery and green plants surrounding the restaurant. There was an oversized picture of a Chinese landscape with a simulated waterfall across the room from them that captured her attention for a short while. Almost a full minute passed before Tina decided to say something to break the silence between them. "Have you eaten here before?"

"Yeah, but it's only been a couple of times. What about you?" he asked.

"I've been here before, too, but it's usually for take-out," she responded, looking around the restaurant.

"Are you uncomfortable being here with me?" he asked, staring into Tina's pure honey eyes.

"No, of course, I'm not. Why would you ask me something like that?"

"Well, I see you're looking around like you're scared that somebody is watching us or something."

"No, that's not it," she replied with a slight laugh. "I just like to be aware of my surroundings when I'm out in public places."

"Oh, is that all it is? Because I don't want you to ever feel uncomfortable with me. In fact, I would like for us to become very comfortable with each other. How do you feel about that?"

"Well, I—I'm not sure." Tina said, stumbling over her words.

"What I'm trying to say is that I already feel really comfortable around you, and I'd like for you to feel the same around me. Is that possible?" he asked, leaning in towards Tina, speaking in a lower sexy voice.

"Of course, it is. If I wasn't at ease with you, we wouldn't be having lunch together now. I like you a lot, and I value your friendship."

"That's a start. I think that we're going to be wonderful friends. You know, when you called me the other night, I was somewhat surprised because I knew that I'd never given you my telephone number. I had no idea that you were interested in calling me."

"You're listed in the telephone directory. And like I said before, I just needed a male's point of view to help me put things into perspective."

"I was certainly glad to be of assistance to you. While we're on the subject, I want to give you my cellular phone number, too," he said, reaching into his pants. Pulling out a small piece of paper with his number already written on it, he handed it to Tina. "Now you'll be able to reach me no matter where I am, my lady."

"Thank you," she replied, taking the paper. "You didn't have to do this."

At that moment, the waitress arrived with their plates and drinks. They continued their light conversation as they both enjoyed their meal. They took their time sipping from their tall glasses of iced tea. When Tina finished her food, she excused herself to go to the ladies room while Debonair took care of the tab.

Debonair was standing in the waiting area at the front of the restaurant as Tina exited the rest room. He reached out for her to take his arm as he escorted her out of the restaurant. He walked her back to the hair salon and stood facing her at the front door while they said their friendly good byes.

"Thanks for treating me to lunch today," Tina said, releasing his arm.

"I have to say that the pleasure was all mine, my lady."

"Why do you always call me 'my lady'?" Tina asked.

"Well, I see you as a lady and maybe someday you'll be mine."

"Debonair, I told you, we can never be more than friends," Tina replied, shaking her head at him.

"I know what you told me, but you can't control my dreams."

"I have to go," she replied quickly, turning away from him. Tina remembered the sensual thoughts she'd had of Debonair last night.

"I'll see you soon, Tina," he said, walking away from her. Upon entering the hair shop, all eyes were on Tina's blushing face.

"So, how was your lunch?" Shenedra asked, eyeing Tina's flushed cheeks.

"It was nice. I'm really full," Tina replied, rubbing her stomach.

"Girl, you need to be careful around him. I know some single women that would knock you out cold to get to that good looking brother," Taneka joked.

"Well, they don't have to worry about me because we're just friends," Tina said, trying to convince herself and them.

"He looks to me like he has a little bit more than friendship on his mind, girlfriend," Shenedra stated, grinning at Tina.

"It doesn't matter what he thinks because friendship is all that I have on my mind. He's a nice person, and I really enjoy talking with him. He has a unique perspective on most situations; he helps me to understand things more from the male point of view."

"Just be sure that you keep him talking when you're together because the second he closes his mouth, you'll be in trouble if you know what I mean."

"I know exactly what you mean, and you can just stop thinking like that right now, Shenedra. He respects me and my marriage."

"All right, all right, I'm done with it. Your six o'clock customer called and said that she needed to reschedule for another day. She wants you to call her at the number on the receptionist's desk."

"Oh, that's great. Maybe I can get home at a decent time and have a long talk with Marty tonight."

"I've been meaning to ask you about him, but I know that this is not the time or the place to discuss your personal relationship."

"Well, just to make a long story short, nothing has changed, which is why we need to have a long talk."

"I see, well, I wish you luck with that one. You know, it's so hard to get men to communicate with us when there are problems in the relationship. They're just not as open with their feelings as we are."

"Yeah, you're right on about that one. I know that we'll work it out. We've been together too long not to get past this," Tina said. In reality, she was beginning to wonder what had happened to the kind loving and affectionate person that she was once married to.

What has become of the man that used to freely share his every emotion and thought process with me? What happened to the man that used to pray and attend church with me on a regular basis? Lord, I don't know what happened, but I've got to get him back.

Chapter 6

Martin thought that it was time to share his problems with his best friend and business partner, Michael Wayne. Two weeks had already passed since he and Tina had their big argument prompting him to walk out on her. He didn't want to go through the entire month of March living in hell. His life was becoming too complicated for him to handle alone.

Michael had asked him several weeks ago what was going on with his personal circumstances, but he wasn't ready to come clean with his partner at that time. Martin thought that he could deal with the drinking and the marriage problems on his own. Now that he knew that his father was in town searching for him after months of horrifying nightmares about his parents, he was ready to confide in Michael.

Marty invited Mike to have lunch with him in his office so that they could talk in private. They ordered subs from a nearby sandwich shop and had them delivered. Both of them had made themselves comfortable by removing their dark business suit coats and rolling up their sleeves. "Marty, are you ready to tell me what's really going on with you?" Michael asked, and then took a huge bite from his hero sandwich, sitting in front of Marty's oversized curved desk.

"Mike, it's not that simple. Besides, I don't know where to start," Marty replied, looking away from him with his hand under his chin.

"Well, I'm listening. The sooner you tell me what's going on the sooner you can move on. Who knows? I might be able to help."

"I don't think that you can help me with this one, buddy. Viagra might be my only solution to this problem."

"What? You're kidding me. What's going on with you and Tina?"

"I don't know, man. I just haven't been able to respond to her lately."

"All men are impotent sometime, Marty," Michael chuckled. "I'm sure this is not the first time that this has happened to you."

"No, it's not, but it's never lasted this long before. We haven't been intimate since Christmas."

"Wow! Now I see why you're feeling concerned. What are you going to do about this?"

"I'm not sure, but that's not all that I have to tell you. I've been hiding something from you since the first day we became friends," Marty replied, turning away from Mike. He remained silent for several seconds, staring out his office window.

"Well, don't clam up on me now. Go ahead and spill your guts. Don't say something like that and then go quiet on me." Michael stared at his friend, hoping that this whole scenario was going to be a joke. Sensing a change in the atmosphere, he sat up straight preparing himself for whatever was about to be disclosed by his partner.

"Man, I—I been lying to you and Tina about my family. I've lied to both of you ever since I've known you," Marty dropped his head.

"What in the world are you talking about?" Mike asked, looking startled. "How have you lied to me and Tina all these years?"

"I told you both that I was an only child and that both of my parents were deceased and that's not true."

"Well, then—what is the truth?"

"Ah, man," he paused. "I just have to spit this out and be done with it." Martin took his time telling Michael the real deal about his life and sincerely apologized for his years of secrecy. His best friend waited patiently while Marty bared his soul to him, trying to suppress his tears along the way. When he was done, Michael slowly rose from his seat; walked behind Marty's desk, and placed both arms around his broad shoulders.

"Man, don't worry about this. Don't let this eat you up any longer. But, you know, you have to tell Tina about this right away. I mean—you know that, don't you?"

"Yeah, I know," he replied sadly. "I just hope that she can forgive me."

"I'm sure she'll be able to forgive you. I can testify about forgiveness. You know exactly what Alese and I went through last year and how she was finally able to forgive me. So, please, let that be the least of your worries because love endures all things and love never fails."

"That's not what I heard the other night. I was told that love don't last always. I guess I'm about to find out if that's true or not."

"Trust me, man, that's a false conception. That's a person speaking who has never experienced real love. They thought they were in love, but they didn't have the real thing, and I'm not referring to Coca-Cola either."

"Yeah, you make a good point," Marty replied, tilting his head to one side, placing both palms on the desk. They were both quiet and in deep thought for several minutes before Michael spoke again, "Marty, I have been worried about you drinking so much lately, man. You know, that could really be the sole cause of your impotence. I think you need to see your doctor as well as cut down on some of the alcohol you're consuming."

"You're right. I know you're right. Although I am seriously thinking about asking my doctor for some Viagra pills, just to help me out in the bedroom for awhile."

"Man, please! Didn't I just tell you that drinking too much could be the problem? Taking any type of pill with alcohol would only make matters worse. Why don't you take my advice, cut back on the drinking, and go get a physical examination to rule out any medical condition?"

"Well, I can do that. But then, I've been having these nightmares lately about my parents. And I honestly think that they are driving me to drink," Marty confessed, smoothing both hands down his face.

"Listen, man, maybe you need to see a psychologist or someone in the mental health profession."

"Oh, so now you're trying to say that I'm crazy or mentally ill or something."

"No, no, I didn't say that," Michael replied, raising both hands in the air. "I'm saying that you have a lot of drama going on right now. It might be beneficial for you to talk to someone that specializes in the mental health field. If you're having terrible dreams and you said yourself that they may be driving you to drink, then it might help for you to talk with a psychologist. You know, he might maybe able to assist you with interpreting your dreams so you can get to the bottom of your problems. I think that's a better solution than Viagra."

"I never thought about it like that. I thought that only insane people needed to see psychiatrists."

"That's another misconception among our people. We think that mental counseling is a taboo subject or it only pertains to unstable people, but sometimes a normal person can be faced with abnormal circumstances that cause them to lose their mental focus. Talking to a trained person in the mental health area might be a possible solution. That's all I'm saying, man."

"Well, you may be on to something there. It all depends on how you look at it."

"The way I see it, you need to explore all available options. It could be due to the drinking, it could be psychological, or it could be a physical problem that you're not aware of. In any case, you need to consult with your doctor first. I don't know what else to tell you, man. I'm not trying to change the subject here, but what are you going to do when your father catches up with you?"

"Now, that I don't know, Mike. I don't even know. I guess I'll just sit down with him and try to have a man-to-man talk with him for once in my life. Maybe I'll get some answers to these questions that I've had all of these years."

"Yeah, I bet you have a lot of unanswered questions. But I wouldn't get my hopes up about him answering anything based on what you just told me about his character. He doesn't sound like the type that will take kindly to being questioned about his actions."

"Well, if he doesn't answer, then to hell with him. He can keep stepping like he's been doing for the last thirty-three years of my life. It's definitely not like I need him. I just wonder what it is he needs from me. He's probably here because he's desperate for some money. He probably got some gangsters on his tail for some heavy dough or something like that. Who knows what the devil Ezekiel Harrison is up to?"

"I'm sure you'll find out soon enough," Mike said, standing up with his lunch bag in his hand, walking towards the trash basket. "I need to get back to my office. Let me know when you need to talk again, my brother. You don't have to take the whole world on by yourself. You have at least one friend that I know of."

"Yeah, yeah, I hear you. Thanks for understanding, man," Marty said as he walked his friend out with his arm around him. He quickly secured his office door and hurried back to the paperwork on his desk.

Martin spent the rest of the day locked in his office reviewing all of their pending accounts for M & M Software Development, Inc. He had instructed his secretary, Katrina, not to interrupt him when he was in his office unless it was an absolute first class emergency. He didn't want to dwell on his personal life anymore than he had to.

It was after 8:00 p.m. when Marty eased out of the office for the day. Everyone else was already long gone as he made his way through the empty parking lot to his black SUV. He couldn't wait to start the car and pop in his favorite mellow CD by Will Downing. Marty loved that song, "A Million Ways to Please a Woman," because it reminded him of all the things that he used to do to please his wife. *Man, it seems like a whole lifetime ago since I met Tina. We were so close and now we're gradually drifting apart and it's all my fault. If I could just confront these demons from my past, maybe I'd stand a chance of saving my marriage.*

Vividly remembering the special joy that he had felt when his sons were born, Marty was happy that he had been with Tina from the first contraction to well after the umbilical cords had been cut. Holding their tiny moving bodies in his hands had been the two high points of his life. He had been so ecstatic that he passed out cigars for almost two weeks after the births of Malique and Jordan. Marty could not begin to phantom how any man could walk out on two precious children and a loving wife like that. His mother had done everything to be a good wife to his father. *How could any man walk out and stay gone for over thirty years, never calling or writing his own family?*

Marty decided that he would stop by the Chauffeur's Lounge just to have a couple of quick drinks to calm his nerves since he wasn't looking forward to confronting Tina this evening. Hopefully, this would give him the strength that he needed to beg her forgiveness for living a lie. She deserved to know what was going on before his father tracked him down and all hell broke loose. *At least Ezekiel has sense enough not to show up on my doorstep upsetting my wife and family. Now that would truly be a disaster for the whole neighborhood to see.*

The music was thumping in the bar tonight, there were party people in every corner having a good time, but Marty felt a strange sensation the second he entered the establishment. He immediately noticed Lucius standing behind the bar trying to give him the eye. He just stopped in his tracks and slowly looked around the lounge, trying to recognize any unfamiliar faces. Marty didn't see anyone that he hadn't seen in there before so he proceeded with caution to the center of the bar and waited for Lucius to come and take his order. "What was that all about?" he asked Lucius as soon as he was within hearing range.

"Hey, man, I was trying to give you the heads up on that old dude that's been around here asking about you. He's over there in the corner booth to my left," Lucius stated, rolling his eyes in that direction without moving his head. "He's been here for over an hour," he continued, anticipating the next question that Marty was going to ask him.

Marty just nodded his head and took a seat at his usual place at the bar. He would have to down at least one drink before he could turn in that direction or even think about who was waiting to see him. "Lucius, bring me my usual, please."

"No problem, man. I'll be right back."

Marty continued sitting at the bar with his fingers entwined on the counter, waiting for his liquor. As soon as Lucius returned with Marty's shot glass of vodka, he quickly downed the contents. Turning around on his barstool, Martin began searching out the man that had been eyeing him since the second he opened the front glass door. He knew Ezekiel Harrison the instant their chestnut brown eyes met, staring holes into each other. Marty slowly slid off the barstool and headed towards the stranger returning his intense stare.

"Well, I was wondering when you would show up," Marty said, glaring down at Ezekiel. His father put his drink down on the table and raised his head up to look into his child's eyes.

"Hi, son, please sit down. I don't like people standing up over me," he said in a husky sounding voice that reverberated in his throat from years of digesting too much strong whiskey.

Marty slid into the booth across from where Ezekiel was sitting and placed both his hands flat down on the table before he spoke, "Look, I'm sitting down, but I don't care about what you like. Let me make myself clear on that," he stated, carefully enunciating each word he spoke while maintaining steady eye contact with Ezekiel. "Now we can talk. Just don't try making no demands on me, alright."

"I don't blame you for being angry with me, but I just wanted to see you. I know how successful you have become and —"

"Excuse me? You know how successful I've become? Is that why you're here, because you want to be paid for being my father?" Marty asked, slightly raising his voice as more anger began creeping through his veins.

"No, no, that's not why I'm here. I would never ask you for money, nor would I ever take any money from you, Martin," Ezekiel stated calmly.

"That's good because you don't ever have to worry about me giving or offering you a single solitary dime, not in this lifetime."

"I just really wanted to see you after all these years, son."

"Why? Why would you want to see me after thirty-three years? Did you suddenly wake up this morning and have an epiphany?"

"Martin, I don't even know what that is. I just know that I wanted to see my sons. I didn't come here to cause you any pain or trouble."

"Then just tell me why you are here. And try telling the truth this time, okay?"

"I told you the first time, I want to see my sons. I've had a long hard life Martin, and I know that I can't make up for what I've done to you and your brother, but I knew it was time to see you both."

"*You've* had a long hard life. What the hell do you think we had — an Easter Day parade?" Martin asked, sounding angry. "Just tell me why you left us and where you have been all this time."

"It's not — I don't have an excuse for what I've done to you, but I am sorry for what I did. I want you to know that. I've always been a rolling stone, son. I thought that getting married and having children would make me want to settle down, but it made matters worse. I was just too young to handle having a wife and kids. Finally, I just couldn't take it anymore, and I had to leave," he paused as his eyes roamed the bar looking at people passing by before he continued in the same slow drawl. "I just travel from town to town looking for pick up work and other odd jobs. Just making enough money here and there to pay for my food and traveling expenses. I've been here for over two weeks and I'm working with this guy that has his own commercial landscaping business. He pays me at the end of everyday that I work, and so far we've managed to stay pretty busy almost seven days a week. I have lived in every state, but I never stay in one town for more than two or three months at a time."

"I'm happy for you. You lived the life that you wanted, even though it meant sacrificing innocent human beings. You should be real proud of yourself for that," Marty stated sarcastically.

Ezekiel sat there, staring at Martin and shaking his head from side to side. Marty stared back at him, observing how much they were alike in physical appearance. They were both about the same height, had the same brown skin coloring, round dark eyes with thick eyebrows over them, and the small slightly protruding ears. However, his father was much thinner than he was; his face had a gaunt look about it; his short cut hair was almost completely white, and his skin was wrinkled. He looked older than his sixty years due to his excessive drinking and reckless lifestyle. Finally, Ezekiel decided to change the course of the conversation. "When was the last time you saw your brother?"

Martin ran his right hand down the length of his face, stretching his eyes before answering. "I don't know for sure, but it's been over twenty years since we saw each other."

"Do you have any idea where I can find him?"

"Look, the last I heard about him was at least five years ago, and it wasn't good news. I was told that he was a street junkie, occasionally camping out in the homeless shelters, but I never tracked him down."

"What happened between you two? You were so close—I thought you would probably grow up being inseparable."

"Well, hey, things change and people change. After you left, Walter changed significantly. We parted ways shortly after mama died when I was eighteen-years-old."

"I guess it shouldn't be too difficult to find him, if what you say is true."

"Well, good luck. I hope you two live happily ever after. Now it's late. I need to get home to my wife and family."

"Martin wait, please. I want to know about your family. Please tell me about them, son." Marty hesitated for several seconds, contemplating how much of his personal life he wanted to share with the father that was a virtual stranger to him.

"I—I've been married for seventeen years. Her name is Antina, but we call her Tina for short, and we met in college. Of course, she's a beautiful woman; she's also a hairdresser with her own hair salon. Tina has a kind loving spirit just like my mama did. We have two sons that we're proud of; Malique is fifteen, and Jordan is eleven. They're typical boys, and they really look out for each other. Both are doing well in school. Malique plays on the football team, and Jordan is a computer whiz. We live in a big six-bedroom house out in Jacksonville Beach. Wh—what else would you like to know?"

"I want to meet your family if you don't mind."

"Hell no, that's out of the question! Don't you ever come near my family or my house. I mean it—don't try me on this, Ezekiel."

His father held up both hands beside his face with the palms out and said, "Son, believe me, I wouldn't do anything against your wishes. If you don't want me to meet your family, I understand. Can I at least see you again?" he asked, placing both hands on the table with one on top of the other.

"I don't know about that. I don't see any reason for us to meet again," Marty replied, standing up to leave.

"Look here, I'm staying at the Motel Six on the south side of town." Ezekiel began, looking up at him. "You can reach me there if you change your mind. I'm already paid up for the month so I can stay in town however long it takes to see both my children."

"I have a news flash for you, old man. We're not children anymore, and we definitely don't need you now. So, ah, you might as well move on to the next town. Good night," Martin said, walking away from his father. He never glanced back, and Ezekiel never took his eyes off the back of Martin's head as he disappeared through the front glass door.

Chapter 7

"Shenedra, this is Tina. I'm on my way to see my doctor for another blood pressure check and the results of my physical exam from last week. I'll be late coming in so I need you to open up the shop for me this morning. I forgot all about this appointment until I woke up this morning."

"Sure, girl. I can handle it while you're out."

"I'll call you back before leaving the doctor's office."

"Don't worry about a thing, Tina. I just hope everything turns out okay. I know how worried you've been regarding those tests. I'm sure that we can manage without you for a few hours."

"Thanks for covering for me. I will be there as soon as I can. I don't know what I would do if it wasn't for you."

"Like I said, don't worry about it. Taneka and I can handle the shop today if you need us to. You just take care of yourself, all right?"

"Yes, ma'am. You have a nice day, bye."

"Okay, bye."

Tina had been worried ever since she completed her physical exam last week. Knowing that something wasn't exactly right with her health, she was afraid to speculate as to what the problem could be and decided to schedule a physical with her primary physician, Dr. Juanita O'Hara. Her blood pressure had been higher than it normally was and the doctor was concerned about it. She had other symptoms that also concerned her physician, like recent weight gain, loss of energy, frequent urination, excessive thrust, increased hunger, and irritability. Of course, she attributed these symptoms to her failing marriage, a busy work schedule, and lack of sexual activity.

Since Tina was aware that her father suffered from high blood pressure and her mother was a diabetic, she made sure to schedule a physical exam yearly. So far, she had been very lucky for a forty-year-old black woman to not have any significant medical problems. Tina had only been hospitalized once in her life, except for her two pregnancies, and she was only twelve-years-old at that time. She suffered from a severe stomach ache and was admitted to the hospital for twenty-four hours of observation. Her doctor feared that she was suffering from an acute appendicitis which turned out to be a false alarm; she was dismissed the next day. She'd never had any surgeries or stitches, and didn't take any prescription medicine besides her birth control pills. And she had even maintained her size twelve figure up until this last year where she gained almost twenty pounds, according to her physical exam last week.

Dr. O'Hara's office was just a few minutes away but every time she stopped at a red light, she reached down into her cosmetics bag for make up. She just couldn't imagine arriving anywhere without at least wearing her favorite shade of red lipstick and one coat of mascara. Since she had to leave the house in such a hurry this morning, Tina just pulled on a blue denim pants suit, stuck on a pair of denim mules, and rushed out the door into the morning traffic.

Luckily, Tina only had to wait ten minutes before they called her back to the inner office area. Upon entering there, Tina removed her denim jacket, placed it on the counter, and kicked off her shoes before stepping onto the scale while chatting with Nurse Howard, a petite woman with dark blonde straight hair. She wasn't exactly happy with her weight but she could live with it for now. Dr. O'Hara had already advised her last week that she needed to start some type of exercise program. Being a workaholic, Tina didn't see how it was possible to carve out time for exercise, even though she had a complete home gym with the latest equipment.

After replacing her shoes and retrieving her jacket, Tina followed the nurse to the examining room in the back. She took a seat on the end of the narrow examining table as the nurse placed a thermometer under her tongue, preparing to take her blood pressure.

Nurse Howard took Tina's blood pressure twice, noticing that it was even higher than it had been last week; she crinkled her brows in wonderment.

"Tina, were you rushing to get here this morning?" she asked.

"Oh, yes, I was. I forgot all about the appointment until almost an hour ago," she replied. "Why, is there something wrong with my blood pressure?"

"Well, I've taken it twice and it is higher than it was the last time you came in. Are you under any type of additional stress?"

Deciding not to share her personal life with the nurse, Tina kept her comments on her professional situation. "I'm just really busy at the hair salon right now."

"Okay, I'll let the doctor talk with you further about that when she comes in. I also need to test your glucose levels this morning. I just need to prick one of your fingers, if you don't mind."

"Why are you doing that? You have never done that in the past."

"I know," replied the nurse, "But we found traces of sugar in your urine last week, and the doctor asked me to check your glucose levels this morning."

"Okay," Tina replied hesitantly, holding out her right index finger. The nurse held Tina's index finger while sticking it with the needle, and then placed the blood on a test strip that was already inserted into a monitor. After five seconds the meter beeped, she recorded the results, and told Tina that the doctor would be in shortly.

Dr. O'Hara entered the room a few minutes later carrying Tina's medical records and charts under her arm. She was taller than Tina with dark curly hair and was exceptionally thin for a woman that had birthed four children. The doctor scanned the papers as she pushed up on the large round-framed glasses she wore. Pulling up a stool, she took a seat directly in front of Tina.

"Mrs. Carlisle, I'm sorry to inform you that according to your recent medical profile, I believe that you need to start taking medication for high blood pressure and adult on-set diabetes right away."

Tina had been holding her breath. She gasped upon hearing this news. "Dr. O'Hara, what are you talking about?"

"Last week your blood pressure was higher than normal and today it's even higher. When I reviewed your lab work, I found sugar in your urine. After pricking your finger today, your glucose levels are well above average, and you wrote on your check-in sheet that you haven't eaten this morning or had anything to drink. Is that correct?"

"Yes, it is," Tina nervously replied.

"Now this type of diabetes is referred to as Type-two and is most commonly found in adults. It's also referred to as onset diabetes because it develops after adulthood. The good news is that this disease can be treated with pills, diet, and an active lifestyle which means that your body is still capable of producing insulin; it just needs some help. We have an excellent nutritionist on staff that you can meet with today."

Tina just sat there staring at Dr. O'Hara. Even with her family background, she thought she had been careful enough to elude both diseases. With the current schedule that she maintained, it was almost impossible to eat right, exercise, and remain stress free. The doctor continued talking and Tina continued staring at her while she spoke, not really processing the information that was coming out of her mouth.

"Mrs. Carlisle. Mrs. Carlisle. Are you listening to me?"

Tina blinked her eyes and snapped her head back before answering. "Yes, doctor, I heard what you said about me seeing the nutritionist, but that won't be necessary. My mother is a nutritionist, and my father is a doctor. As you know, my mother is also a diabetic and my father suffers from high blood pressure so I'm aware of both diseases and the special diets that are required for both."

"I understand. Then I'm sure that I don't need to explain the dangers of you having the two most deadly diseases found in African-Americans today. You need to have the prescriptions filled so that you may start taking both medicines right away and schedule an appointment to come back for a check up in about three or four months. By then, we should be able to tell whether or not the medicines are working properly, okay?" the doctor asked, handing her three prescriptions.

"Yes, Dr. O'Hara, no problem," Tina replied, reaching for the prescription papers.

"In addition to taking the pills, you need to monitor your glucose levels approximately three times a day. Once in the mornings before you eat breakfast, approximately two hours after you've eaten lunch, and then again at bedtime. The third prescription that you have is for the blood glucose test strips. The receptionist will give you the monitor that goes with those strips on your way out free of charge. Now you'll have to purchase the blood pressure testing kit yourself at any of the local drug stores. It's very simple to use, especially if you buy one with a digital monitor. You're not really what I consider overweight but losing anywhere from ten to twenty pounds would probably help both of your conditions a great deal. So do you have any questions for me?"

"No, I really don't. I'm just sort of stunned right now. I didn't see this coming. I mean—I've tried to be so careful. There's been so much stress in my life lately—I just don't know."

"What type of stress are you talking about? We have a counselor here that I'd be happy to refer you to if you need to talk to someone regarding personal problems."

"No, thank you. It's not that serious right now. I'll keep that in mind over the next few months in case things don't get any better for me, though."

"All right, it's your decision to make. Just let me know if you need that referral at any time. By the way, the exercise program that we talked about last week is even more important now. As a matter of fact, I suggest that you take the rest of the day off and go home to get some rest and then start setting up a personalized exercise program." Noticing that Tina was still looking a bit discombobulated, she added, "This is quite a bit to digest in one day. From now on, you have to be aware of your stress levels and try to keep them under control as well. I think that monitoring your glucose levels and your blood pressure on a daily basis will assist you in altering your lifestyle. I'm going to give you a chart so that you can record both of your readings everyday and bring them back to me on your next visit, okay?"

"Thanks, doctor. I'll make an appointment to see you again in four months, and I will definitely start exercising more."

"All right, that's it for today unless you have some additional questions for me," Dr. O'Hara stood, waiting for Tina to respond.

"No, doctor, I don't have any more questions. Thank you for your time."

"I look forward to seeing you in four months. If you should have any problems between now and then, feel free to call my office," she stated, turning to leave the room while looking back at Tina.

"All right, Dr. O'Hara thanks again."

Tina slowly slid each arm through her jacket, looking around the room, feeling like she had suddenly entered the twilight zone. Desperately hoping this whole episode was a joke being captured by hidden cameras, she quickly scanned the room searching for the flashing red light. Finally realizing that she wouldn't be that lucky today, she slowly walked out of the examining room. *How could I have both diseases? How am I going to deal with both of these major medical problems? This can't be happening to me. My parents are going to be really upset when they hear this news. I'd better wait until I can tell them in person.*

Tina called Shenedra on her cellular telephone to let her know that she would not be in for the remainder of the day, stopped at the pharmacy for her prescriptions, and then drove straight home. She had to reassure her friend several times that she was all right but just needed to relax in the comforts of her home.

"Tina, do you need me to bring over anything, girlfriend?" Shenedra asked.

"No, I told you, I'm fine. I just need to take it easy for awhile and get my blood pressure down some. You know what all I'm dealing with right now. But don't worry, girl, you'll see me tomorrow."

"I'm looking forward to it. Call me later tonight."

"All right, I'm home now. See you later, bye."

Before exiting her car, Tina leaned her head back against the headrest, *I'm going to take a super long hot bubble bath in the spa tub and just relax by myself for a change. I deserve to have at least one day for myself and today will be the day.*

Upon opening the front door, Tina was immediately met with the sound of loud rap music coming from upstairs. It was so loud that she could even make out the nasty words to the song even though she didn't know who it was, but it sounded like one of those ghetto female rappers. They talked even nastier than the male rappers.

What in the world is going on here? Malique is supposed to be in school, she thought, climbing the stairs making a disgruntled face. She was so angry and upset that her body temperature had already elevated several notches as she mumbled to herself. *This boy better have a darn good excuse for being in my house in the middle of the doggone day. I'm not playing with him either because I need to be relaxing for once.*

Even though the door was closed, Tina was so furious that she didn't bother to knock. Grabbing the doorknob, she quickly turned it to the right, and boldly stepped in the room ready to display a mean and nasty attitude. Tina took two steps into the bedroom and stopped abruptly. Freezing instantly, her eyes almost bulged out of their sockets.

Malique was lying across the bed sideways with his pants bunched around his ankles, and his arms sprawled out to the side. Another boy was in the bedroom on both knees with his face buried between her son's legs. Tina screamed, placed her hands over her pounding chest, and sucked in extra air to keep from losing consciousness. "No! No! I don't believe this! This is not happening in my house!" she yelled, covering her eyes and stomping her feet.

Pushing the boy away from him, Malique jumped straight up, reached down, and quickly pulled up his pants. Appearing to be the same age as Malique, the thin young fella was so shocked that he stumbled to his feet, ran right past Tina without uttering a word, bolted down the steps, and slammed the front door on his way out. Marching over to the portable CD player, Tina pushed the button so hard to turn it off that it tumbled from the shelf, making an awful crashing sound as the CD popped out and rolled around the floor. Turning to look at Malique with fiery eyes, Tina was so consumed with anger that her facial muscles and mouth twitched to the point that she was unable to verbalize her thoughts. Sensing his mother's dilemma, Malique immediately started stammering and pleading with her. "Ma, please—please listen to me. Ma, I—I'm sorry. Ma, I'm really sorry. Please don't tell dad about this," he begged.

"You have some nerve. You're home in the middle of the day, having sex with another boy, and all you can say is you're sorry and don't tell your father!" she shouted, looking at him in bewilderment with her arms folded across her chest. "Are you gay?"

"What? No! I'm not gay. He was just doing me."

"And you think that means that you're not gay! You were involved in homosexual activity! That makes you gay in my book!"

"Well, I'm not gay, ma. This is just something that I wanted to try, and he asked me to let him do it to me. Come on, you know I like the honeys," he said, trying to smile as if this could possibly be humorous to Tina.

"So you're bi-sexual, then?" she asked, looking confused.

"No, ma, I'm a try-sexual. I was just trying something different."

"What is wrong with you? Why in the world would you agree to let another boy go down on you like that?"

"I don't know—I just wanted to see how it felt with another male."

"Get out of my face," Tina replied between clenched teeth, "And get your butt back to school right now. Don't you say another word to me, all right? Get out now!" she screamed, pointing at the opened bedroom door.

"Okay, okay, I'm leaving," Malique said with both hands in the air, backing out of the room. He turned and ran down the stairs without looking back at his mother. Tina couldn't move until she heard the front door slam shut, and then she slowly, meticulously went down the stairs holding the wooden side rails for support.

Chapter 8

With the drop-top down, the sun beaming on her face, and the mellow sound of Maxwell singing, "This Woman's Work," Tina cruised out to her parents' home past the west side of town on Highway 90 heading towards Tallahassee. It wasn't considered the country, but the homes were far enough apart to give each estate a feeling of seclusion. She wanted to make it out there and back before night fall since what was supposed to be a day of relaxation had turned out to be everything except that.

Tina intended on being home tonight to talk with Malique and hopefully talk to Martin about her health as well as his son's sexual behavior. Eliminating stressors in her life was going to be more than a challenge for the middle-aged hairdresser, homemaker, and mother. Instead of reducing the stress in her life it seemed that more was being added on a daily basis. *What could possibly be next?*

Whenever the burdens of city life became too heavy to bear, she could always rely on her stable parents' warm comforting love. They lived only fifteen miles outside the city limits in a huge older Colonial style two-story home with five spacious bedrooms, four full bathrooms, one-half bath, and a four-car garage filled to capacity. Dr. Sloan loved all his vehicles so much that he had to have enough enclosed space to keep them covered. He even employed a mechanic to visit their house on a monthly basis to clean the cars and keep them all running in tip-top condition. He owned a nineteen sixty-five red Ford Mustang sports car, a nineteen eighty white Mercedes Benz sedan, with a new black Lexus LS430 sedan for him, and a brand new silver Mercedes ML500 sports utility vehicle for his wife. Malachi hated the new SUV's and couldn't imagine how anyone would chose that over a luxury automobile, but whatever Delilah wanted is exactly what he got for her.

The house was painted white with black trim including a white picket fence expanding around the entire perimeter of the ten-acre property. With a welcoming, wraparound front porch and a handsome terrace out back, this house offered versatility for outdoor entertaining. Tina enjoyed the benefits of being their only child and having the lavish estate to herself. They had hosted many parties for their daughter inside the house and outside over the years of her development into adulthood. This was also the ground where she'd wed Marty on their special day. The place had been beautifully decorated that day and half the city was in attendance, including the mayor. Not that she really noticed because she only had eyes for Marty on that day.

After turning off the main road, she had to drive almost a quarter of a mile just to pull-up in the front of the house. Tina had called to make sure that her mother was home before making the long drive out there. Detecting the urgency in her daughter's voice over the telephone, Delilah was quick to assure Tina that she was leaving work to meet her daughter for a late lunch at the family house. Although they weren't especially close, she needed her mother's professional expertise today. Her mother considered her to be a spoiled married woman and was usually very straightforward with her advice. Even though Tina didn't appreciate being called "spoiled" or the recipient of the "tough love" techniques that Delilah practiced, she did appreciate the common sense commentary from an older, experienced parent.

Just as she suspected, Delilah was standing in the front doorway, anxiously awaiting her only child's arrival. The small woman was wearing a causal blue pants suit with her graying hair pulled back into a chignon. She greeted her daughter with a smile, a gentle hug, and a kiss before pulling her on into the house. The immense great room featured a fireplace, a media center, and two sets of French doors that opened to the inviting rear terrace. They walked across the tiled entryway through the warm colored living room, decorated in rich browns and turquoise along with several shades of green, and headed into the newly remodeled kitchen. The well-planned area included a built-in desk with an extra telephone line. She had installed all the latest gadgets, including updated stainless steel commercial-grade appliances and natural wood cabinetry. An island bar made it easy to serve casual meals on warm summer days. They each sat in a high back chair pulled up to the Santa Rita granite countertop bar and shared a tall glass of diet soda filled with ice. Looking out the kitchen window, Tina admired the professionally landscaped yard with gorgeous palm trees strategically placed in all the right places.

"Okay, baby, I'm listening. I know you came out here to talk," Delilah stated, crossing her legs, clamping her hands together on the bar after taking a sip of her diet drink.

"Now, what makes you think that I have something to talk about?" Tina asked, smiling at her mother.

"Well, I know that you didn't drive all the way out here in the middle of the week just to check on us, now did you? I also heard the tone of your voice on the telephone. You know, a mother always knows when her child needs help."

"Yeah, you're right, mom. I have a lot on my mind right now, and I really needed to talk to someone that knows me. I don't think that anyone knows me better than you do."

"I certainly agree with you on that. So what's going on? Is there a problem with you and Martin?"

"Yes, Marty and I are having a rough time right now, but that's only a part of what's wrong. I really don't know where to begin, mom. It's like my whole perfect world is crumbling apart before my eyes, and there's nothing I can do to stop it."

"All right, sometimes it seems that way because we don't like for things to change. You know sometimes change is a good thing."

"I know that but in this case it's not," Tina looked down at the folded hands in her lap.

"We're both grown married women. You can tell me anything, Tina."

"I know. It's just not easy to talk to your mother about personal things, you know."

"I guess that means that you're having problems in the bedroom, huh?"

"Well, that's part of it. Martin and I are not getting along too well right now. He's been working late every night and then going out drinking before coming home. Now we can't...we can't even make love anymore because he's impotent. I keep telling him it's from the alcohol, but he won't listen to me. I can't get him to go see his doctor or visit a marriage counselor. I had made an appointment with a male therapist, but he got so upset that I had to call back and cancel the session." Tina let it all out with her mother in one long breath. There was no need in holding back any longer. Heaving a sigh of relief, she relaxed her shoulders, waiting for Delilah to respond to her openness. She had to share this with a woman full of wisdom.

"Oh, baby, that's terrible. I can't believe that Martin is being so stubborn about this. You've got to come up with a strategy to get him to listen to you. There's got to be someway for you to get through his stubbornness. I'm sure that if we put our two heads together, we can think of something. I know that Martin is a reasonable person, we just need to guide him through the darkness into the light."

"Then, I had my physical exam last week with Dr. O'Hara. I went back to see her today for my test results, and the news that I received is not good. She tells me that I have high blood pressure and adult on-set diabetes. Now I have to take two prescriptions every day for that, test my blood glucose levels three times a day, and check my blood pressure daily, too. I mean that's enough to stress a person out right there. She also wants me to keep a record of each reading for the next four months until I see her again."

"Sweetheart, I was hoping and praying that you would not inherit these diseases from your father and me, but at least you've caught them early. With the proper diet modifications and exercise you'll be all right. You're going to have to make some changes and sacrifices in your life immediately. It's not going to be easy given your present state of mind. Once all of this sinks in, you'll realize that you don't have a choice if you want to get better. Then, you can focus on making the proper adjustments. Hopefully, you'll be able to come off both medications with a little time and effort," she stated softly, patting Tina's hand.

"Yeah, I know that. It's just going to be difficult with so much stress in my life right now. I mean the shop is very busy. It's already difficult finding time to exercise and eating right is almost impossible. I haven't even been home to cook a decent meal in I don't know how long."

"Well, nothing is impossible if you plan it out right. You just have to do a better job of planning your work schedule as well as your meals for the sake of your health. Making time to exercise won't be easy, but it's possible to fit it in either early in the morning or late in the evening. You have to get your priorities in order, and as far as I'm concerned, your only priority is your health. I've lived with diabetes all of my life. I've always been a working mother, and I've managed just fine without ever having any household help besides your father."

"Yes, you're right, mom. Maybe I can hire more help at the shop. Shenedra asked me the other day about hiring someone to do the bookkeeping and accounting. Anyway, it's something for me to think about."

"Now what else is bothering you? I know that you haven't told me everything," Delilah said, eyeing her suspiciously.

"Mom, this one is very—I don't know if I should tell you about this one. It's so embarrassing until I'm really ashamed to talk about it."

"Antina Latrice, you can tell your mother anything. We're both grown women, now keep talking, and don't you dare be embarrassed to tell me what's on your mind."

Tina still hesitated while searching for the right words to convey the earlier main event of the day. After a heavy sigh, she finally spoke in a barely audible voice. "When I came home from the doctor's office this morning, I caught Malique upstairs having sex with another boy, and I freaked out over that."

"Honey, when you reach my age, you've heard of everything. I know Malique is only fifteen, and he's confused about a lot of things right now and trying to find his way. You know teenagers experiment with different things sexually."

"But, ma, he was with another boy. I would still be upset if it was a girl but a boy, I can't believe that my son is a homosexual."

"I know, and I understand what you're saying, but listen to me. Now we both know it's wrong, but don't make a big deal about this with him. And please don't try talking to him while you're upset because that will only worsen the matter. Did he tell you that he was a homosexual?"

"No, he didn't. He claimed that he was just trying something different."

"Then don't pressure him about the incident. Trust me, Tina; he's probably embarrassed enough as it is."

"You don't think I should talk to him?"

"Of course, you should talk to him after you have calmed down, just don't make it a major issue, or he will shut down on you completely. I told you, teenagers will try different things when it comes to sex. Keep assuring him that he can come to you and talk to you whenever he's ready to deal with that part of his life, and you must be willing to listen to him without making quick judgments when the time comes."

"How can I not judge him when I know that it's morally wrong, mom?"

"You can let him know that it's wrong without preaching to him, baby. I tell you this—you don't want to lose that child. Give him some space and time. I promise you that he'll come to you when he's ready to communicate. Then you'll have the opportunity to voice your inner feelings," she stated, pausing briefly.

"Now going back to Martin, you have to be really patient with him, baby. This is a very sensitive issue for a man, and you must treat it as such. You can't attack his manhood regardless of how you feel about the situation."

"Mom, this is very frustrating for me. I don't know how much longer I can take this."

"What do you mean by that? You don't have any other choice unless you plan on being unfaithful to your husband, and I know you're not foolish enough to do that."

"Of course, I'm not crazy enough to go that far, but how much longer do I have to go without sex before I become attracted to someone else?"

"Well, you sound like you already met someone, and you're ready to jump into bed with him," she stated with furrowed eyebrows.

"I'm not saying that, mom, my goodness, give me a break will you. It's just that we haven't had sex at all this year. I'd just like to know how much longer I'm supposed to wait."

"Now don't you start talking like that, Antina Latrice. You have to stand by your man, be patient, and wait on him to confide in you about what's troubling him. You have to get to the root of his real problem. The drinking is just a symptom of what's really bothering him…"

"Is that my baby girl's car out there?" Malachi Sloan shouted, entering the kitchen doorway. His tall figure took several long steps in their direction as he reached out for Tina and Delilah. Gracefully giving each of them a peck on the cheek, he then warmly embraced his daughter.

"Yeah, it's me, daddy. How are you?" Tina slid off the high chair and returned her father's tight hug.

"Baby girl, I'm doing fine. I'm doing fine. Are you going to stay and have dinner with us tonight?"

"No, daddy, I can't," Tina said, glancing down at her watch. "I need to get home and check on the boys. They should be home by now."

"Did your mother tell you that we're planning to take the boys with us to Fort Lauderdale the first of May and spend two weeks down there at the time-share duplex?" Malachi asked, walking over to the refrigerator for a drink.

"Yes, she did, and I certainly appreciate that. I know that they're looking forward to it already."

"We're hoping to have a good time visiting family and seeing the sites down there. We'll be gone on your birthday so you don't have to worry about them while you're having that big birthday party you're planning."

"Well, that sounds great. I'm sorry that you and mom will be missing my party, but it sounds like you all will be having a lot of fun."

"That's what we're counting on, baby girl," he replied, hugging Tina again.

"Mom, thanks for all your advice, I'll call you later," she said, standing up and heading towards the living room.

"Oh, baby, that's the reason that mothers were put here on earth," she said, standing up.

Tina stood at the front entrance and hugged both her parents before leaving. Once she was in her car and buckled in, she looked up at her parents and waved good-bye as she pulled out of the long circular driveway. When she checked the rear view mirror, they where still standing in the doorway with their arms wrapped around each other watching her drive away.

"What's going on with our baby girl, Delilah? I know she came out here to talk to you about something," he questioned his wife while she remained silent. "Well, are you going to tell me what's going on or not?" he asked, following Delilah back to the kitchen.

"She's having some problems with Martin and just needed some motherly advice."

"Well, I hope that you told her to divorce that no good husband she married. I don't see what she ever saw in him; he's not good enough for our daughter, I tell you. I don't care how rich he is, he has no home breeding. That man has no idea about how to make my baby girl happy."

"Malachi, Martin has been a good husband to our daughter. You should be grateful that he married her since you have spent so much time spoiling her rotten. It's amazing that any man puts up with her demanding attitude. She's lucky that Martin is rich enough to support the lifestyle you think that she deserves to have."

"I didn't spoil her rotten so that she could spend her life working in a hair salon and married to somebody with no class. She deserves to have a lot more than that, but she'll never get it as long as she's tied down to that punk."

"She's been with him for seventeen years now, and I don't think that she's going anywhere. So you might as well finally accept him and be done with it. Every marriage has its share of problems but that doesn't mean that you have to rush to divorce court. Where would you be if I drew up divorce papers every time we had this argument?"

"Well, I don't have to worry about that, now do I? Is that all she wanted to talk to you about? I really don't want to have another discussion about my imperfect son-in-law."

"No, actually there was something else. She got the results of her physical exam today, and she has high blood pressure and Type-two diabetes. So she was upset about that, too. I guess they both kind of slipped up on her since she has such a chaotic life right now, you know."

"Goodness, Delilah! All of the stress she's been under has finally caught up with her. I was hoping that it wouldn't come to this. She's got to take better care of herself. It might be time for her to let that hair shop go."

"Don't worry, she'll be fine. She knows how to handle herself, you'll see. There's no way that she's going to give up that hair salon though. You're wasting your breath if you even mention that to her. She's enjoyed braiding hair since she was four-years-old."

"Well, I hope she finds a way to make the necessary changes or I'll have a talk with that husband of hers," was all he could manage to say. Malachi turned away from his wife and climbed the stairs to their room. Delilah picked up the two glasses that she and Tina had used and carried them to the sink while praying silently that her daughter's marriage and health would be all right. She wasn't pleased with the way that Tina sounded or looked this afternoon. *Lord, please don't let her do anything stupid where her marriage is concerned*, she prayed. Delilah knew that temptation had ruined many good marriages. Hoping that her daughter would be strong, she vowed to check back with Antina real soon. This situation was too sensitive to let it go unchecked for a long period of time.

Chapter 9

It was dark by the time Tina made it back to her beach estate. After seeing her loving parents and playing soothing music all the way back home, she felt better than she had all day. There was nothing like a long drive with the top down to help clear a sister's head. Her mother's words were deeply etched in her psyche as she recalled all of her advice. Tina hated to admit that her mother was right on every point they had discussed. She needed to be more patient with her husband and her son. They both needed her to be steadfast and nonjudgmental of them. As the mother and the wife, it was her duty to hold the family together no matter what.

The only lights in the house where coming from upstairs. She checked for Martin's car as she pulled into the three-car garage beside her Acura RL. When Tina entered the house tonight it was quiet for a change, so she climbed the stairs to investigate. She opened the door to Jordan's bedroom first and found him sitting on the floor playing a video game. "Hi, Jordan, your mommy is home now."

"Hey, mom," he replied, barely glancing in her direction.

"Did you all eat anything yet?"

"Yeah, Malique made us some ham and cheese sandwiches with potato chips about an hour ago."

"All right then. Are you okay, do you need anything?"

"No, I'm fine, mom."

"Okay, I'll check on you around bedtime."

"Sure, mom," he replied, keeping his attention on the television screen.

Tina walked the few steps over to Malique's room. She decided to knock before entering his bedroom this time as flashes from earlier in the day darted through her mind. He didn't get up to let her in; he just yelled for her to enter the bedroom. "Hello, Malique," she said calmly, walking over to where he was sitting and standing at his side.

"Hi, ma," he replied, sitting at his desk staring at the computer monitor. He was diligently surfing the Internet for something.

"Are your all right? Do you want to talk about what happened this morning?"

"Nope, I sure don't. I'm surfing the net right now for a research paper that's due in my African-American History class tomorrow."

"Well, at some point, we will have to discuss this but let me say something before I leave, okay?"

"Ma, please, can we not do this tonight?" he sounded irritated.

"Look Malique, I know that you don't want to discuss this with me, but I don't want you having sex with boys or girls at this point in your life. Plus, you're too young to be doing sexual experiments. You'll have plenty of time to try different things when you're much older. Do you hear me?"

"Yes, ma'am, I told you that I was sorry about today. I know that I disrespected you and myself. I promise you that it won't happen again, ma."

"Baby, I accept your apology. I want you to come to me whenever you're ready to talk about this further, all right? Now I trust you to do as you say you're going to do so I won't bring this up again."

"All right, ma. I'll see you later."

"Good night, baby," Tina said, turning to leave the room.

She walked down the stairs and went straight to her master bath room remembering that she never did get the long soaking bath that she had planned this morning. While Tina was running the hot water in the tub, she poured a generous amount of vanilla scented bubble bath into the flowing water and lit several candles around the perimeter of the garden tub. She thought about calling Martin and asking him to please come home right this minute so they could talk about her day, but she was tired of begging him for the least little shred of attention. So Tina simply undressed, turned off the water, and then slid into the luxuriously scented bubble bath hoping for some of her troubles to fade away.

Relaxing her head against the small inflatable bath pillow, her mind began to wander into dreamland as she closed her dreary eyes. *Imagining that she was still soaking in the jet tub, she looked up to see Debonair walking towards her through the opened doorway completely naked, except for a luscious, thick burgundy towel wrapped around his midsection. His locks were pulled back into a long ponytail with a few falling around his face, and his skin was glistening like he had showered in baby oil. The fine hairs in the center of his chest were lying flat against his yellow toned skin. He didn't speak and neither did she; they just smiled at one another as he entered the bathroom and gently closed the door. The sparkle in his dark rum eyes told her that he was on a mission to please her in ways that she had never imagined before. Once he licked his lips, her insides were engulfed in flames, burning with sexual desire for him.*

He seemingly floated over to her, knelt down on the side of the huge tub, and wrapped his chiseled arms around her. Then, he took his left hand and placed it under her chin and lightly tilted her face up towards his magnetic eyes. They held that pose for several seconds just gazing at each other as he lowered his face closer to hers. Tina could barely breathe; she couldn't really tell if she was breathing or not because all her breath was suddenly gone from her. She could feel the heat permeating from his lips before they ever touched hers. Suddenly his lips were on top of hers so tenderly that she immediately felt an insatiable hunger for the taste of him. She slightly parted her lips and slipped her tongue inside his mouth, searching for the passionate energy that was exuding from him. They dined on each other's tongues as if this kiss was their last meal, licking each other lips for the tiniest speck of sugar they each could find. Sliding his hands underneath the water, he cupped her slippery breasts while smoothing the soapy suds across her pointed nipples, gently squeezing them. Enjoying the hardness of each nipple between his skilled fingers, he continued massaging her to ecstasy.

Debonair tried to pull his head away from Tina, but she put both hands behind his head and pulled his lips closer to hers as she continued feasting on his sweetness for several more seconds. Finally he reached up, unclenched her tiny fingers, and eased her hands down into the water while he slowly pulled away and stood up. Still looking down at Tina, maintaining eye contact with her, he reached for the side tuck on the towel and ripped it from his waist.

"Tina! Tina! Where are you?" Martin shouted before opening the bathroom door and peeking in. Tina woke up and splashed in the water from being startled by her husband. "Baby, were you sleeping?" he asked, giving her a strange look.

"Yeah, I guess I did fall asleep," she said, sitting up in the tub and staring at Marty with wide eyes, breathing heavy.

"Baby, are you all right? You look funny," Martin asked, looking concerned.

"Oh, I'm fine. You just startled me. You know, I didn't hear you come in."

"Well, I'm home. You can finish your bath because I'm going to bed."

"Martin, wait a minute," she said, getting out of the tub, reaching for her white terry bathrobe. "Marty, I really need to talk to you about something."

"Look Red, I'm tired, and I've had a rough day. So if you don't mind, I'd like to get some sleep, please."

"You're not the only one that had a rough day today, Marty. I went to the doctor today for the results of my tests from last week, and I have high blood pressure and Type-two diabetes."

"What? Baby, I'm sorry to hear that. You're going to be all right, aren't you? What else did the doctor say?" he asked, walking towards her.

"She just gave me a prescription for each condition, told me to monitor my diet and exercise. I also have to check my blood sugar three times a day and take my blood pressure daily."

"Wow, Tina. That's something. I don't know what to say, baby. Is there anything that I can do?" He had his arms around her now.

"Well, there's nothing that you can do for me. I just need your support with eliminating some of the stress out of my life."

"Babe, I'm here for you. Anything that you need me to do is already done."

"It's going to be up to me to monitor my condition. I need to work on maintaining a better diet and putting that state of the art exercise room to good use. But you can talk to your son, Malique," Tina stated, looking up into his face.

"Okay, what's going on with Malique?" he asked with furrowed eyebrows.

"I came home after my doctor's visit today and found him in his room with rap music blaring while having sex with another boy. Actually, the other boy was on his knees giving Malique head while he was sprawled across the bed enjoying himself."

Martin's eyes popped, his bottom lip fell down as far as it could possibly go, staring at Tina in disbelief as he began shaking his head from side to side. "You're kidding me, right? There's no way that I can believe that. Malique has five girlfriends, and you're telling me that he's gay."

"He says that he's not homosexual, and he was just experimenting with this gay guy out of curiosity."

"I see, well, we'll just see about that," Marty stated, marching out of the master bedroom.

When he opened the door, Malique was coming down the stairs carrying a plastic bowl with a few leftover popcorn kernels. Martin stopped right in his tracks as soon as he spotted Malique; he stood there glaring at his son with his arms folded and his nostrils flaring. Malique didn't notice his father staring at him until he reached the last step and then he stopped in place when he saw Martin. His eyes were fixed on his father for two seconds before he glanced over at his mother's startled facial expression. Tina's eyes immediately went to the floor knowing that she had disappointed her son by sharing his personal details with Martin. Malique's eyes suddenly bulged in horror at the sight of them standing there. He didn't know if he should continue his journey to the kitchen or run back up the stairs before either one of them had a chance to respond.

Martin didn't say a word; he just turned on his heels, walked past his son, and headed for the front door. Tina cried out to him, "Marty, where are you going? Marty, come back here now!"

He kept walking out the front door. Malique looked at Tina with hatred in his eyes. "Ma, you told him didn't you? I asked you not to tell him!"

"Malique, he's your father. I had to tell him."

"No, you didn't," he cried, running back up the stairs.

Tina stood there looking shocked at what had just transpired between her husband and her son. She glanced at the front door and then glanced upstairs at Malique's closed bedroom door before turning to go back into her bedroom and closing that door, too. Throwing herself across her king sized bed; she put a pillow over her head to muffle her tears while she cried out in agony.

It had been awhile since Tina had prayed, but she felt that tonight was a good time to kneel and speak to the man above. All of her life she'd had a close personal relationship with the Lord but lately her time had been so consumed with worldly concerns that she hadn't made time for Him either.

Once upon a time she and Martin could have been named the "perfect Christian couple," attending Sunday school and church services every Sunday with their two sons in tow. Now over a year had passed, and neither one of them had seen the inside of a church, nor had they prayed together in several months. Tina missed the solace that she used to receive from the Lord and her husband. Martin had once been a man of deep faith, whom she admired tremendously, and a praying father.

Knowing that she wouldn't be able to make it on this journey alone, Tina began to pray from her heart. *God, how did we get to this point? God, how can we ever get past this hardship in our lives? I need answers and direction from you. My life is falling apart and I don't know what to do. Please save my son and my marriage.* Then Tina took her time and recited the Lord's Prayer before climbing into her bed and pulling the comforter over her trembling shoulders.

All of a sudden, she recalled the detailed fantasy about Debonair. *Oh, God,* she began to pray again while lying in bed. *Please take away any desires that I might have for this younger man and give me back my husband. Amen.*

Chapter 10

"Girl, can you believe that we're in Atlanta, standing on Peachtree Street, getting our shop on?" Taneka glanced from Shenedra to Tina and then back to Shenedra. She was beaming with excitement from being with her girls in one of her favorite places on earth.

They were looking at purses being displayed by one of the street vendors on the sidewalk. Dressed in authentic African attire, he had a whole table lined up with different designer knock-offs. "Hey, look at this Prada purse. It looks just like the real thing," Taneka said, holding up the brown and gold purse for her friends to see. They were all wearing blue jeans, colorful tops, and their designer shades to shield their eyes from the glaring sun. Even though it was late March, the weather was cool enough for them to wear jackets while the sun beamed brightly against their faces. But it had warmed up considerably since their arrival around noon that Thursday.

"It sure does look real," Shenedra said, snatching the small bag from Taneka.

"Let's go to Lenox Square Station where we can do some serious shopping for the real stuff," Tina interjected.

"Well, excuse me, but not everybody can afford to shop at Macy's, Rich's, and Neiman Marcus," Taneka replied, pulling out thirty dollars to pay for the fake purse.

"Yeah, yeah, I hear you. Just pay for your cute pocketbook so we can go to the mall," Tina replied with a hand on one hip.

By the time they made it to the mall, they were all ready to eat and decided to have lunch at Ruby Tuesday's before hitting any of the major stores. They enjoyed themselves while waiting for their orders by chatting and teasing each other the entire time. Shenedra and Tina decided to partake of the salad bar before indulging in their entrees. Taneka skipped the well-stocked salad bar and waited for her food because she had planned on treating herself to a tall order of strawberry shortcake after her meal.

Shopping in all the major department stores was more fun for Tina than her accompanying friends. They mainly watched Tina buy one expensive outfit after another while they encouraged her to keep trying on different clothing. She had a charge card for just about every store that they stopped in and didn't hesitate to use each one of them.

Later that evening, after they had loaded the car down with all their shopping bags, they decided to take in a movie at the Magic Johnson Movie Theatre before retiring for the evening. It was after ten o'clock when they left the theatre heading for their rooms at the Crowne Plaza Hotel. They would have a full day tomorrow at the World Natural Hair Expo filled with classes, hair shows, and entertainment at the Georgia International Convention Center in College Park in the greater metropolitan Atlanta area.

Tina was the first one to rise, take a shower, and get dressed the next morning. She was excited about participating in the natural hair show and creating one of her spectacular hairstyles in front of the other stylists that were coming from all over the country. They had adjoining rooms, but Tina had her own suite while Shenedra and Taneka decided to share a room and split the cost. Tina was used to having her privacy but still wanted to be close to her girlfriends. She leisurely applied her make-up before putting on her new gold and olive stripped georgette tunic set with sheer sleeves and a distinctive crisscross V-neck. The solid gold palazzo pants were lined and felt very comfortable for the long day ahead. Her gold hoop earrings and thick cuffed bracelet perfectly set off her ensemble. She was ready for the day as she left her room to see if her friends were ready for breakfast.

They had all decided to attend separate workshops so that each could focus on their area of expertise. Then they would get together in the afternoon and watch the hair show extravaganza. Since Tina enjoyed doing locks she chose to attend the seminars on doing yarn locks, silky locks, and wrapping locks. Shenedra mainly attended the workshops pertaining to braids and weaves. She wanted to learn how to do the new cobra stitch and infusion weaves with no lumps, bumps or damage to clients' hair. And Taneka loved working with twists so she attended the Senegalese twists and the new kinky twists classes. On Saturday, they were scheduled to have a fashion show, a funky old school jam, and a pool party. Then on Sunday, they would check out of the hotel at twelve and head back to Jacksonville.

"Tina, are you hyped about participating in the hair show and creating one of your original designs?" Shenedra asked, eyeing her best friend after taking a bite of her flaky croissant with strawberry jelly.

"Yes, that is all that I could think about last night. I hope that I can find a volunteer with decent looking locks to work on." Tina had her fork fiddling over her plate of eggs, sausage, and pancakes.

"I know that's right because you can only work so much magic," Shenedra responded, laughing at herself.

"Well, it's almost time for us to get over to the convention center. We don't want to miss our first workshop for the day," Taneka interjected.

"All right, now remember the plan," Tina began, "We're going to meet up for lunch at 1:00 p.m. and then attend the hair show together in the main exhibit hall, right?"

"That is the plan, now let's get going," Shenedra stated.

They all loaded on the free shuttle bus provided for the conference and chatted with other hairstylists as they traveled to their destination. Everybody was dressed to the nines and admiring each other's outfits, hair and make-up. You could hear ladies talking about the shopping they had done or were planning to do before leaving the lovely city this weekend.

It was almost noontime and Tina had attended the three workshops on her list. She was tired because she hadn't slept much the night before, but it was time to meet her friends for lunch. There were so many people in the dining hall that there was no way she could find Shenedra and Taneka for lunch so she just decided to sit wherever she could and eat. Just as she was finishing her meal, Shenedra and Taneka spotted her and they walked to the main exhibit hall together.

Tina sat there squirming in her seat from the fascination of seeing all the beautiful natural hair creations. She was hoping that they would call her number soon before she lost all her nerve as well as her creativity. All of the hair designers had been assigned a number when they registered and the numbers were being called randomly for each stylist to come center stage. They called five at a time and they only had thirty minutes to create a winning style. At the end, when the judges tabulated all the points, the designer with the highest average would receive a one thousand dollar check. Just as she was about to rise to go to the bathroom to freshen her make-up, Tina's number was called.

"Girl, that's your number," Shenedra said, jumping up to hug Tina. "Now get out there and show them what you working with."

"All right, I got this," Tina said with confidence.

Tina walked to her assigned station, picked up the microphone, and requested a volunteer with locks for her creation. Before she could even put the microphone down, she saw a figure approaching her from the left and turned to see the handsome Debonair Jenkins walking towards her booth dressed in all black. She started looking around, trying to figure out where in the world he had come from. It was as though he just materialized right in front of her eyes out of thin air.

"Are you surprised to see me, my lady?" he asked, smiling from ear to ear.

"What are you doing here?" Tina asked with her mouth still opened.

"Well, apparently I was sent here to help you out since you did ask for a volunteer. Now will I suffice, or are you just going to stand there with your mouth open?"

"Boy, just sit down," Tina said, closing her mouth, pointing at the seat.

Debonair sat down per her instructions. Tina instantly started working her magic on his gorgeous long locks that she had twisted and colored deep auburn less than a month ago. Approximately thirty minutes later, she had him sporting a fabulous designer creation. She had divided his hair into three sections in the front and had each of those sections braided in a crisscross style directed to the back of his head. Then she braided several long plaits in the back, took some of those and wrapped them around the others so that he had a thick bun with a few fat braids extending from it. Everyone thought that it was a marvelous quick style.

Even though Tina didn't win any prizes for her creativity, she was delighted that her work could be showcased at such an extravagant event. Shenedra and Taneka were so elated that she even had the nerve to get up there in front of so many people, that they decided to take their boss out to dinner after the hair show. She was still the number one stylist in their book.

"Debonair, are you going to join us for dinner at Anthony's Restaurant?" Shenedra asked, admiring his body hugging outfit.

"Well, if that's an invitation, then the answer is yes. You know, I'm ready to show off my new hairstyle," he replied, rubbing his hand over his hair.

"And just what is that supposed to mean?" Tina inquired, giving him the eye.

"I'm just saying—I want everyone to see your handiwork, my lady."

"All right, you're saved," Tina smiled.

Debonair offered to chauffeur them to the restaurant over on Piedmont Road Northeast. Anthony's was an elegant restaurant housed in a stunning antebellum mansion on three acres in Buckhead, just minutes from downtown. It was definitely the ultimate culinary experience with twelve unique dining rooms providing a scenic view of Atlanta. Tina and Debonair each dined on filet mignon, grilled prime filet of beef with béarnaise sauce, while Shenedra and Taneka each decided on the grilled gingered salmon, seasoned with fresh ginger, and served with lime cream sauce.

After dining on the finest cuisine at Anthony's Restaurant and savoring the first class service, Debonair drove the ladies back to their hotel around eleven o'clock Friday night. As they entered the building, they heard soul music coming from the lounge and decided to go have a drink together. They laughed and talked until it was almost midnight. Debonair did a killer Jamie Foxx impersonation after reciting all the jokes he'd learned from watching BET's Comic View Show nightly. He had memorized some of the best lines from the most popular comedians.

"All right, you guys, I'm going upstairs for the night. You know, I have a young daughter, and I'm not used to these late night hours," Taneka stated, rising from the table.

"Well, I'm walking up with you because I'm beat, too," Shenedra replied, covering her mouth as she yawned.

"I can't believe this," stated Tina, looking at her friends, "Both of you single women are going to bed before me. It's early yet," Tina teased them.

"Yeah, right, Ms. Party-All-The-Time. We'll see you in the morning," Shenedra said, rising to walk out with Taneka.

"Now that just leaves the two of us," Debonair stated, giving Tina an alluring smile.

"Not really because I was just teasing with them. I'm tired, too. I was up most of the night thinking about that hair show."

"Are you sorry that you didn't win?"

"No, I just entered for the fun of it. Although it would have been nice to have a thousand dollars in my pocket right now to help cover some of the shopping that I did today."

"I know what you mean. A thousand dollars looks good anytime. Well, I guess I'll say good night. May I walk you up to your room, my lady?"

"No, thank you. Tell me, what are you doing in Atlanta?"

"Honestly, I heard you talking about coming here for the hair show and just decided to drive up by myself to see what would happen."

"Is that right? You weren't planning to meet me here?"

"No, I wasn't planning on it, but I was hoping that I would see you or run into you while I was here."

"Yeah, right."

"Look, Tina. I wouldn't be a gentleman if I didn't walk you to your door."

"All right, but don't even think about an excuse for entering my room."

"Hey, I promise," he said, raising both hands in the air, laughing at himself.

They took the elevator to the second floor where Tina's room was located. Even though there weren't any other people on the elevator, they were standing very close to each other with their bodies almost touching. She could smell his cologne and the essence of his body blended with the woodsy scent he was wearing. Tina recognized the fragrance of Issey Miyake cologne as being one of her favorite male scents and she was becoming intoxicated by it. As they stood side by side, both staring at the elevator doors, Tina clutched her purse because she needed something to do with her hands. The thought of reaching out to feel his warm scented body was slowly driving her to the brink of madness.

When the doors to the elevator opened, Tina snapped to attention, and quickly stepped out into the hallway. She was walking briskly, not looking back to see if Debonair was on her heels or not. As she approached her room, she took out the key card, slid it through the slot, and opened the room door. But before entering the room, she turned to speak to him. "Debonair, thanks for helping me out today."

"It was my pleasure," he replied, stepping closer to her, easing his right arm around her waist. "Did I tell you how beautiful you look today, my lady? You are glowing in that olive and gold outfit," he whispered lightly in her ear.

"Ah, thank you," she replied, gasping for air and swallowing. She took a step back, gently pushing his arm away. "Good night, Debonair."

"Good night, Tina. I'll see you tomorrow," he said as he placed an index finger to his lips, kissed it, and then he pressed that same moist finger to her lips.

Tina quickly backed into her room and closed the door in a prideful attempt to resist the dreamy young man. She walked to the sink and splashed cold water on face, wanting to believe that she was dreaming. But after realizing that she was wide awake, she started undressing and thinking to herself. *What am I going to do about this man? I can't sleep with him. I will not sleep with him. I hope that I don't even see him tomorrow.*

Chapter 11

The Saturday workshops were basically a continuation of the ones from the previous day, and they lasted for another half a day. During the lunch hour, they had an Ebony Fashion Fair Show featuring the latest clothing by some of the top African-American designers in the business. Tina, Shenedra, and Taneka were able to get a front row seat at a table together for this event. They shared their comments, along with the professional commentator regarding each garment displayed.

Later that day, they had an old school concert starring Maze featuring Frankie Beverly in the main gathering area of the convention center. The band stayed on stage for over two hours and the crowd still wanted more so the group came back and played for almost another hour before leaving the stage for the evening. They could have listened to Frankie and the band donning their signature white outfits, sing all night because he sung everybody's favorite tune. Tina stayed on her feet for most of the concert swaying from side to side, clapping her hands along with the mellow music, but she really broke out in a dance when they performed, "Before I Let You Go," for the last song.

It was almost 9:00 p.m. by the time they made it out of the concert. Of course, they were all famished by now and decided to look for a place to eat.

"Well, ladies, where would you all like to dine?" Shenedra asked, opening her car door.

"I heard about a great Caribbean restaurant on Auburn Avenue Northeast, but I can't remember the name of it. Do you know what I'm talking about, Shenedra?" Taneka asked, climbing in the back seat.

"Yes, I believe I do. It's not that far from here if that's where you all want to go," she started the car and then looked over at Tina.

"That's fine with me," Tina replied.

The Caribbean restaurant served the best jerk chicken, curry chicken, and brown stew chicken that they had ever tasted. The peas, rice, and cabbage were absolutely delicious. They also had plenty of Jamaican ginger soda to go with their dinner. It had taken them almost an hour to be served and finish eating, but they all left completely satisfied.

Leaving the restaurant shortly after 10:30 p.m., they noticed a line of sharply dressed people waiting to get inside the club upstairs.

"That sounds like reggae music," Tina stated with enthusiasm in her voice.

"It sure does. Let's go see what's going on," Shenedra replied, walking in that direction.

Tina touched a lady standing in line, who looked to be about thirty-years-old, on the shoulder, "Excuse me, Miss. Do you know the name of this club?"

"Yes," the lady replied, "It's *Royal Peacock*, and it's a reggae dancehall style club. It opened at ten o'clock but the party doesn't start until after midnight," she added with a wide smile.

"Well, what time does it close?"

"Honey, it doesn't close until four in the morning, and they keep it pumping the whole time, too. But it's really packed tonight for the 'Reggae Jam Down,' the lady replied, bopping her head.

Once they finally made it inside *the Royal Peacock*, it was standing room only. The music was so loud you couldn't even hear your own thoughts, but they loved it. Tina looked around the club noticing the four walls splashed with the signature Rastafarian colors of red, yellow, and green. Flags representing island nations flowed from the ceiling of the dimly lit, incense-filled dance hall to create a genuine Caribbean party feel. They offered tropical libations and island beers to top off the theme.

There was hardly any room on the wide-opened dance floor so Tina and her girlfriends just danced with each other right where they stood. Tina had her eyes closed while she was swaying to the music and lip synching to the familiar songs. When she opened her eyes a few seconds later, she had to blink several times before she was able to focus on the smiling face of Debonair Jenkins who was dressed in white from head to toe. Tina even reached up, briskly rubbing her eyes, not believing that his fine body had materialized in front of her again. She tried to speak to him, but the music was too loud for either one of them to hear.

He just eased closer to Tina, moving to the rhythm of her body as she loosely grooved to the music. They danced non-stop for almost two hours, bumping and grinding with each other to the sounds of the gritty reggae music. He held Tina's hips with both hands as he gently swayed his torso against hers in sync with the beat.

Quickly realizing that she was dancing with temptation, Tina told herself that she was in control of her libido and it was only a dance.

So she continued rubbing her sweaty body against Debonair's, imitating some type of dance hall steps that could have easily been filmed for a video clip.

Seconds later, Debonair placed his arms around her upper parts and then slowly brought his hands down over her sweaty forearms. Tina's body was so wet that her white satin, above the knee strapless dress, with the flirty bottom was adhering to her baby soft skin. Showing off her muscular dancer legs, Tina did a two-step tango with her talented partner as if they were the only couple on the crowded dance floor.

Dancing provocatively to every tune with Tina, Debonair moved his agile body gracefully to the pulsating reggae beat. They were both tired and sweaty by the time they left the dance floor around one o'clock in the morning. He had removed his white coat and loosened the collar around his satin white shirt. Since Tina was so exhausted that she couldn't keep the beat anymore, she finally took Debonair by the hand, leading him outside into the fresh cool air. Shenedra and Taneka swiftly followed them out into the open parking area.

"What are you doing here?" Tina asked, suspiciously eyeing her dance partner, noticing the sweat dripping from his handsome forehead.

"Well, I thought that I was dancing with you," he replied, sounding cocky.

"I mean — how did you know that I would be here?"

"I didn't know. This just happens to be one of the best clubs in Atlanta. I always party here when I'm in town."

"Yeah, right, I believe that."

"I'm serious, but if you want to believe that I'm following you then so be it. I'm just glad I got to see you again. You were amazing on that dance floor."

"Well, I like reggae music, too. You see I knew every song."

"Hey, I was impressed. I thought the only music that you listened to was Maxwell."

"Now you know, don't you?"

"I guess I do. Listen, do you ladies need a ride to your hotel?" he asking, looking at Shenedra and Taneka.

"No, I drove my car tonight," Shenedra replied.

"Are you two ready to go or do you all want to go back inside?" Tina asked.

"Girl, there's no way you'll get me back inside that club. I cannot hang with these Atlanta party folks," Taneka said laughing.

"Well, I'm with you on that one, and I'm ready if you all are," Shenedra added, searching in her purse for the car keys.

"I'm definitely done. I haven't stayed out this late in years," Tina stated.

"All right, ladies. I'm going back inside for a little while longer. What time are you all leaving tomorrow?" Debonair asked Tina.

"We're checking out around twelve and heading straight to Jax."

"Then I'll see you all back in Jacksonville next week," he leaned over and lightly hugged Tina and then said good night to Shenedra and Taneka. He walked away from them and headed back towards the club.

On the ride to their hotel, Shenedra and Taneka both teased Tina about the way she was dancing with Debonair. "Girl, what was up with you and Mr. Debonair at the club tonight? You two were so close together I couldn't tell where you end and he began," Shenedra laughed.

"Child, please, he is just a boy. What would I want with him?"

"Hello, he is not a boy, and I know that you are not blind, Tina."

"No, I'm not blind, I'm just married."

"Okay, Ms. Married Lady. That fine young thang has the hots for you, and that I know. Taneka and I don't even exist when you're around him. He stares at you like you're a king sized chocolate candy bar."

"Oh, whatever," Tina said, waving her hand. "He's just a good friend and I know that he's probably infatuated with me, but I can handle that."

"I hope so because I don't want you to break his heart."

"Girl, please, he's probably got five or six girlfriends right now."

"That's true, I would certainly believe that," Shenedra said. Taneka had already fallen asleep in the back seat.

Once they made it safely back to their hotel rooms, Tina headed straight for the bathroom. She had sweated so much at the dance hall until she was desperate for a soapy lukewarm shower. It was a really quick one being that she was exhausted from the day's events. Sitting naked on the side of the bed, she spread creamy cocoa butter lotion over her entire body before slipping on a short silky animal printed night gown. Listening to the smooth rhythm and blues station on the radio, she wrapped her hair up into a black night scarf.

Tina lay on top of the bedspread, meditating on the melodic voice of Brian McKnight singing, "Anytime," when she heard a light tapping at the door. Slightly raising her head, she listened for a second but didn't hear anything, so she laid her head back down. Then she heard the light tapping sound again.

Tina reached for her robe and put it on before she tipped over to the door. "Who is it?" she whispered.

"Tina, it's me, Debonair."

"What?" she asked, cracking the door open. "What are you doing here?"

"I'm sorry for disturbing you, but I really would like to talk to you."

"Look, it's very late, and we can talk tomorrow."

"Please, it'll only take a few minutes, I promise."

Tina hesitated and then against her better judgment, she pushed the door on open and told him to come in. He slowly entered the room with his hands in his pockets; he turned to look at Tina as she eased the door shut. Debonair sat down on the side of the bed facing the door as Tina walked over and stood in front of him with her hands at her side. "Well, what is it that you want to talk to me about?" she asked in an even tone. "It's almost two o'clock in the morning."

"I have to tell you how I feel about you. My feelings for you won't let me wait for you any longer," he whispered, looking up at her serious face. "You see, I'm falling—I'm falling in love with you, and I can't help myself."

"Debonair, please, don't do this."

He gradually stood up, placed his arms around her shoulders, and tightly pressed his body against hers before whispering, "Do you feel that, Tina? Do you feel how rapidly my heart is beating for you? Do you feel my throbbing hardness against you?"

Tina couldn't speak. She could feel his heart pounding against her chest and his manhood pressing between her legs. Tina had missed being held and feeling the hardness of a man against her aching, love-starved body. She returned his hug as they embraced each other and then slowly dissipated into his arms with tears in her eyes. As much as she really wanted to stop, it was useless to think that she could. The point of no return had already been crossed, and it was too late to reverse her burning libido.

"I'm crazy about you, Tina. I think about you all during the day, and I dream about you all during the night. I can't get you out of my mind. I constantly think of you," he said softly. "I know that you're attracted to me, and I think that you're the most beautiful woman that I have ever seen at any age."

Tina stood still with her eyes closed and head tilted upward, clenching his shirt at the waist with both hands to keep from falling. Debonair gently licked from her lower neck all the way to the top of her forehead without stopping as Tina began shivering.

"I want to see your magnificent body," he said, sliding her light silky robe and her thin nightie off her shoulders. "Tell me whatever you want tonight. I'll do anything you tell me to do for as long as you want me to do it."

Calmly pushing the garments down as he lowered himself down with them, he kissed her tingling body all along the downward journey. Bending on his knees, he reached up for her black satin panties and slowly eased them over her round buttocks, her thighs, her knees, and then her ankles as she stepped out of them. His face was level with her moist center; he inhaled her natural feminine scent and smiled with pleasure as he looked up at her contorted face. Tasting the object of his desire, Debonair savored her unique flavor.

Tina, being too weak to speak or to stand any longer, turned her body and eased down onto the bed. Thinking that she might lose consciousness from the intensity of the moment, she leaned up slightly on her elbows to watch Debonair undress his masculine muscle filled body.

Looking down at her, he promptly unbuttoned his shirt, and then tossed it to the floor. He slid his pants and underwear down then stepped out of them. Laying his naked body on the bed beside Tina, he looked into her watery eyes. They were both propped up on their elbows with their heads turned towards each other as they engaged in a kissing contest, feeling the fire from their tongues while their minds soared to blissfulness. Suddenly he rolled over and straddled Tina, took her face into his hands, and leisurely sucked her rosy cheeks prior to moving on down to her swollen C-cup breasts.

Tina's hands roamed over his solid back, down to his firm butt and onto his muscular thighs, searching for the male stiffness that her body was so desperately craving. Not wanting to make her wait any longer, Debonair gently raised up her legs and put one on each of his shoulders before connecting their bodies together. He succulently licked around her ankles in a circular motion while easily stroking back and forth. "Baby, I'm not going to stop until you tell me to, until you beg me to," Debonair declared.

Moments later, Tina squeezed his torso and pulled him deeper into her wet mound, releasing all the frustrations that she had felt over the last three months. Then, she softly begged him for more as he willingly complied with her wishes. Once they were both expended again, he skillfully moved his sweaty body to her side, collapsing onto the bed.

After minutes of heavy breathing and trying to catch their breath, they passionately kissed each other over and over again. Neither wanted the night of joy and pleasure to come to an end.

"Tina, ever since the first day I saw you walk in the coffee house four months ago, I've wanted to be with you," Debonair stated, holding Tina in his arms.

"Is that why you were flirting with me everyday?" she teased.

"Yes, it is. It was innocent and playful at first but over time, I really started to care about you and looked forward to seeing you come in every morning. I didn't understand how one little lady could hold so much coffee," he joked, letting out a slight laugh.

"I love my coffee, and I have to have it every morning as soon as I get to work."

"I tried to contain myself every time I saw you. Even while I was driving here this weekend, I thought that I would be able to admire you from a distance. Then when I saw you in need of a volunteer for your hair show, I had to step to the plate."

"Well, thank you for being my knight in shining armor."

"No problem, my lady," he responded, kissing Tina on the forehead while holding her hand. He brought her delicate manicured fingers to his mouth and sucked each one of them like a cherry Popsicle melting deliciously down his throat. Tina's fingertips were hypersensitive from sticking them with a needle three times a day to test for her diabetes so this particular move really heightened her euphoria. She was tingling and shivering with desire as she eased herself up on top of him, lowering her breasts down to his face. Tina watched as Debonair caressed and licked each one going back and forth between the two until she was ready for him to satisfy her again. She gently straightened her back, placed both his hands over her protruding chest, and traveled with him to ecstasy as he sweetly moaned her name several times.

After their third climax together in less than ninety minutes, Tina was exhausted. She rolled over on the bed face down as Debonair continued kissing her back and shoulders, trailing kisses all the way down to her tingling spine and then coming up again to engulf her earlobes with his hot lips. He turned her body over to face him as he gathered her into his warm embrace, not wanting to let her go. Every time she moved in the bed, he moved right along with her and never let her out of his arm's reach.

Another hour and a half passed before he woke up and stared down at Tina's somber face. Knowing that this might be their one and only night together, he had to feel her heat again. Rubbing his hands all over her flaming upper thighs, he quickly found the moistness between her legs that he'd help to create. Tina was still in a dreamlike state, but she could feel the pleasure flowing through her body again as she squeezed his neck and moved her body in sync with his finger rhythm.

Just as she opened her mouth to let out an orgasmic sound, he placed his lips over hers, taking her voice away with his passionate kiss as he felt her twitching in his hand. Feeling completely relieved, Tina relaxed in his arms for the remainder of the short night. She was too overwhelmed with passion to feel the slightest twinge of guilt from her adulterous actions.

Relaxing his body beside hers, Debonair began drifting into a quiet sleep with the scent of Tina on his body and the taste of her in his mouth. He was more satisfied at this moment than he'd ever dreamed of being with anyone. Hoping that this was the beginning of a truly romantic relationship, he didn't let the fact that she was married cross his mind or his heart. All that mattered was the fact that they were here together in a city famous for making fabulous dreams come true.

Chapter 12

"Thanks for bringing me home Shenedra," Tina said, taking her bags from the trunk of her best friend's car. "I'm sorry that I wasn't much company on the trip back. I was just really tired and needed to get a nap."

"Hey, you don't have to tell me. I think that we're all very tired and deserve to have the day off tomorrow. I know that I have a lot of things that need to be done around my house."

"Well, I have a lot that needs to be done around here, too, but I'm planning on getting plenty of rest tomorrow. At least we made good time coming back—it's only seven o'clock."

"Yeah, it's still early. You can call me later tonight or just call me whenever you get up tomorrow so we can chat, all right?" Shenedra asked, slamming down the trunk of the car.

"I'm just glad that it didn't rain the entire trip back," Tina stated.

"Yeah, I am, too. But it's looking like we're going to get some rain here tonight," Shenedra responded, glancing up at the evening storm clouds.

"I don't care. It can rain as hard as it wants to tonight. That way I'll really get a sound night of sleep."

"I know that's right. Girl, tell Taneka good-bye so we can get home before it starts storming," Shenedra said, walking Tina back around to the passenger's side of her car.

Tina reached up and hugged her girlfriend good-bye then reached in the car and hugged Taneka good-bye, too.

Pretending to be asleep, Tina had been thinking about the previous night on their ride home. She was the first one in the car after they checked out of the hotel around 12:00 p.m. wearing her comfortable stretch jeans and blue knit jersey top so she would be comfortable in the back seat. Sure, she was tired and exhausted, but she also wanted an excuse to be quiet long enough to think about her night of passion with Debonair Jenkins, deliberating over what the possible consequences could be for her marriage. While she did feel guilty, she couldn't help but feel a sense of total satisfaction, for he had stirred desires in her that she thought were gone forever. He took his time, asked her what she liked, and then proceeded to do whatever she wanted. Debonair didn't mind taking directions. He was like a willing student behind the steering wheel on his first day in a driver's education class, and she was the domineering instructor. The young man was delighted to move as slow or as fast as she wanted to go, hit the brakes whenever she said, and turn left or right at a second's notice. Her toes were still tingling from the amazing sensations he had awakened in her dormant body.

"Mom, mom, I'm glad you're home," Jordan said, running to hug Tina the instant she opened the front door.

"Well, thank you. I'm glad to see you, too," she replied, hugging him back, and kissing his face.

"Dad made dinner, and he said that we couldn't eat until you got here."

"Oh, he did? That's wonderful, baby. What did he make for us?"

"Ah, he made spaghetti, Italian garlic bread, and corn on the cob. And I'm hungry."

"Yeah, well, I am, too," Tina walked with Jordan to her bedroom and tossed her bag inside the door. They strolled towards the kitchen together arm and arm, smiling at each other.

Martin was wearing his white chef's apron over his blue jeans and short sleeved T-shirt as he looked up at Tina and Jordan entering his domain. "Hey, babe," he said, putting down a glass, walking towards his wife and son. "I'm glad you're home."

"Well, what a nice surprise. I wasn't expecting you to be home, and I certainly wasn't expecting you to have a hot meal prepared."

"You know, we don't always get what we expect, sometimes we get more and sometimes we get less," he said, placing his arms around Tina, lightly squeezing her.

"How long have you been in here cooking, Marty?"

"It only took me a couple of hours to pull this little meal together. It's no big deal."

"All right, Mr. No Big Deal. I'm going to go wash up, and then I'll set the table for us to eat in the dining room tonight," she said, giving him a peck on the cheek.

"That's cool, baby, because I am ready to get down tonight on my special secret recipe homemade spaghetti," he bragged and clapped his hands one time.

"Jordan, baby, go upstairs and tell Malique that it's time for him to come down to eat dinner with us," Tina instructed him, pointing toward the stairs.

"Okay, mom. I'll be right back because I'm really hungry," he whined, running for the stairway.

"Look, baby," Martin said, pulling Tina into his arms, "After dinner, we'll take a bubble bath together and spend a relaxing evening in our room. How does that sound?"

"Ooh baby, that sounds wonderful," Tina replied, wrapping her arms around his waist, pulling him closer to her as they shared a quick kiss.

The meal was delicious as Tina knew that it would be. The one thing that her man could make perfectly every time he stepped into the kitchen was spaghetti. She decided to make this a special family night by having everyone eat in the formal dining area. Tina even set the table using the real china instead of the paper plates they normally ate from every night.

Dinner went as smoothly as she could have hoped considering the tension she felt between Malique and Martin. She wondered if anything had transpired between those two since she left but didn't dare to bring up the subject. Malique was pretty quiet for the whole meal and only spoke when he was spoken to and even then he only replied with very short answers. He kept his head turned downward towards his food and barely made eye contact with anyone.

Tina was just so thrilled to be home with her family and having a meal with all of them together that she didn't want anything to spoil the mood. She kept going around the table, trying to pull everyone into a lighthearted conversation while she nibbled on her food.

Malique was the first one to finish his dinner so he politely stood and asked to be excused. Tina didn't really want him to leave that soon, but she gave him permission to exit the dining room. She would have to talk with him again privately so they could move on away from this episode in their lives. Tina had made a decision to adhere to her mother's advice as far as Malique was concerned, only she wasn't sure if Marty would feel the same. She was positive that the embarrassment from being found with another male and then having his parents find out, was punishment enough for now.

Shortly after Malique left the dinner table, Jordan finished his food and also asked to be excused. So Marty and Tina quickly cleared the table, placed the dirty dishes in the automatic dishwasher, turned it on, and then headed for their bedroom.

Entering the dimly lit bedroom, Tina stopped the second she spotted the dozen long stem yellow roses in a box laying on her side of the bed. "Oh, Martin, you didn't have to do this. Baby, this is so sweet," she said, picking up the roses, inhaling their fragrant scent.

"Well, nothing is too good for my, baby. You know that, don't you, Red?"

"Yes, Marty, I know that, and I appreciate you very much."

"And I appreciate you being patient with me for the last few months, too. But I have something to tell you."

"Yeah, what is it, Marty? Is it good news?"

"Yes, I think so. I went to see Dr. Chatman for a physical exam on Friday, and you were right. He thinks that my impotence is due to the fact that I've been drinking more lately. He advised me to join a local chapter of Alcoholics Anonymous. So, ah, I'm not drinking anymore, and I've decided to attend AA meetings on Tuesday nights at 6:00 o'clock."

"Oh, Marty!" Tina exclaimed, tightly hugging his neck, "Baby, that is good news. I am so proud of you."

"Thank you, thank you," he replied hugging her back. "But look, ah, I'm going to run us that bubble bath that I promised you, all right?"

"Sure, baby. Let me get undressed, and I'll be right in," Tina replied, suppressing the guilty feelings creeping through her veins. She needed a few minutes to gather her composure before engaging in intimacy with her spouse. *What if he's able to tell that I've been with someone else?*

"Okay, take your time. I'm not going anywhere," he stated, walking towards the master bathroom.

Sharing a lovely long hot bubble bath, Marty held Tina in his arms, whispering sweet words in her ears. "I missed you this weekend. I'm glad you're home, babe," he cooed, tickling her breasts.

"Me, too," she replied in a sultry tone. Reaching her hands backwards to embrace his neck, she pulled his face closer to hers. Martin leisurely washed every inch of her body with the soft bath sponge and then helped her rinse away all the soap. He had rose scented candles of various sizes burning throughout the bathroom as they relaxed in the water until all the bubbles disappeared. Slowly, they exited the tub and dried each other off with fresh towels before making their way to the bedroom holding hands.

They stood on the side of the bed, holding each other's faces in their hands while searching for each other's quivering lips. Marty kissed Tina all over her face several times before he moved down to her neck and began nibbling on it passionately.

"Baby, baby, I want you. I want you right now, Red," Marty whispered.

"I want you, too, Marty," she responded.

"Baby, let's get in the bed and make this happen," he said, pulling back the covers as Tina climbed into the bed and then he eased in behind her. They resumed their kissing feast while their hands roamed each other's body as far as they could reach.

After more than thirty minutes of foreplay, Marty gave up on the prospect of making love with his wife tonight. He sighed loudly in disgust, "I don't believe this! I have never wanted you more in my life, and I can't do it."

"Baby, it's all right. Please don't worry about this. Its okay, Marty, you can just hold me close, and I'll be satisfied," she stated, resting her head in his arms. Secretly, Tina was rather relieved that they hadn't made love. She was worried that Marty might somehow be able to tell that she'd been unfaithful if they had actually had sex tonight.

"No Tina. This is not right."

"Marty, what do you mean, this is not right? It's going to take some time to get the alcohol out of your system before you can resume your normal sexual activity. Let's just be patient."

"That's not what I'm talking about, Tina," he said, sitting up on the side of the bed, holding his head in his hands.

"Well then, what are you talking about, Marty? Please tell me what's going on so that we can deal with this," Tina stated as she moved to sit beside him on the bed and placed her arm around his shoulders.

"It's not that easy. It's just not that easy. If I tell you why I'm really like this, you might leave me."

"Why would I leave you, Marty? I would never leave you. Baby, you can tell me anything. Believe me, you can tell me anything."

"I know that, Tina, and I know it's time that I told you the truth," he said, staring deeply into her eyes.

"You know it's time to tell me the truth about what, Martin?" she asked, eyeing him suspiciously, not knowing what to think.

"I have to tell you the truth about my past. Now I just need you to listen and let me get this out before I lose my courage."

"Okay, Martin, I'm listening, I won't say another word until you're done."

"I lied to you about my family when we first met. I told you that both of my parents were dead and that was a lie; I told you that I was an only child and that was a lie. I told you that I didn't have any family living here in Jacksonville, and that was a lie, too."

"Oh, my Lord!" Tina exclaimed, quickly covering her mouth.

"I'm sorry, baby. I'm sorry for lying to you during our entire relationship. But after meeting your bourgeois family and seeing where you lived, I couldn't tell you the truth. It was easier to tell you a lie, and eventually, I started to believe the lie myself." Martin could tell that Tina wanted to intervene and ask questions, but he held up his hand for her not to speak as he continued his story. "Now what I told you about my mother was the truth. She was killed in a car wreck shortly after my eighteenth birthday. But my father wasn't in the car with her like I told you. He had already deserted us nine years prior to that. You see, I was nine when he left and my brother, Walter, was eleven. Anyway, after daddy left us, mama had to work two jobs just to keep a roof over our heads, and then Walter turned to the street life. He moved out when he was about sixteen and got a place with some of his hoodlum drug dealing friends. But after mama passed, I never saw him or my daddy again," he stopped talking and just looked at Tina, waiting for her to react to his words.

"Martin, I don't know what to say. I'm absolutely speechless."

"I know that this is a lot to digest, but that's why I've been having these nightmares lately, too. Almost every other night for the last four months, I've been dreaming about mama and daddy. I can hear them arguing really loud and throwing things at each other in the living room of that old apartment we had in the projects. I can't make out what they're saying, but I know they're both angry and yelling at each other. Then, I hear the front door slam really hard. I mean it slams so hard that the entire complex is shaking. Then mama starts crying and calling daddy's name like she's in serious pain. I'm lying in my twin bed with the covers pulled over my head, too scared to move and go help her. I'm just lying there in my bed crying like a baby until I can wake myself up."

"Martin, I had no idea that you were having these nightmares."

"I started drinking more after each dream, trying to make it go away, but it kept coming back. Now that's it. That's everything about my past that I didn't tell you before we were married."

"Marty, I'm sorry that you didn't feel like you could tell me this when we first met each other. But, baby, we've been together for seventeen years. You don't trust me by now?"

"Yes, I do trust you. I was just never able to tell you this because I was so afraid of losing you. And then, after awhile, it didn't matter to me. It really didn't matter to me because it felt like they were really dead. I hate to say that, but that's just how it felt."

"So what about your other family here in the city? Do you know where they are?"

"Not really. My mother has a sister that lives here. Her name is Rhoda Ingrams, but I haven't seen her since my mother's funeral. She never got married, but she used to work as a nurse's aide at the same nursing home with my mama. She had two children and both of them were older than me. Her son's name was Ethan, and her daughter's name was Susan. We used to all play together when we were kids, but they had both moved away by the time I graduated from high school. And, ah, as far as my daddy is concerned, he moved here from some part of North Carolina, and we never met any of his family. I figured if I changed my last name and pumped up my thin body, no one from my past would recognize me."

"Martin, this is an incredible story. I am just shocked to think that you have been living with this for all this time. This is unbelievable."

"Well, that's still not the end of the story, baby. I saw my father about a month ago."

"What did you say?"

"I saw my father last month at the bar where I hang out after work. He had been in there asking about me, and the bartender told me about it. Then a few nights later, he showed up at the bar, and I confronted him."

"You did? And what did he say?"

"He didn't say very much—not very much at all. He claimed that he just wanted to see his children again."

"You don't believe him, Marty?"

"Hell no, I don't believe him. You know he wants money or something. Even though he didn't mention that—that's got to be it."

"Well, what about your brother, Walter?"

"What about him?"

"Well, where is he now? Do you know?"

"The last I heard, he was a junkie living on the streets around the city or staying in the homeless shelters whenever he could."

"Marty, that's terrible. You mean to tell me that you haven't tried to help your brother, and he's living right here in the same town as us?" she asked, sounding disappointed in her husband.

"I didn't know how to help him, Tina. What was I supposed to do, bring him here so he could steal from us to support his habit? I don't think so."

"You didn't have to bring him here, but you could have helped him get some type of treatment."

"Tina, you can't help people unless they want to be helped. You think he wants to be rehabilitated? If he wanted that, he would be clean by now and trying to live a decent life. I'm just surprised that he hasn't been here begging for money."

"Marty, what are you going to do? I want to know what you plan to do about this. Our sons need to know their history."

"I know, babe. I know you're right. And I've decided to see my father again if he hasn't left town already."

"What did he say that he's been doing all these years? Did he tell you why he left like that?"

"Well, he said that he's basically been a rolling stone all of his life and was unable to settle down with any one woman. He tried it with mama, but it didn't work out, and he had to leave us."

"That is just—that is just, I can't even say it."

"I know, Tina. There's nothing to say."

"What is your father's name?

"His name is Ezekiel Harrison."

They sat on the side of the bed in silence for several minutes, each engaged in their own train of thoughts. Finally, Marty spoke, "Tina, I don't want you to leave me behind this."

"I'm not leaving you, but this is a lot to deal with right now. How could you live a lie for seventeen years with your sons and me? Every time that I asked you about your family, you outright lied. I'm your wife, I deserve better than that, Marty."

"I know. I know you do. Please try to understand how I was feeling at the time. I was still dealing with a lot of hurt and pain. Your father already didn't like me. I figured if he knew about my past, he'd convince you not to marry me."

"Don't you know better than that? There was nothing that my father could have said to stop me from marrying you."

"Do you really mean that, baby?"

"Yes, I mean it, but it's going to take some time for me to accept that you could be so deceitful."

"I didn't think that I was being deceitful. I was just protecting you all from the ugly past that I had."

"You should have told me, Martin. You should have told me long before now. What are we going to tell the boys?"

"I haven't figured that out yet. I have to talk to Ezekiel and see where his head is before I involve my sons in this mess."

"Your sons are already involved. Can't you see that? They have living family members that they don't even know exist right here in Jacksonville. God forbid if they should happen to date one of their cousins and not even know it."

"Baby, I'll make this up to you. I promise." Marty said, reaching for his wife. Feeling unable to return the embrace, Tina swiftly stood and made her way into the bathroom with a sheet wrapped around her body. She needed some time alone to deal with her own guilt and deceitfulness as well as Martin's startling confession.

Chapter 13

A few minutes past five o'clock on a lovely Friday afternoon, Martin rang the bell for service three times at the Motel Six on the south side of town. He was about to say forget it and walk away but quickly changed his mind. Martin decided to follow through with the real reason that brought him to the motel on this bright, spring April Fool's Day. Well, he certainly felt like a real fool for coming to this side of town just to see a man that deserted him over thirty years ago. What could he possibly gain from another conversation with his father?

Martin hadn't been able to fully concentrate on his job since confiding in Tina about his family problems four days ago. So he left work a little earlier than usual today heading straight to the motel wearing his charcoal gray business suit. Marty was relieved when a tall lanky gentleman suddenly entered the room.

"Yes sir, may I help you? Are you looking for a room today?" the clerk asked. The tall super thin man greeted Martin with a wide smile across his copper toned face.

"I don't need a room for me, but I am here looking for someone. Can you help me out with that?"

"Well, who are you looking for?"

"I'm looking for Ezekiel Harrison. He's an older black man, around sixty, and he's about my height with a much smaller build. He told me about a month ago that he was staying at this motel. Is he still here?"

"Ah, yes sir, I believe he is. Let me call his room and see if he's in there."

Martin waited patiently while the motel clerk rung Ezekiel's room and informed him that someone was at the front desk looking for him. "Sir, he's in room one-twenty-six, and he said to tell you to come on around."

"All right, thank you very much for your time."

"You're welcome, sir."

Martin thanked the clerk again before turning away. He didn't know what he was going to say or how he was going to feel about seeing this man again. He only knew that he needed some closure in his life. And the only way for him to do that was by confronting his father and making him answer his questions.

When Martin made it to room one-twenty-six, the door was already slightly ajar so he just gave it a gentle push and walked right on in. Martin noticed the Kentucky Fried Chicken box on the round table by the door as soon as he entered the room. Smelling like a combination of musk mixed with greasy fried chicken, he crinkled his nose as he stepped into the room and eased the door shut. Then he saw that Ezekiel was sitting at the foot of the bed with his legs crossed wearing a pair of wrinkled khaki pants without a belt and a brown knit shirt, holding the remote control in his hand. Watching "Oprah" on the nineteen-inch color television, he mumbled a greeting to his son.

Glancing up at Martin, he returned his attention to Oprah. Still standing, Martin answered his father's greeting with a weak one of his own.

"I was wondering how long it would take you to come see me," he said, still staring at the television.

"Ah, I'm really surprised that you're still here. I thought that you were looking for a room to rent somewhere."

"Yeah, I was. But I decided to stay here a little while longer just in case you came looking for me. I worked out a deal with the manager so he allowed me to keep this room."

"Well, I'm here, and I'm here because I need some answers from you right now," Martin stated, eyeing his father.

Ezekiel stood up, pushed the off button on the remote control, and put on his apple cap. "Whatever you want to ask me will have to wait. Right now we need to go somewhere."

"What are you talking about? I just got here. Where is it that you need to go?"

"I said *we* need to go somewhere. We need to get down to the Duval County Medical Center right away. Your brother, Walter, is in the hospital. He was shot three times last night, and he's listed in critical condition."

"Let's go, my car is right outside," Martin said, walking toward the door.

Martin blazed through the traffic as he questioned his father about the circumstances surrounding his brother's shooting. Ezekiel didn't know very much about the incident, but he told Marty everything that he had been told.

"How did you find out that he was in the hospital, and what do you know about the shooting?" Martin asked.

"I finally located Walter about three days ago in a homeless shelter and spoke with him there. Of course, he was sky high and didn't pay much attention to what I had to say, so I just left him alone. Anyway, I went back to the same shelter to look for him last night around eight o'clock and some woman told me that the ambulance had left there taking him to the hospital less than an hour ago."

"Ah, man, I don't believe this. This is not happening."

"It's happening all right. I just hope that we're not too late to see him alive one more time," Ezekiel said, staring straight ahead at the road.

"Well, we're almost there now. Did you come to the hospital last night?

"Yeah, I came, but they had already taken him into surgery, and they told me that there was nothing for me to do, so I just went on back to my room and prayed for a miracle. My mind just told me to stay in my room all day and wait on the Lord."

"Oh, so you're Mr. Religion now?"

"No, no, I ain't saying that. I'm just trying to say that I am older and wiser now. I still take me a stiff drink when I have a mind to, but I am wiser in the Lord."

"All right, we're here now," Martin drove into the hospital parking space and turned off the engine to his vehicle.

They jumped out of the SUV and walked briskly towards the hospital's main entrance. Ezekiel was struggling to keep up with Marty's fast pace, but he told his son to keep going without him.

Martin swung the heavy glass door open, held it until his father arrived, and then rushed over to the lobby desk in the center of the entrance area.

"Excuse me, Miss. Can you tell me what room Walter Harrison is in?" Martin politely asked the elderly female attendant.

"Yes sir," she said, looking at the directory, "He's in room one-seventy-eight. That's on the far side of the hospital. Go straight down this center hallway and turn left. You should see the signs directing you to the critical care unit from there."

"All right, thank you very much," Marty replied, heading in that direction with Ezekiel trailing closely behind him.

When he made it to the room, he abruptly stopped outside and waited for Ezekiel. Marty could see Walter lying in the hospital bed through the huge glass window. He recognized the name on the door as that of Walter Harrison, but he didn't recognize the man lying unconscious in the narrow bed. His brother had tubes running to and from almost every part of his small body. Walter was a thin, frail, gaunt looking man. In fact, he looked to be about the same age as their father, and he appeared to be several shades darker than Marty remembered him being.

He recognized the heart monitor, the blood pressure monitor, and the life support machine, but didn't know what the other equipment and tubes were for. Marty could see the respirator and hear it making that sound as it breathed air in and out of his brother's still body. He stood there staring through the clear window in a frozen state with his mouth agape, too scared to move for fear of losing his balance and stumbling to the floor. Ezekiel came slowly to the window and stood beside Marty. His breathing immediately became exasperated as he grabbed Marty's arm for stability. "Hey, are you okay?" Marty asked, grabbing Ezekiel's by the arm, trying to hold him up.

"I—I don't know. I need to sit down."

"All right, let me help you to this chair over here right behind us," Marty stated, holding his father's hand and wrapping the other arm around his shoulder, leading him to an armchair.

"I'll be all right," Ezekiel stated after breathing deeply several times from a sitting position.

"Are you sure? You want me to get you a nurse or a doctor?"

"No, no. That won't be necessary. I just wasn't prepared to see him in that condition, that's all. Why don't you go on in there and see about your brother. I'll be okay right here for a few minutes."

Martin slowly stood up and walked towards the hospital room. He looked back a couple of times to make sure that Ezekiel was all right before entering the room across the hall from the small waiting area. Marty could hear his heart beating as he cautiously walked towards the hospital bed. Looking down at his brother, Marty was suddenly overcome with memories from their childhood. Recalling all the times they had played together, all the hopes and dreams they had shared, and the loneliness of living apart from one another, he broke down to his knees, and chokingly cried at Walter's bedside. With tears streaming down his face, Marty reached out to touch his sibling's hand.

"Sir! Sir! No one is supposed to be in here except for family. Are you family?" the short thin nurse asked, walking towards a bent down Martin.

Martin looked up and wiped his face with his hands before speaking, "Yes ma'am, I'm his only brother. My name is Martin Carlisle."

"I'm Nurse Paxton, and I'm glad that someone has come to see about him. He is in critical condition. His physician's name is Dr. Bill Matheson, and he will be here shortly if you'd like to speak with him."

"Ah, yes ma'am, I definitely want to talk with the doctor. Can you tell me anything about his condition?" Martin sniffled, rising to his feet.

"All I know is that he's lost a lot of blood. He suffered three gunshot wounds at close range, one to the chest and two to the stomach. The doctors were able to remove all of the bullet fragments from his body. I'm sorry to tell you this part, but the police believe that it was some type of drug related shooting," Nurse Paxton looked at Marty sympathetically. She had witnessed first hand how drugs had destroyed many families in this city. Even her own family had been touched by this same type of tragedy on more that one occasion.

"Do the police know who shot him?"

"Well, if they do know, they didn't tell us, and we didn't ask any specific questions regarding the crime."

"Thank you, Nurse Paxton. I know you probably can't say for sure, but what do you think his chances are for making a recovery from this?"

"I really don't know. You'll have to talk to Dr. Matheson about that. I'm sorry, but I have to go check on the other patients. Please ring the nurse's station if you need anything," she said, walking towards the door. The doctor would have to share that piece of bad news with the family. She wasn't willing to accept that as part of her responsibilities, not after seeing the sad look in that gentleman's eyes.

When the door opened again, Martin looked up to see his father walking towards him. "What did the nurse say?" he asked.

"She said that he was shot three times and they got all the bullets out of him, but I'll have to talk to the doctor regarding his condition if I want to know more."

"Yeah, they don't usually tell you too much. But we can tell from all of these contraptions that they have him hooked up to that it's not going to be good. I just hope that he regains consciousness long enough for me to talk to him. I should have tried harder to talk with him before this happened," Ezekiel slumped over on the bed as tears flooded his face. Martin reached for a chair, pulled it up to Ezekiel's knees, and helped him sit down.

"You just have a seat right here, and let me go find out how long it'll be before I can talk with the doctor."

"All right, son, I'll be right here."

Fifteen minutes passed before Martin returned to the room and pulled up a chair to sit down beside his father. "Were you able to speak with the doctor?" Ezekiel asked.

"Yes, I was. He said that Walter has about a twenty to thirty percent chance of recovery if they can keep him stabilized. He'll be in intensive care for another day or so before they move him to a regular room. Hopefully, they'll be able to tell us more at that time."

Ezekiel starting sobbing so hard that Marty didn't know what to do. He didn't know if he should comfort the man or leave him alone with his grief. After a few seconds of thinking, Marty decided to gently pat him on the back and wait for him to stop crying as he wiped away his own tears with his other hand.

"Is there anything that I can do to make you gentlemen more comfortable?" Nurse Paxton asked, reentering the room.

"No, ma'am, we're fine. We'll just be a few more minutes, and then we're leaving for the evening."

"Well, I just need to check and record his vitals before the next shift comes in. I'm really sorry about your brother. Is this your father?" she asked, referring to Ezekiel.

"Yes, ma'am, he is."

"It's so good that the two of you could be here for him. I know how hard this has to be on both of you, but God will see you through. Just trust in Him and His grace will see you through."

"Thank you for your kind words, Nurse Paxton. I'd like to leave my name and telephone number at the nurse's station in case there's any change in his condition. Someone can call me at anytime."

"That's a great idea. I'll be right back with a pen and a sheet of paper, and I'll take care of that myself before I go off duty."

"I'd really appreciate that," Martin replied as the nurse hurried out of the hospital room.

Following the nurse out into the corridor, Martin removed his flip style cellular phone from his pants and dialed Tina's mobile number. He wanted to share this latest development with his life partner. Tina answered after the third ring, "Hi, Marty, what's going on, baby?"

"You're not going to believe this, but I'm at the hospital with my father."

"What happened? Is your father sick?"

"No, he's fine. It's my brother, Walter. He's been shot three times, and it doesn't look good. So I'm going to be here for awhile."

"Oh, no. I'm sorry, Martin. I'm on my way. You don't have to say another word, okay?"

"Thanks, baby, I'll be waiting on you," Martin replied, closing up his flip phone. *Tina always has my back. I'm glad that she's coming. Now I won't have to face Ezekiel alone for the rest of the evening.*

Chapter 14

"Thanks for letting me come over on a moments notice," Tina stated, entering Debonair's apartment shortly after eight in the evening wearing a pair of hip hugging white pants and a floral designed top with short sleeves. "I just really needed someone to talk to, and I wasn't ready to go home after work. It's been a very long and exhausting day; I'm not up for the drama that's going on at my house."

"Have a seat and I'll fix us a cup of coffee or would you prefer a glass of wine, my lady?" he asked, waiting quietly for a response. Tina observed how cute and casual he looked in his gray loose fitting cotton pants and a white T-shirt with one pocket on the chest.

"Umh, I think that I would rather have a glass of white wine."

"Okay, one glass of white wine is coming up," he turned towards the small kitchen that Tina could see from the living area. Tina noticed that his one-bedroom bachelor pad was actually clean and well maintained for a man living on his own. The only pieces of furniture were a green cloth sofa and a small entertainment center across the room with a nineteen inch color television set, VCR/DVD combo player and a collection of movies stacked on both sides of the unit. She glanced through his music and video collection while he returned to the front room and poured two glasses of wine. Tina wasn't much of a drinker. She occasionally enjoyed the sweet taste from a bottle of good spirits, though.

"Well, would you like to share with me what's going on in your life right now?" Debonair asked, sipping from his glass.

"It's just so much, I really don't know where to begin. My marriage is really in sad shape. Ever since that Atlanta trip last week, Martin and I have barely spoken to each other."

"Oh, yeah, and why is that?"

"When I made it home that night, he finally told me the truth about his past and how he's been lying to me for the entire length of our marriage. You see, I thought that he was an only child, and both his parents were killed in a car accident when he was a teenager, but now I've learned differently." Tina went on to explain the details of her marital situation and her health issues to Debonair. He listened quietly for several minutes as she poured out her heart to him.

"So as you can see, this has not been a very good time for us and especially me. I just needed to share this with someone that wasn't going to judge me and after the night that we spent together in Atlanta, I knew that you wouldn't do that. I still think of you as a good friend and what we shared was very special to me," Tina stated, staring into his dark rum eyes.

"It was special to me, too, Tina. You'll never know how truly special our time together is to me. You deserve to be happy, and I'll do anything and everything in my power to see that you're satisfied in life."

"You're so sweet. I appreciate having you as a friend right now. You're a very good listener, you know."

"It's easy to be a good listener when you enjoy hearing the melodic sound of a lovely voice like yours. I bet you can sing, can't you?"

"Ah, I've been known to carry a tune or two around the house and in the shower."

"Well, I've got a shower in the back; I'd love to hear you sing."

Tina raised her eyebrows then decided to brush off his suggestive comments. "No, no, I don't feel like singing tonight. You know, I have to feel the songs that I sing about and what I feel right now is nothing but the blues. And I know that you wouldn't want to hear the blues on a beautiful night like this."

"I don't know. I bet you could even make the blues sound uplifting with that pretty voice."

"Maybe some other time, Debonair, thanks for listening to me tonight. I'd better get going before it gets late," she stated, looking at the timepiece on her wrist. Tina pulled her braids back. Rubbing her neck with one hand, she was holding the almost empty wine glass with the other.

"What's wrong, my lady? Is your neck sore or something?" he asked, sounding concerned as he rose and moved behind her on the sofa.

"Yeah, I haven't been sleeping well, and I've had this crook in my neck all day."

"Here, let me see if I can help you out," he stated, reaching down to massage her neck and shoulders with both hands. "I can feel a kink in your neck and the tightness in your shoulders."

"Umh, that feels like heaven. I used to get massages on a regular basis, but I haven't had one in ages."

"You're in luck tonight, my lady. Full body massages are my specialty, and I would love to give you one right now," he whispered softly in her ear.

"I would love that, but I'm not looking for any more troubles than I already have. I don't want you to get the wrong impression by giving me a massage that I want more than that from you, Debonair."

"Hey, I'm not into taking advantage of women. I won't touch any part of you that you don't want me to touch. I would just like to see you relaxed and not looking so stressed out for a change. I think that I can help you out, if you're willing to trust me, Tina."

"I trust you, but I don't know if I can trust those magic fingers of yours. I've already felt the power that you have in them," she eyed his hands.

"These," he replied, holding up all ten fingers, slowly flexing them. "These are for pleasing, teasing, and stress relieving," he joked. "Now, let me show you to my room, and I can start with just an upper body massage. We don't have to go any further than that if you're not comfortable with it."

"All right, I could use that. I feel a difference just from the little bit you did while sitting here."

"Well, let's get started. My room is right down the hall to the left. You can go ahead and get settled while I heat up a little bit of scented oil."

Minutes later, Tina was lying across his full sized heated waterbed face down on top of a brown and black striped comforter. Surveying the bedroom, she quickly surmised that this was a single man's haven. It was sparsely decorated with only a night table and a coordinating chest. She had stripped down to just her pants and panties with both arms at her sides. The waves from the bed had her body floating back and forth as if she was on a luxury ocean liner at sea. Debonair entered the bedroom carrying a blue plastic bowl with scented hot oil filtering throughout the perimeter of the small room. "Wow, just the scent of that is relaxing. Is this some type of aromatherapy?"

"Yes, this is lavender oil which is considered calming. Aromatherapy can relax your mind and body, soothe the senses, and even improve some internal functions. You know, I also like different fragrances. I've always been into a variety of aromas especially on a woman's body. I think that the smell of a woman is the most exhilarating scent in the world," he inhaled deeply.

"You sound like you've had some practice at this before. Am I just another knot on your bedpost?"

"Oh, no, don't even go there. I'm no playboy or Casanova if that's what you're trying to imply. I just mean that when I'm into a person, she has all of my attention, and I'm willing to go above and beyond the call of duty to please her. That's all I'm saying. Now, let me put on one of your favorite artists while you relax and let me work out some of those kinks in your back."

Debonair turned on the CD player on his bedside nightstand and waited for the sound of Maxwell singing, "Fortunate," to filter through the room. He poured several drops of oil into his hands, vigorously rubbed them together, and then gently touched her back. Tina completely relaxed with the soothing music as his warm fingers masterfully caressed her neck and back. All of her problems and pains quietly floated right on away as she became totally engrossed in his slippery masculine hands. "Now you're cheating. You know that I'm in love with Maxwell's voice. I could listen to him sing all night long," Tina chimed.

"I make it my business to learn all that I can about you. I want to know all of your likes and your dislikes so that I can fulfill you every desire."

"Thank you for caring so much for me. I haven't had anyone to go out of their way to please me the way that you have in a long time. This is an amazing experience for me—just being with you is amazing."

"You're welcome; I enjoy our time together as well. Are you ready for the next stage, my lady?" he asked, whispering sweetly in her ear after several minutes of rubbing her entire back.

"Yes, I am. I'm at your mercy now," she replied, basking in pleasure.

He took his time concentrating on her upper back at first in the area between her shoulder blades. With slow gliding hand strokes and applying deep circular finger pressure, he tenderly kneaded her back muscles until the tension from each one was released into his fingertips. Methodically, he made his way down to her lower back, listening for the muffled moans of desire escaping her lips.

Debonair lifted her midsection just enough to slide down her pants along with her satin bikini panties. He proceeded to do a full body massage, pouring oil down the center of her back all the way down between her honey buns before gently slithering the liquid all over her backside. Then he continued pouring the warm oils down the center of each leg, massaging her inner thigh muscles, the back of her knees, the calves in her legs, and then a strong foot massage where he drenched each of her toes with oil as he manipulated them individually.

By the time he finished massaging her from the neck down to the tips of her painted pink toe nails, she felt and looked like putty in his hands. She didn't have the power left to resist his charms because every single nerve in her body was on fire and tingling with lust for him. Debonair slowly removed his clothes and laid his steaming naked body on the comforter next to hers. Lying on his side, he rolled Tina over on her side with her buttocks against his hips in the popular spoon position.

Their rhythm together started out at a slow steady pace. He wrapped both arms around Tina's body, cupping her tender breasts between his slick fingers. Tina lifted her braids up so that he could nuzzle her neck while she ran her hand over his smooth face. Finally, with both of them stretching their necks, they shared a deep passionate tongue lashing kiss. His tongue was so long that Tina could almost feel it going down the back of her throat before she pulled away from him. Caught up in the rapture of his loving, she was no longer able to control her excitement. Tina released all of her turmoil as she gripped both of his hands, entwining his moist fingers with hers.

Burying his mouth into the nape of Tina's neck, Debonair felt an explosion in his midsection like a burning thrill he'd never experienced before. This time, he held onto her hands for dear life as his body slowly relaxed against hers after several seconds of uncontrollable contractions. "How do you feel?" he asked, holding Tina in his arms several minutes later.

"I feel absolutely wonderful," she responded, turning to face him.

"Good, I want you to always feel this way," he stated, touching her smooth chin, staring deeply into her loving eyes.

"You were absolutely amazing. I don't think that I've ever experienced pleasure that intense before in my life. I hope that I'm not becoming addicted to you."

"Well, I hope that you are because I'm already addicted to being with you like this. I think about you every second of the day whether I'm asleep or not."

"You know, it just dawned on me that I don't know anything about you. I don't even know how old you are or your birthday for that matter."

"No problem. I'm thirty-years-old, and my birthday was March twenty-seventh."

"Wait a minute. You mean the night that we made love in Atlanta was your birthday?"

"Yes, it was, and thanks for being my birthday present. I drove up there to celebrate by myself, but after seeing you, I couldn't resist going back to your room that night even if it meant that I had to beg and plead with you to see me."

"I wish that I had known that was your thirtieth birthday. Now I really want to know more about Debonair. You can start with telling me about your job at the coffee shop."

"Let me see, I've been employed at the Insomnia Coffee House full-time for over a year now. I worked there part-time for two years while I completed my degree at the local community college. Before that, I just worked at the mall in different department stores while I went to school off and on until about three years ago. That's when I decided to earn an Associate's of Arts degree in Business Management. Shortly after graduating, the assistant manager moved out of state, and they offered the job to me."

"Do you like working there?"

"Yes, I do. If I wasn't working there, I probably would not have met you so you might say that I love my job. You certainly made it worthwhile the first time that I saw you walk in. I tried to make it to the cash register to check you out, but one of the waiter's beat me to it. I spoke to you on your way out, but you barely noticed me as you spoke."

"Oh, I noticed you all right. I just didn't want to show how much I noticed you, but I saw you eyeing me. Now what else is there that you'd like to share with me?"

"There's not really a lot to tell. What you see is what you get with me. My life is basically an open book."

"Yes, but I want you to tell me what's inside the book behind the shiny gorgeous cover that I'm looking at right now. What about your parents? Do you have siblings?"

"My parents are divorced. They have been divorced since I was about twelve-years-old. My mother, Katherine, works in the janitorial department at one of the state buildings downtown. My father, Franklin, owns a service station over on the south side of town. My uncle owns a chain of local barbeque restaurants. Have you ever been to Jenkin's Restaurant?

"Of course I have. Everybody in the state of Florida knows about Jenkin's famous mustard based barbeque sauce."

"I guess you're right about that. I love that sauce myself. You know, he has four locations throughout the city. I used to work in the one on King's Road with my cousins after school everyday and during the summer when I was a teenager. But after awhile, I got tired of smelling like charcoals and smoke all the time."

"That's funny," Tina said, laughing with him. "Finish telling me about your family."

"Sure, I have one older sister. Her name is Karla, and she works for an insurance company up in Atlanta. Her husband's name is Harold, and he's a real estate investor. They have a ten-year-old son named Andre. Now, we're really close. He's one of the smartest kids that I've ever met in my life. And then last but not least, I have a five-year-old daughter named Eboni."

"What? You're kidding me! You have a five-year-old daughter?"

"Yes, I do. She's my heart, too." Debonair placed his right hand over his chest, circling the area around his heart.

"Why haven't you told me about her before?" Tina inquired, sitting up in the bed with the sheet covering her breasts, leaning against a pillow propped against the headboard. Debonair rose up on one elbow, responding to Tina.

"She never came up during our conversations. We haven't discussed my personal life at all. But yeah, she's five-years-old with pretty brown skin, big bubbly brown eyes, long pretty ponytails, and an innocent smile that can brighten any day. I don't get to see her as much as I would like, though, because her mother, Pamela, is tripping all the time."

"How do you mean?"

"She can do some crazy stuff. She's still mad at me for breaking up with her so she uses the child to try and punish me every chance she gets. If I tell her that I want to spend time with Eboni, and I'm coming to pick her up at a certain time, she'll agree to it but then when I get there, she'll pretend like she doesn't know what's going on. You know, just outrageous things like that. I remember one time that I went over there and Eboni was supposed to be ready at 6:00 p.m. I got there almost an hour early, and the child was not there. Pam claimed that she told me that Eboni had a sleepover at a friends' house. I was so mad that day, that I could have physically hurt her. Sometimes I think that's exactly what she wants. She wants me to hit her or something stupid so she can have me locked up."

"Well, can't you take her to court and tell the judge what's happening?

"I've tried that, and she doesn't care about that. Pam is going to do whatever she wants to do as long as it makes me miserable."

"Why did you really break up with her?"

"It just wasn't working for me. I tried to make it work for the sake of my daughter but after awhile I just couldn't deal with all the drama. And Pamela is the drama princess, it has to be her way right now or all hell breaks loose over the simplest things. I couldn't live like that, not knowing what was going to set her off at anytime and anyplace. One time we were at my mother's house, Pam got mad at me for some remark that I made about her weight and she started breaking up dishes. You know, my mother is just as crazy as she is, and she almost went ballistic on Pam. I had to drag her out of there kicking and screaming before my mother body slammed her."

"That is some drama! I can't imagine you being with someone like that. How did you ever meet her?"

"We met at a local night club. She was basically a buck wild party girl, and we had a lot of fun together. Then when she got pregnant, we tried living together and were talking about getting married. In my heart, I knew that would never work out, but I was willing to give it an honest try. Well, she wanted me to do all the caring for the child while she looked pretty and continued doing whatever she wanted to do."

"That's ridiculous. Now tell me about some of the things that you like to do," she prodded.

"I like to do anything that's spontaneous. I like going places on the spur of the moment. You know, I don't like to go anywhere and have a routine. I like being free to do as I please."

"Oh, my goodness, look at the time! It's almost ten o'clock, I've got to get home," Tina read the digital clock on the nightstand, scrambled out of bed, and searched for her clothes. Debonair followed behind her, pulling on his underwear and pants while watching her get dressed.

Suddenly the doorbell was ringing and someone was banging at the front door. "Are you expecting someone?" Tina asked, sliding on her shoes.

"No, I'm not expecting anyone at this late hour. You stay in here while I go see who that is," he whispered.

"All right," Tina responded nervously, bending to sit on the edge of the bed.

Debonair closed the door as he exited the bedroom and headed towards his front door. When he swung the door open, there stood Pamela dressed in a short black lace see-through dress, holding his daughter by the hand.

"What are you doing here dressed like that and riding my daughter around with you?"

"Well, I'm dressed like this," she stated, moving her hands down the length of her body, "because I'm on my way out, and I need you to baby-sit your child until I return unless you got some ho up in here that you're banging right now."

"Come on in, Pam, and stop talking like that in front of this child. Don't you have any respect for yourself?"

"I have plenty of respect for myself, but you on the other hand, seem to be lacking in some self respect. Which ho you got up in here tonight?" she asked, walking in the room, pulling the child by the hand behind her.

"Why didn't you call me and let me know that you wanted me to watch Eboni tonight?"

"Because you're her father, and I shouldn't have to call and ask for your permission if I want to go somewhere. You should be able to keep her."

"I didn't say that you had to ask for my permission to go anywhere. I'm saying that you could give a brother some notice when you want him to keep a child on a Friday night."

"Well, just consider yourself notified right now because I have to go. My girls are waiting for me in the car."

"And how did you know that I would be home on a Friday night?"

"I didn't know that you were going to be home; I just decided to take a chance on you being here. It was either that or taking her to the club with me."

"I know that you have better sense than to take a five-year-old out to an adult night club, Pamela."

"And I know that you have better sense than to question anything that I do. Baby, come give your mama a hug and a kiss good night so that she can go," Pamela reached for Eboni and pulled her into her thin arms. Then, she abruptly turned on her four-inch heels and stepped out the door.

Moments later, Tina eased the bedroom door open and peeped out around the corner to see Debonair sitting on the sofa with a beautiful little girl dressed in blue jean capri pants and a white smock top. Her hair was neatly braided with white and clear beads on the end of each one as she watched television sitting next to her daddy. Clutching her purse, Tina walked into the living room, and coughed lightly to make her presence known. They were so busy watching the, *Sponge Bob*, cartoon show that they didn't notice her entering the room.

"Tina, this is my daughter, Eboni. Sweetheart, I want you to say hello to my friend, Miss Tina," Debonair introduced the two of them.

"Hi, Miss Tina, how are you?"

"I'm doing fine, Eboni, how are you this evening?"

"I'm fine, thank you, and I'm five-years-old," Eboni stated proudly.

"Yes, you are. Your father already told me how old you were. It's very nice to meet you. Look, Debonair, I have to run. I can see that you have your hands full for the rest of the night."

"I'll walk you to the door," he replied, rising from the sofa.

Once they were on the other side of the door, Debonair continued the conversation. "You see, this is the kind of craziness that I was telling you about earlier. When she wants to go out barhopping, suddenly I can see my daughter, but it's never when I want to see her on my terms. I didn't make a scene about it because I didn't want to hurt Eboni's feelings like that."

"Well, you did the right thing. Don't ever confront Pam in the company of your daughter because she'll feel like you don't want her to be here. It's sad, but I understand your predicament."

"Thanks for understanding, and thanks for coming by. I've enjoyed every second that you spent with me. You can come over whenever you want. You don't have to call or anything. In fact, I'm going to have a key made for you so that whenever you need a quiet place to come and relax after work, you can come right in."

"You're the sweetest man that I've ever met in my life. I can't believe that you would do that for me. Thanks again. Now I really have to go." They kissed quickly as Tina turned and walked out the door. She was almost running to her car in the dark.

Chapter 15

"Good morning, ladies," Shenedra beamed, rushing into the hair shop with her arms full of shopping bags, letting the door slam shut behind her on a sunshiny day.

"Good morning," replied Tina and Taneka. Tina was braiding a young lady's hair at her station, and Taneka was sitting behind the receptionist's desk reading a *Braids & More* hair magazine.

"I'm running late this morning because I had to pick up my boyfriend and let him hold my car today. His car wouldn't start this morning, so he's got to borrow mine. Then, I had to stop at the hair supply store to pick up some products before coming in," she stated while taking supplies consisting of B & B hair spray, molding gel, Hot Six oil, moisturizing shampoo, hair pins, and other grooming items out of the bags, organizing her work area.

"That's all right. Your first client already called and said that she would be a little late this morning. So you still have a few minutes to finish getting set up and relax, girl," Tina replied, reaching for more synthetic hair.

Suddenly the shop door opened and a tall dark brother walked in dressed in dark jeans, a white jersey trimmed in red, and carrying a brown Claiborne purse in his hands. All the women in the salon turned to behold his masculine build and smooth full lips as his eyes quickly scanned the room and landed on his lady friend.

"Shenedra, you left your purse in the car, darling," he said in a deep throaty voice, handing her the bag.

"Oh, thank you, Carson. I want to introduce you to my co-workers," she sat the purse down in her empty chair, grabbed his hand, and walked towards Tina. "Carson, this is the shop owner and my best friend, Tina Carlisle," he and Tina exchanged greetings, and then she lead him to Taneka.

"And this is my co-worker and friend, Taneka," he and Taneka spoke to each other and shook hands.

"Okay, darling, I've got to run to see about getting my car repaired today. I'll call you later," he pulled her towards him and planted an electrifying kiss on her inviting lips.

"All right, I'll see you later today," Shenedra replied, watching him walk out the door.

"You go, girl!" Taneka exclaimed. "Now a fine brother like that could pull me back into the dating game!"

"Yes, yes, yes! He is my man, and I am proud to say it loud!" Shenedra bragged. "It's been a long time since I had a good man. He doesn't have any children; he has a steady job; and he knows how to handle his business, if you know what I mean."

"Well, I am not mad at you, girl," Tina said laughing. "I hope that he's the one for you because he certainly looks the part."

"Yes, he does. But he's not just good looking now; he's a very kind and considerate person. He takes me anywhere I want to go; he buys me nice jewelry, and he's always fixing things around my house. You know, that saves me a lot of money on home repairs. He's a very handy man to have around for real."

"That's great, Shenedra. Girl, I am so happy for you," Taneka chimed in.

"Thank you, ladies. I plan to make him very happy for a very long time," Shenedra said, raising her head, smiling happily.

Around lunch time, Tammy, the receptionist came in and met Shenedra coming out of the bathroom holding her stomach and complaining that she wasn't feeling very well. Apparently, she had eaten some spicy foods the night before that were not agreeing with her digestive system.

"Girl, do you want me to take you home?" Tina asked, looking concerned.

"Well, I don't know—I'm going to try and make this next appointment."

"If you're not feeling well, then there's no reason for you to stay. Your health is more important than work," Tina insisted. "See if you can reach Carson and ask him to come pick you up."

"Umh, maybe I better because I'm starting to cramp up now," Shenedra stated, bending over, holding her stomach.

"Look, I'm caught up for awhile. I can drive you home," Tina reached for her purse and pulled out the keys. "Let's go."

"All right, you don't have to boss me around, you know."

"You're so stubborn that I have to be firm with you. I know how you are, remember?" Tina took Shenedra's hand and led her to the door.

They were heading towards Shenedra's house when she suddenly asked Tina to drive by Carson's single story quadruplex. "Tina, turn right on the next street for me, please. I want to see if Carson made it back to his place yet. You can drop me there and go back to the shop if he's home; I know you have another appointment coming in soon."

"All right, but it's no biggie either way. You don't live that much farther, anyway."

"Yeah, but I'd rather be here with my baby instead of going home to be alone since he's off today."

"Whatever you say," Tina replied, pulling up beside Shenedra's steel blue Mitsubishi Eclipse with the windows down.

"Well, it looks like he's here," Shenedra stated, opening the car door.

"I'll walk with you to the door just to make sure that he's here," Tina said, opening her car door, too.

Tina helped Shenedra down the sidewalk, making light conversation as they approached the front door. Shenedra rang the doorbell several times before hearing someone stirring inside. She was about to push the button again when a short tiny woman with a tangled weave opened the door wearing a thin white cotton housecoat with no shoes.

"May I help you ladies?" she asked, looking from Shenedra to Tina.

"Where is Carson Forde?" Shenedra asked, sounding irate.

"He's still in the shower, what..." Shenedra quickly forgot about her stomach ache, raised her right leg, and kicked the door on open, stepping past the woman into the living room. "Who the hell are you?" Shenedra demanded, standing tall with her hands on her hips. She looked the young lady up and down from head to toe and figured that the girl couldn't possibly be a day over eighteen-years-old.

"I'm Carson's girlfriend," she replied, clenching her housecoat together and looking scared. Shenedra quickly turned on her heels, heading towards the hallway. When she turned the corner, she walked right into Carson standing there dripping wet, wearing a blue towel around his waist, and a totally shocked look on his face. His eyes and mouth were both wide open, staring at Shenedra. He snapped his mouth closed, swallowed hard, and softened his facial expression.

"Hey, darling, what are you doing here?" he asked sweetly.

"Never mind what I'm doing here, Carson. Who is this young heifer answering your door and claiming to be your girlfriend?"

"Look, Shenedra, don't trip on this, okay," he tucked the towel in on the side and then reached for Shenedra. "Darling, she's not my girlfriend. I can explain this, all right?"

Shenedra snatched her arm out of his reach, slapped him across his left cheek with the other hand, and then shouted, "No! It's not all right, and there's no way for you to explain what I've already seen with my own eyes!" She exclaimed, turning sharply on her heels, and walking back into the living room. The girlfriend was still standing in the same spot with Tina glaring at her as she tried to apologize to them both.

"Honey, don't waste your breath apologizing to me," Shenedra raised her hand to block the girl's face as she continued speaking. "What you need to do is get the hell away from this trifling ass Negro. Baby, he don't mean you or me any good, alright," then she turned to Carson, who was standing behind her, rubbing his sore cheek, and eyeing all the ladies in the room. "Give me my car keys right now you low down lying snake in the grass son-of-a-bitch!"

Carson walked to the table by the door, snatched up the cars keys, and held them out to Shenedra without saying another word. She looked at him with the most disgusting twisted face that she could muster before saying, "Now I should give you and your young girlfriend a good old fashioned beat down, but I'm not in the mood for going to jail today. So let me give you a little piece of advice, brother man—from now on you better sleep with one eye open and the other eye *wide* open." Shenedra grabbed the keys from him and marched out the door in front of Tina.

Tina followed Shenedra the rest of the way home, she wasn't about to leave her best friend alone at a time like this. While she dialed the number to the shop to let Taneka in on the latest development, her mind wandered back to the other evening that she had spent with Debonair at his apartment. He had truly made her feel alive again by being so attentive to her every need and doing sensual things that she had only dreamed about. Yes, she felt guilty for cheating on Marty and promised herself that she would not let it happen again, but Tina was slowly losing her focus on reality. She was becoming addicted to sin.

"Hello, Braids and Lock Shop, Tammy speaking."

"Hi, Tammy, how are things at the shop?"

"Well, it's not real busy right now, but someone is waiting for Shenedra and your one o'clock is running late."

"Okay, I need to spend some time with Shenedra so please ask Taneka if she can cover for us or ask the clients to reschedule."

"Is everything all right, Tina?"

"We have a problem that I can't go into right now. I'll try to be in the shop within the next hour or so, okay?"

"Yes ma'am, I'll speak to Taneka and see if the client wants to reschedule."

"I'll call you when I'm on my way back to see how things worked out."

"That sounds good, Tina. Bye."

Tina pulled her Corvette in behind Shenedra's car in the single driveway of her two-bedroom brick house. Shenedra was already out of the car and opening her front door with heavy tears streaming down her face as Tina exited her vehicle.

Rushing into the living room, Tina could hear Shenedra flushing the toilet in the bathroom as she walked to the doorway. Shenedra was standing in front of the mirror washing her face with a wet washcloth.

"You know what, Tina. I don't know why I'm tripping on this. I should have known that he was just too good to be true, but I didn't see this foolishness coming."

"Girl, I'm sorry. I'm so sorry to see you going through this. I can't believe he had that child up in his place like that."

"I know, she looked like she was still on breast milk. Tina, I'm sick of these grown men messing with these immature naïve girls. I mean its bad enough that he's messing over a grown woman, but leave the babies alone, please."

"It's just sickening and unbelievable," Tina stated, following Shenedra into her bedroom. Shenedra took off all of her clothes and threw them in the closet. She slipped on a blue nightshirt that was lying across the bottom of the bed, climbed on top of the navy and white plaid comforter, and laid flat of her back with her hands over her stomach. Tina sat in the chair beside the bed, leaning forward with her right hand under her chin, staring at Shenedra.

"What?"

"It's nothing. I'm just worried about you, that's all."

"I know you're worried about me, but I'll be all right. He's not the first man to do me wrong, and I'm sure that he won't be the last. But you know what? A thirty-seven-year-old Foxy Brown looking sister like myself is about ready to give up on black men. For once, I'd like to find a decent man so that I can have a portion of what you have with Marty. You know, you are one lucky sister."

"Yeah, I know." Tina said, barely audible.

Shenedra rose up on her right elbow and looked over at Tina. She had the strange sensation that something was not quite right with her girlfriend's marriage.

"Tina, is everything all right between you and Marty? Is he still impotent?"

"Yes, he is."

"Are you still upset about him lying to you about his family?"

"No, I'm over that now because I can see how much pain he's been in lately with his family, especially with his brother being comatosed in the hospital for almost two weeks. But I haven't told you everything either."

"Well, what is it that you haven't told me? I thought you told me everything."

"I didn't tell you that I slept with Debonair while we were in Atlanta for the hair expo."

Shenedra jumped up off the bed and stood over Tina. "I knew something was going on between you two! Why are you just telling me about this, Tina?"

"I just—I just couldn't tell anyone. And that's not all."

"What more could there be?"

"I've also been with him once since we returned to Jacksonville."

"Tina! Girl, are you insane? Why are you having an affair with this man? Sure, he's thirty, but he's still too young for you to be playing around with. Tell me how this happened," she demanded.

"There's not much to tell. When we were in Atlanta, he came to my hotel room that Saturday night after we left the reggae club, and you all were gone to bed. I was so sweaty that I took a quick warm shower. Then, I was about to go to bed when I heard him knocking at my door saying he really needed to talk to me. I let him in and one thing led to another. My body was in dire need of sexual healing, and he was more than eager to satisfy my every craving."

"Okay, I can see you being weak for him that one time, but how did you sleep with him again?"

"After we got back that evening, Marty and I tried to make love, but we couldn't, and then he told me about his family. At first I was upset and hurting so much that I wasn't speaking to Marty. So I called Debonair a couple of days later just to talk, and he invited me over to his place. We started having a conversation about my life and how unhappy I was, and then we ended up having spectacular sex; I just wanted to forget about my problems with Marty for that night." Tina sighed before continuing. "He made that possible for me."

Shenedra plopped down on the side of the bed, shaking her head at Tina. "Girl, this is a mess. This is one fine mess you have yourself in."

"I know that, but I don't know how I'm going to get out of it. You see, he gave me this hot oil full body massage, and I just dissolved on his sheets as all my problems faded away. He had every nerve in my body tingling from my fingertips, up to my shoulder blades, and then down to the tips of my toes, not to mention the reeling sensations that were shooting to the top of my head. There was no way for me to resist him once I let those magical fingers touch me that way. It just felt so good to have all of my worries gone for awhile, especially with such a willing young man."

"That's just it—they faded away for awhile, not permanently. You still have the same problems you had before you laid down with him, maybe even more. No! You definitely have more problems now because you're not stable enough to be doing this, and he's too young to understand the depth of his actions."

"I don't know how I'm going to get out of this relationship with him. He's really been there for me; he's so supportive and sweet to me."

"I know how you're going to get out of this. You're going to break it off with Mr. Debonair and rededicate yourself to your husband. Marty is a really good man. He does anything and everything for you, Tina. Just because he's having some sexual problems right now is no reason for you to leave him or do him like this. If I had a husband taking care of me like Martin takes care of you, I'd wait more than a year to have sex with him."

"That's easier said than done. Once you've been married as long as I have you just get used to having regular sex and when you're cut off like that, you go through withdrawals just like a drug addict."

"Well, you need to learn other ways to please yourself. It only takes a few minutes to masturbate."

"Girl, please, I am not into touching myself," Tina replied, sounding disgusted.

"Then you better help your man learn other ways to please you before your sexual addiction costs you everything you've gained in life. I mean it, Tina."

"Marty doesn't believe in alternative sex methods. We have never had oral sex. He doesn't do toes, and he's never even given me a foot massage. He's one of those old fashioned brothers. Besides, he's not even interested in trying new things." Shifting her body in the chair, Tina's tone suddenly became energetic. "But Debonair is a totally uninhibited lover, and I've never had that before. He is so fine that he oozes sex appeal, and he has the goods to back it all up!"

"So what you're telling me is that this relationship is just about getting your freak on with another man."

"No, that's not all it's about. We genuinely care for each other or we couldn't do the things that we do."

"All I know is that sleeping with Debonair is not going to save your marriage."

"I know—I know. I have never found myself attracted to any other man besides Martin, but Debonair is different. I can't help that I'm drawn to him like a magnet. He's such a gorgeous guy, and he's in love with me."

"Tina, you need a strong taste of reality. Didn't you see what happened to me today? That man probably got three or four other women besides you. If he's sexing you, then he's sexing them, too. There is no way that a young freaky man is going to be happy satisfying just one woman. Surely you don't think someone that fine and single is going to be faithful to a married woman. I don't think so. You better check yourself before you wreck your whole life. And as far as him being in love with you, he doesn't even know you well enough for that. He's just in love with your body."

"I know what you're saying is true, Shenedra. I want to leave Debonair alone; I just don't know if I can. Every time I close my eyes, I see his face and hear his voice calling out my name."

"Tina, at least Marty is trying to get some help for his condition. Please come back to the light and focus on your marriage, girlfriend. He's stopped drinking, and he's coming home at a decent time every evening. I hope you can work it out with him and leave this young fella alone. He can't be anything but trouble for you, Tina, and that's real. There's no way for your situation with him to ever work out. I just hope that he's not one of those foolish fatal attraction men."

"No, he's too nice for that. I can't see Debonair as a stalker."

"Girl, you never know about these young men now. I just hope and pray that he's not, for all our sakes. I hope he's not that foolish. Tina, please promise me that you're not going to see this man again."

"Shenedra, I wish that I could promise you that. All I can say right now is that I will try to stop seeing him. I honestly will try," she said softly, still thinking about him. "Anyway, I've got to get back to the shop. I promised Tammy that I would be back over an hour ago. I will check on you again after work today." She left Shenedra's house telling herself that it was over with Debonair, only the increasing moistness between her legs told her otherwise.

Chapter 16

Martin's brother, Walter Harrison, lived on life support for almost three weeks before they decided to disconnect the machine. Dr. Matheson hadn't given them much hope for his recovery since the day they had first discussed his condition. The twenty to thirty percent chance for survival that they initially gave him rapidly descended to zero after they discovered a lung infection. It was nothing short of a miracle that he had managed to live that long in a comatose state. Walter never regained consciousness, but Martin and Ezekiel were by his side everyday holding his hands and talking to him about their childhood memories. They had both shed tears in the small hospital room and tried to comfort each other over the last few weeks. Martin still felt much bitterness towards his father, but he was slowly learning to forgive Ezekiel for the past the same way that Tina was trying to forgive him. Michael had told him that he would have to forgive his father if he ever expected Tina to forgive him for his lying and deceitfulness; he was trying to work it out with Ezekiel because he desperately needed his wife to stay with him.

All they had learned from the police investigation was that Walter apparently had snatched some drugs from one of the young runners of a well-known dealer, Romeo Sinclair, also known as Kingpin, and fled with them to the homeless shelter. He was out in the alley behind the building sharing the dope with some of his friends when the drug dealer pulled up and started blasting. Walter and one other man were fatally wounded in the shooting spree.

Romeo Sinclair had already posted bail and had been released from police custody over two weeks ago. Martin hadn't received any word of a trial being set for the notorious criminal.

The small funeral service was conducted at 10:30 a.m. on a Saturday at the Smith and Steele Funeral Home and attended by Martin, Tina, Malique, Jordan, Ezekiel, Michael Wayne, his pregnant wife, Alese, and their four-year-old daughter, Bianca. Everyone in attendance wore black clothing and carried a white facial tissue in one hand.

It was pouring down rain as the thunder crackled outside and the lightening flashed all through the windows of the tiny chapel. Pastor Karema Wright, dressed in a black robe with a white collar, only said a few words, read a couple of Scriptures, and prayed for the surviving relatives and friends that had come to pay their respects to Martin's brother. She was a renowned woman of God who had agreed to conduct the services on behalf of her best friend, Alese Wayne. Since Martin and Tina had not attended church together in over a year, they weren't comfortable asking the new reverend at the church they had once attended on a regular basis to be in charge of the funeral. So Tina asked Alese if it would be possible to get Pastor Wright to perform the service for them. They had attended her church several times before with the Wayne's and were quite impressed with Pastor Wright's knowledge and powerful delivery of the Word.

Martin didn't bother trying to notify any of his other family members. He made a solemn vow to himself that he would contact his Aunt Rhoda and find out about her family sometime before this year was over. And maybe, just maybe he would travel with Ezekiel to North Carolina to meet some of his side of the family. But that was a big maybe.

Due to the fact that Walter's body had deteriorated even more during the last two weeks that he was hospitalized, Martin decided to have a closed casket funeral. However, he and Ezekiel still picked out a navy blue suit with a white shirt and a striped navy and maroon necktie for his burial. Martin had one of Walter's childhood pictures in a solid gold heart shaped frame sitting on top of the bronze casket featuring a huge spray with orange and red flowers draping over the sides.

Martin cried throughout the length of the short service as he sat with Ezekiel on his right and Tina on his left with each of them holding one of his hands. Tina sobbed with him and tried to keep both of their tears wiped away. Their two sons, Malique and Jordan, sat between Michael and Alese on the row directly behind them. Alese had an arm around Jordan's shoulders and the other arm around her young daughter; Michael had his arm over Malique's shoulders though neither one shed a tear. Their father had told them two weeks ago about their uncle and grandfather, but today was their first time ever meeting Ezekiel.

Prior to coming to the services, Martin picked his father up at the motel and introduced them to his family. Ezekiel wept tenderly as he hugged each family member, being too emotional to speak a word of greeting to them. Tina held him in her arms and told him that it was okay.

By the end of the program, the rain had passed over and they were able to proceed with the burial on the other side of town, which was unbelievably dry. Martin had purchased a plot for his only sibling at Riverside Memorial Park Cemetery on Normandy Boulevard. He also picked out the upright smooth-top tombstone to be placed at the head of the grave. They only spent a few minutes at the graveside after Pastor Wright prayed. Then the funeral attendants lowered the casket into the ground and began filling the grave as everyone dispersed.

After the burial, Ezekiel asked Marty to take him directly to the Greyhound Bus Station. He was ready to leave Jacksonville.

"Look, Ezekiel. Why don't you at least stay on another week at the house with us?"

"Thank you, son, but I'm not ready for that. I can't handle being here any longer. I promise you that I'll be back later on in the year, and I'll stay with you then. Right now, I'm headed to North Carolina to see my folks and let them know about my family. You know, I told you that I have a brother and a sister there and two aunts and one uncle living."

"Yes, you told me. Maybe by the time you come back, I'll be ready to bring my family up there for a visit to meet your side of the family."

"That's a great idea. It's never too late to get to know your kinfolks," Ezekiel smiled.

"I guess you're right about that, Ezekiel," Marty replied, trying to smile, too.

"Now take your family and go on home. I'll be all right until the bus gets here. I need a little time to myself, anyway."

"You have a safe trip, and you can call me collect anytime. I mean it."

"I know you do, and I certainly plan to call you, but it won't be collect."

Ezekiel gave Marty, Tina, and both his grandsons a big bear hug and held them for several seconds before releasing them. He really considered staying at that point but didn't want to intrude in their lives at a time like this. He felt it would be better to keep in touch with them from a distance for awhile and then come back at a later date for a more personable visit.

Later that evening while they were relaxing in the family room with the boys upstairs, Tina approached Marty regarding her birthday party on the following week. Tina was sitting in the brown leather chaise and flipping through an *Essence* magazine feeling comfortable in a leopard printed caftan. Marty was wearing navy shorts and a blue short sleeved shirt, leaning back in the coordinating leather recliner watching his favorite station, ESPN, on the widescreen television.

"Marty, you know, if you're not up to it, we can cancel the party for next Saturday."

"No, Tina, why would I want to do that? We've been planning this party since the New Year. Anyway, haven't you paid that professional party planner a lot of money for this event?"

"Yes, I have, but I just thought that with everything you've been through in the last three weeks with your brother and father, you might not be up to partying."

"Well, I don't feel up to partying today, but the party is not happening today. I'll be all right by next Saturday. Besides, I've resolved my issues with my father and my brother."

"I'm happy to hear that Marty — I mean the part about your family. Are you still having those nightmares, baby?"

"No, they're finally gone. I'm able to get some rest at night now."

"I'm glad to hear that."

"Listen, Tina. I want to thank you for being so patient and understanding with me during this turmoil in my life. You have been an absolute Godsend to me, baby. And I thank you for that. One thing that I've learned from attending those AA meetings every Tuesday is that having a supportive family is the most critical part of recovering from any illness."

"You don't have to thank me for anything, Marty. We're a family, and we're going to always be a family no matter what happens."

"You got that right. Now let's finish up with the details for your birthday celebration so we can go to bed and get our groove on."

"Marty, you are so crazy. But if you're serious, the party details can wait another day," she said, tossing the magazine on the table, gazing at Marty. Tina hoped that her husband really had his groove back this time. If he was willing to try, she was all for it. After desperately trying to resist Debonair's charm, her body was in need of some fine tuning.

"Then what are we waiting for? Let's get this party started right now," he teased, sweeping Tina up into his arms, heading towards the master bedroom.

Carrying her in his arms as they entered their room, Marty gently placed Tina down on the bed, leaned his body over hers, and smothered her glowing face and warm neck with liquid lava kisses. Tina returned his urgency while clenching the bottom of his shirt, lifting it over his body, and tugging it off his ears. Marty rolled over on his side, immediately pulled down his elastic waist shorts and Calvin Klein briefs, then kicked them across the floor. He nervously watched Tina stand up, glide the silky caftan over her head, and then wiggle out of her black string bikini panties before playfully tossing them onto the bed. She purposely waltzed towards the master bathroom, pretending that she was moving her body to a slow love song as she seductively smiled back at her fully aroused husband. *Yes, yes, this time it's real! It's going to be so good,* she said through her eyes, flashing a sensuous smile at Marty.

Her sexy body language and alluring lips were commanding him to follow her into their cozy bath facility. "Oh, I see. You want to play games with Big Daddy now that you see I got my groove back," Marty teased, following her into the bath.

"That's right, Big Daddy, I want to be a naughty girl with you tonight," Tina replied in her sexiest low voice.

Backing her naked body against the marble countertop between the his and her sinks; she placed her hands at her side, using them to slide her bottom up on the counter. Lifting her legs and stretching them out to embrace Marty's torso, she pulled him closer to her.

With the blood rushing ferociously to his head, Marty was engrossed with his own image in the mirror, clinging to Tina's soft welcoming body. Admiring the image of them being joined together, his arms roamed the curve of her back.

Tina clasped her feet together as she squeezed him tighter between her thighs, lightly scanning the length of his back with her long manicured nails. As the intensity of their long overdue love making increased, so did the pressure of her nails digging into his perspiring skin. They were so emotionally enthralled with each other that it didn't take long for them to complete their anticipated love session. After a mind soaring kiss, Marty tightened his grip on Tina as he leaned his head backward, opened his mouth wide, and unleashed his pleasure.

"Baby, that was the best. That was absolutely the best," Marty stated, between deep breaths. "Maybe I should make you wait another four months before we do that again."

"That's very funny, Marty. I don't think that you ever want to go that long again, sweetheart."

"Baby, you got that right," he replied, conquering her lips with his mouth while smoothing his hands around her hips and backside.

Seconds later, he tenderly held her tranquil face in his hands and said, "Seriously though, Tina. You know, you were my first love."

"Marty, what are you talking about? You're kidding, right?"

"No, I'm not kidding. You were the first and only woman that I have ever made love to, baby."

"Please, Marty. You need to stop playing with me. I don't believe that I was your first."

"That's because I'm so good at what I do, you didn't even know that I was a virgin," he joked, holding Tina's hands. Marty felt that he'd kept enough secrets from his wife and from now on, he wanted to be open and honest with her about everything. This would be the final secret he had to share.

"I sure didn't. I guess I was so excited the first time we made love, I didn't notice. After all the long conversations that we've had over the last seventeen years, why haven't you ever told me this before?"

"Because, baby," he replied, kissing her fingers. "It's a difficult thing for a man to admit that he's a virgin. I knew what to do because it just felt so right between us."

"Okay, Martin, what other secrets do you have? I guess what they say is true, you can live with someone for twenty years and still not know everything about them."

"You know that I love you, and I have always loved you, right?"

"Yeah, I know that," Tina stated, smiling at him.

"Look at that," Martin stated, looking down at himself. "You got me all excited again. Now meet me in the bedroom for round two, girl. Big Daddy is not done with you yet," he laughed, and lifted Tina down from the counter, smacking her on the bottom as she sashayed out of the bathroom.

Reaching inside the cherrywood hand-carved nightstand drawer on his side of the bed, Martin pulled out a plastic-wrapped surprise for Tina and handed it to her wearing nothing but a sly grin on his brown face. Sliding his firm naked body into bed beside her, he was ready to continue their first night of making love after several months of abstinence.

"What is this? Why are you handing me a condom?" she asked with a chuckle, reading the green package out loud. "Gently raised spirals for maximum stimulation. Marty, have you lost your mind? Where did you get this?" she asked, straining to resist the smile forming on her rosy lips.

"Come on, baby, I just bought a little something to help tickle your fancy. I promise you that it won't hurt," Martin teased in a whisper, leaning back against a plush pillow. He clasped his hands together behind his head, waiting on his lady love to cover his solid maleness in lubricated latex.

Smiling devilishly to herself, Tina was happy that the old sexy "love machine" Martin had finally returned to their bedchambers. They made love at least two more times before they welcomed in the Sunday morning sun creeping through their window panes, shining on their contented faces as they lay adjacent to one another. Life was almost as good as it should have been for both of them.

Thinking that after last night, it would definitely be easier to stop lusting for Debonair; Tina opened her eyes and then fell asleep again with her head resting on Marty's right shoulder. She was thankful to have her husband's virile body returned. It was amazing what a month of sobriety could do for a man's sexual functions.

The next morning, Tina got up, changed into some exercise gear, and made the necessary telephone call to her ex-lover, Debonair. Knowing that he wouldn't take the break-up news lightly, she was very stern with him. "Look, Debonair. I can't see you anymore..."

"But, Tina, listen to me..."

"I've decided to make it work with my husband. Please don't call me again," she insisted.

Although he kept trying to interrupt her train of thought, Tina hung up the telephone as soon as she made her point. At that moment, she also knew that she'd have to stop going to the coffee shop every morning because it was time to make some changes in her lifestyle anyway.

After checking her blood pressure and glucose level, which were both normal, Tina smiled at her results. She was beginning to get used to this morning routine even though she still dreaded pricking her fingers three times a day.

Tina entered the exercise room and climbed onto the stationary bicycle. *It's time to start taking better care of myself. The combination of diabetes and high blood pressure is a serious matter. I have to start eating right and exercising at least twice a week as of today.*

Chapter 17

Tina was almost ready to slice her birthday cake in front of the hundred or so guests that were gathered in the great room to celebrate her forty-first birthday. Just as the crimson sun was setting, she welcomed the final guests into her home. It had been a magnificent May Day for a party that extended from the six-bedroom house out into the well-maintained back yard. Ethnically dressed in a beige and gold trimmed pants suit with a matching hat, she appeared to be a happily married woman.

Skimming the room, admiring all of the guests that were likewise wearing their African attire in accordance with the cultural theme of the party, she was astonished at what a magnificent job the professional party decorator had done with her immaculate home for this special occasion. From the colorful printed banner hanging over the entrance way to the table donned with African violets, Tina was amazed.

Suddenly Tina felt her flip-style cellular phone vibrating against her waist. Noticing the loud music thumping along with her heartbeat to the sound of Mary J. Blige singing, "It's a Wrap," she reached down to check her phone. She reviewed the second text message that she'd received this evening: "Baby, please meet me outside for your birthday present."

Gasping for air, she quickly erased the message from her cell phone. Tina looked up, trying to conceal the panic on her face, and scanned the room for her husband. There he was in the corner, having a lively conversation with his friends Michael, Ralph, and Terrance. *I could sneak out the front door for just a few minutes since everyone is inside and waiting for me to cut the cake. This man is probably not going to leave unless I meet him outside soon.*

With her heart pounding and the blood racing through her veins, she took another look at the extra large birthday cake on the far end of the table. It was decorated with one of her most recent portraits recreated in the center of the cake. She was wearing a striped sundress in her favorite colors of orange and green. There were many small orange flowers with green leaves along the perimeter of the frosted cake surrounding her smiling face. It had one layer of chocolate cake and one layer of yellow cake with extra buttercream icing, just the way she liked it. Tina hadn't eaten any sweets in months so she decided to splurge on the cake. Right now, she wished that she could go back to the day that she had taken that picture over two months ago before she started this affair with "Mr. Smooth," Debonair Jenkins.

Tina and Martin had been planning this elaborate bash since the beginning of the New Year, and she wanted it to be a stone cold blast. However, this was not exactly the type of blast that she had anticipated having today. This was her first time having a birthday party in all of her adult life. She had wanted to have one for her fortieth birthday, but Martin and she were just too busy with their friends, Alese and Michael Wayne, who were separated at the time. Anyway, that was over with now and all of her friends and neighbors were there to congratulate her on reaching this milestone in her successful life.

"Tina, girl, are you all right? You're not looking too good. Is something wrong?" Shenedra was touching Tina's arm and searching her best friend's eyes for an answer. She sensed that something wasn't right.

"Shenedra, Debonair is outside. He just sent me a text message on my cell phone that he's waiting for me. Girl, what am I going to do?" Tina stretched her panic filled eyes in horror.

"Girl, I know what you better not do. You better not even think about going out there to see that young man. I thought you said that you told him it was over," Shenedra stated, eyeing Tina suspiciously.

"I did tell him that, but he's been calling me and sending me text messages every day for the last seven days straight."

At that very moment, Tina felt her phone vibrating against her waist again. She knew who it was but still reached down to read his third message for the evening: "Baby, please meet me—I'm waiting outside."

Shenedra arched her thin eyebrows and stretched her gray catlike eyes as she spoke to Tina. "Please don't tell me that was him contacting you again."

"Yes, it's him. This is his third time sending me a message in thirty minutes, and I don't think he's going to stop unless I go outside to see him. He claims that he has a present for me."

"Well, I know somebody else that's going to have a present for you if you get busted tonight. Now you stay right here and let me go talk to him." Shenedra turned to walk away but Tina grabbed her by the left forearm.

"No, Shenedra. I can't let you do that. Besides, I want to see what he got me for my birthday. Keep your eyes on Martin while I slip outside for just a minute, okay?"

"Tina, don't even try..." Before she could finish her statement, Tina had already checked to make sure that Martin was still preoccupied with his friends as she walked towards the door heading outside.

When Shenedra looked towards the corner where she had seen Martin engaged in conversation a few seconds ago, he was gone. Before she could block his path, she caught a glimpse of the back of his head as he walked toward the master bedroom. *Oh, my God! The master bedroom is adjacent to the front door!*

Tina slipped outside and eased the front door shut. She was sure that no one had seen her tipping out, and she would have a few minutes to secretly spend with Debonair. Although she had successfully avoided sleeping with him since confiding in Shenedra, her heart was beating triple time at the prospect of seeing his handsome face again. As soon as he saw her opening the door, he headed in her direction, and they met in the middle of the extended entranceway.

"Happy birthday! Baby, I'm so glad you came out to see me!" he said, embracing Tina, giving her a smooch on her luscious lips.

"Ummhh, you know this is crazy, don't you?" Tina asked, looking up at his dark rum eyes. Licking her lips, she savored the taste of him. Her heart was still thumping rapidly from just knowing that they could be busted at any second.

"All I know is that I had to see you on your birthday so that I could give you this," he stated, pulling a long thin box from behind her back and placing it in Tina's sweaty palms.

"What is this? You risked coming here just to give me this?" Tina asked, stretching her eyes in amusement.

"Yes, I did. I wanted you to have this today, not tomorrow."

Tina lifted the top off the package, opened the burgundy and gold trimmed box revealing an emerald birthstone bracelet.

"Debonair, it's absolutely stunning. Out of all the jewelry that I have—I've never owned a birthstone bracelet. It is so beautiful."

"I want you to wear it just for me, and only when we're together," he said, pulling her to him again and hungrily devouring her tasty lips.

"Debonair, please, you're a sweet man, but I've told you that we can't be together like that again, all right? I mean it. We can't see each other anymore after tonight," she stated, taking the bracelet out of the box and dropping it into her pants pocket. Then she handed the box back to him.

"I understand," he said pitifully. "Just let me have one more taste of your sweetness, and I won't call you anymore," he said, covering her lips with his trembling mouth.

Entering the master bedroom in search of his new Olympus digital zoom camera, Marty headed straight to the seven-drawer cherrywood dresser. It was almost time for Tina to cut the birthday cake, and he definitely wanted to have his new camera ready to capture that picture perfect moment.

Standing in front of the double-mirrored dresser, near the window overlooking the front lawn, Marty thought he heard the sound of voices coming from outside between songs. Out of curiosity, he tiptoed over to the window, gently pulled back the curtain, slightly bent forward, and peeped outside. He observed a man and a woman embraced in a romantic kiss outside on the lighted walkway. Although he didn't recognize the man, he did recognize his wife as her hands were caressing the locks pulled behind the man's head.

Oh, no! Marty snapped his head back upright as he quickly released the curtain. Feeling as if a blood vessel had popped in his head, evil thoughts raced to his brain. *What the hell is this? I don't – who the hell is that kissing my wife? I will kill that mutha…*Marty's brow was still furrowed when he turned around and stared dead into Shenedra's horror stricken face; he instantly knew that she was somehow a part of this conspiracy to deceive him.

"Oh, my God! Marty, please don't go out there!" Shenedra begged as Marty approached her standing in the doorway.

"Get the hell out of my way!" Marty shouted, rushing towards her with his eyes narrowed, nose flaring, and hands balled up into fists. Shenedra saw something in Marty's eyes so dangerous that she slammed herself against the door to get out of his path. Marty zoomed past her without even looking her way. She could see the perspiration on his forehead and the blood-filled veins bursting against his skin as he zipped by.

Martin made his way through all of the invited guests, marched up to the front door, grabbed the handle, and violently swung it opened shouting his wife's name. "Tina! Tina! What the hell is going on out here?"

Debonair had just pulled away in his car. Tina was heading back towards the front entrance when she inhaled deeply at the sight of Marty walking through the door screaming her name. She was still holding her breath, too stunned to speak as Marty fired off at her. "You heard what I said, dammit! Who was that nigga with his tongue down your throat?"

"Marty, please, calm down," Tina begged, finally exhaling. At that point, he was completely out of control. Martin's hands flew up, grabbing Tina by the throat in a frightening death grip. Tina was beating his hands with her fists, trying to make him release the hold that he had on her. She felt the blood draining from her face while gasping desperately for air.

"Don't tell me crap about calming down! I want to know what's going on right outside my front door! I will kill you right now, right here if you don't tell me something!" he shouted, still holding her by the throat.

Shenedra rushed to her friend's aide yelling and screaming for help. She began clawing at Martin's fingers, kicking his legs, trying anything to make him release Tina. By this time, Michael and several other male partygoers rushed through the doorway and headed straight to Martin. Using all his strength, Michael was able to force Marty's hands away from Tina's throat as she collapsed into Shenedra's arms, fighting to remain conscious.

Alese and Taneka walked outside looking horrified, kneeling to help Shenedra get Tina in the house. They carried her directly to the master bedroom and locked the door.

"Marty, what's going on out here, man? What is wrong with you?" Michael asked, wondering what in the world had caused his best friend to turn against his own wife so suddenly.

"Man, I don't believe this," Marty said in tears, spinning around in a circle, holding his head. "Tina was out here kissing some light skinned nigga with dreadlocks."

"Marty, that can't be true. You must be imagining things."

"Don't tell me what can't be true! I saw it with my own two eyes! I was in the bedroom, and then I looked out the window when I heard voices. By the time I made it out the house, he was pulling off in a white car," Marty cried, sitting on the grassy lawn.

Most of the guests were outside by now feasting on Martin's misery. Some of them had already left and others were heading for their cars in silence. Shenedra and Taneka came out of the bedroom and began escorting visitors out of the house, apologizing for the commotion going on outside. About thirty minutes later, Alese walked out explaining that Tina was fine and wanted to be left alone.

Martin had spent all of this time sitting in his home office with Michael, crying his heart out to his best friend. "I can't believe that Tina would do something like this," he stated between sobs.

"Marty, you still don't know everything. Just give her a chance to explain, man. Stop jumping to conclusions."

"You didn't see what I saw. I know she's been with him; I can feel it in my bones. Now please leave me alone."

"I'm leaving your office, but I'm not leaving your house until I know that things are straight," Michael replied, walking through the doorway.

Finally around midnight, Martin gathered enough composure to saunter into the family room where their remaining four friends were assembled, standing in a semicircle. They had put the untouched cake into the oversized deep freezer and packed away the leftover party food into the stainless steel refrigerator. Shenedra turned in the opposite direction when she saw Marty approaching the room with a scowled face; she could feel what was coming next.

"How long have you known about this?" he boldly asked her.

"Marty, I—I can't discuss this with you. Tina will talk to you after you have calmed down."

"What is his name?"

"Marty, please—don't do this. Tina will talk to you later."

"Get out of my house! I want everybody in this room out of my house now!" Marty shouted, pointing at the door.

"Look man, we're not going anywhere with you acting crazy like this. Alese and I are going to spend the night here or at least stay until you calm down some."

"Why is everybody telling me to calm down? I have a right to know what's going on with my wife." Martin lowered his voice, looking into space as if he was talking to himself.

"If you relax for a second, I'm sure Tina will explain all of this to you," Michael replied. "If you keep up the loud screaming, one of your neighbors might call the police. Believe me; you don't want them out here in your business."

"All right, all right, I'm calm. See, look at me, I'm calm." Martin replied, tapping his chest. "Now will everybody please leave my house?"

"What are you going to do, Marty?" Michael asked.

"Ah, I'm going to stretch out here on the sofa until Tina decides to come out of the bedroom and talk to me. I know that I was wrong for grabbing her, but I lost my mind after seeing the way she was kissing..." Marty eased down on the sofa, resting his face in his hands.

Michael put his arm around Alese as he walked all the ladies to the door. "Come on," he told them, "Maybe its best if we leave them alone to work this out. We can come by and check on them tomorrow."

They both walked out with Michael and Alese. Suddenly Shenedra broke down into tears as she reached out for support. Taneka grabbed her hand and placed the other arm around her sobbing friend's shoulder, leading her into the night atmosphere.

Martin spent the remainder of the night on the rustic brown leather sofa in the den, although he didn't really sleep. There was no way humanly possible for him to slumber after this disastrous evening. By 5:00 a.m. he had made himself crazy with thoughts of Tina and the other man. He wanted to know everything, and dammit he wanted to know right now. This bedroom seclusion game had gone on long enough; it was time to dance to the music or pay to the piper. He stormed to the bedroom door and began banging on it. "Tina, open this door, or I swear I'm going to bust it down!" Marty backed up from the door, preparing to kick it in when he saw the doorknob turning and heard it click open. He cautiously stepped to the door and pushed on it before entering.

Tina was sitting there on the side of the bed, hunched over with a wet towel up to her puffy red face. She was too ashamed to look up at Marty as he entered the dreary room.

"Just tell me how you could do this to me, Tina. Tell me why you would totally disrespect me in my own house this way."

"Martin, I never meant for this to happen. I never wanted to hurt you. You have to believe me."

"Believe you! What the hell do you expect me to believe?"

"I need you to believe that I love you, and that I want to be with you no matter what."

"Well, I certainly don't believe that. Now tell me who he is and exactly how this elicit affair got started."

Tina wiped her face with the cold towel as she purged her soul to Martin. He bombarded her with questions about Debonair that she rapidly answered in an attempt to show him that she was being honest and forthright. After almost two hours of heated conversation, Marty pulled two black suitcases and a garment bag from the closet and began packing his things. Tina slung herself at his feet, hopelessly trying to convince him to give her a second chance through her tears and shameless begging.

Martin had listened to all that he could stand. He didn't know if she was telling the truth or not; he didn't know if she loved him or not; and at this point, he didn't care anymore. All he undoubtedly knew was that he had to leave his house now, before somebody got hurt really bad. In Marty's deepest moment of anger, he realized that it was a good thing that Tina had persuaded him not to ever bring a gun into their home. If he'd owned a firearm right now, he wouldn't have been legally responsible for his actions.

Marty drove around for hours in his SUV, not knowing where to go or what to do. He grew tired of his cellular phone ringing constantly and clicked if off. He wasn't in the mood to talk to anybody or see anybody on this early Sunday morning when most happy couples were rising and preparing to go to church service somewhere. As his mind focused on the fact that it was the Sabbath, and the fact that he hadn't been to church in over a year except for his brother's funeral, he began to wonder if that had something to do with his pathetic life right now.

His best friend, Michael, was always witnessing about the Bible to him and praising God for his anointing and blessings, but Marty had never really gotten into the Word of God. Sure he attended services with Tina for awhile after the boys were born. He wanted to have the perfect family and that included attending church together on most Sunday mornings. Then, Tina and he used to pray together almost everyday. Actually Tina did most of the praying except for the marriage prayer that he liked to recite with his wife.

Marty could distinctively remember going to church with his mother and brother as a child. During that time in his young life, it was just strictly entertainment for him, watching the preacher prance around the church huffing and puffing while the elder women shouted for him to "Preach on!"

But after Ezekiel left them and Cora Lee had to work two jobs, there wasn't much time for churching. There was only time for sleeping and working.

He made it to Michael's house just as they were walking out the front door on their way to church around 10:30 a.m. Marty was feeling dingy and scroungy compared to the three of them wearing their Sunday best clothes. But he perked up when Bianca ran towards him yelling, "My Uncle Marty," no sooner than he exited his vehicle.

"Hello, baby girl," Marty said, swiping her up into his arms.

"Hey, Marty, are you okay?" Michael asked, looking concerned as he walked towards Martin.

"Yeah, I'm all right," he responded halfheartedly. "Hi, Alese, how are you doing?"

"Good morning, Marty, I'm doing well. Did you get any sleep last night?"

"If I did, I can't remember."

"Well, I want you to go on into our house and lie down in the guest bedroom until we return from church," Alese stated, pointing to the front door.

"Ah, I don't want to impose on you all. I'll be all right. I just know that I can't go back home anytime soon."

Alese smiled softly, "You're not imposing. Now I insist that you stay here and rest until we return, and then I'll fix you something to eat." She figured he definitely would be hungry by then. "I know that you and Tina have a lot to work out so you're welcome to stay here with us for as long as you like."

Michael chimed in, "Alese is right, Marty. At least stay here until we get back from church. Take you a hot shower and try to relax for a little while. We'll work out the rest later on this evening."

"All right, all right. You all better get going. I don't want to be the cause of anybody being late for church on such a gorgeous day."

"That's fine because pretty soon you'll be coming to church with us," Michael stated, smiling at his buddy.

Martin silently returned the smile, but in his mind he was thinking, *I wouldn't count on that if I was you, partner. I certainly wouldn't count on that.*

Michael was already praying for a miracle in his friend's life as he and his family drove away in his sunlit copper Nissan Murano. *Whether Martin knows it or not, he's going to be our house guest for awhile if he's not ready to return home. It might take a little bribery, but my best friend is staying with us.*

After Marty left the house in anger with his bags packed, telling Tina that he was through with her and never wanted to see her whorish behind again, she called her best friend, Shenedra, and asked her to come over right away. While she was waiting on Shenedra to make the twenty minute drive to her house, Tina walked through the great room wearing a green housecoat with matching slippers and eyed all of the beautifully wrapped unopened presents from last night. She searched for the tag on each present, looking for her gift from Marty. He had told her that it would be special and something that she had always wanted.

Just as she was reaching for the last bag, Tina heard the doorbell ring and walked to the front entrance to let Shenedra into the house. "Tina, you look terrible. How do you feel?" she inquired.

"Believe it or not, I feel much worse than I look," she replied, gravitating towards her bedroom. "Girl, come on in my room where we can relax." Tina entered her bedroom, sat down on the side of the bed, and motioned for Shenedra to join her there.

"Okay, but where is Martin?" Shenedra asked, looking around before sitting next to Tina on the bed.

"He packed his things and left me over an hour ago."

"Tina, no! Did you ask him to stay?"

"Of course, I did. I not only asked him, I begged him on my hands and knees. After I confessed and told him everything, he said that it was just too much for him to bear, and he had to leave. He said he'd be back to talk with the boys when they come home next weekend but other than that, we were through."

"Tina, I'm so sorry that it had to come to this. He doesn't mean what he said. I knew that Debonair would be trouble for you. I can't believe he had the nerve to show up here last night. What did he give you for your birthday, anyway?"

Tina had totally forgotten about the present from Debonair as she reached behind Shenedra, lifted up the pants lying across the foot of her bed, and pulled the emerald bracelet from the front pocket. "Well, it's certainly beautiful, but is it worth your marriage?"

"No it's not. I hate myself for ever allowing this affair with Debonair to happen." Tina relaxed back onto her king sized pillow and thought that it felt a little lumpy. She rose back up with the pillow in her hand and fluffed it several times before looking down to see a white envelope with her name on the front, printed in Marty's handwriting. She picked up the package, pulled out the contents, opened them up, and then threw herself back on the bed screaming out in total despair.

"Oh! My goodness, Tina! What's wrong? What's in that envelope?" Shenedra asked, looking startled.

Tina was too emotionally warped to answer the questions. She just handed the envelope to Shenedra as she continued her gut wrenching crying episode.

Pulling out the two first class cabin tickets for a seven-day cruise to the Bahamas, Shenedra dropped them on the bed, and just shook her head at Tina. *She had everything that most women only dreamed about and here she was pissing it all away,* she thought, bending down to comfort her girlfriend.

Chapter 18

Over a month had passed since Tina and Marty separated after her super birthday bash. Tina was swamped at the hair salon with it being the height of the summer season, everyone wanted to show their natural hair including new braided styles, twists, or locks. She was happy to have an ultra busy work schedule as a reprieve for her unhappy home life during this time. Of course this didn't stop Debonair from blowing up her cellular phone until it got to the point where she changed the number. And she stopped going to his place of business and asked him to stop coming to hers. So far, he had obeyed her wishes. Tina simply made her own coffee at home every morning before leaving for work or stopped at the nearest Starbuck's since she didn't have any desires to ever see Debonair Jenkins again.

Finally, growing tired of lying to Malique and Jordan about their father being on a business trip or working late nights week after week, she decided to tell them the truth. Marty hadn't shown up since he'd left the day after her birthday party or called to speak with the boys like he'd promised.

After gathering them in the family room one night preceding dinner, Tina patiently explained the dire situation to her sons. Telling them that it was best that she and Martin spent some time apart, they listened quietly as she spoke. "Where's Daddy staying, mom?" Jordan asked.

"Ah, he's living with Uncle Mike and Aunt Alese right now, baby."

"Well then, when is he coming home?"

"We haven't worked that out yet, so I'm not sure. I won't know that for awhile."

Jordan lowered his head, leaning against Tina's chest as they sat next to each other on the sofa. Wrapping her arms around her baby boy, she eyed Malique leaning back in the recliner, waiting for his teenage response. He just sat there carefully pondering the situation before speaking. "Hey, Jordan, I've got a new video game on my dresser you can borrow."

"Oh, yeah, what's the name of it?"

"It's a surprise, but I bet you'll love it."

"All right," he replied, dragging himself away from Tina. As soon as he disappeared from sight, Malique slid over on the sofa next to his mother.

"Ma, I know that you probably don't want to tell me this, but I have to ask you something."

"Sure, sweetheart, you can ask me anything. I'm listening."

"Ma, have you and dad been arguing about me and, you know, my gay experience? Is that why daddy moved away from us?"

"Oh, sweetheart, no, that's not it. Your father's leaving had nothing to do with your sex life, which I hope has been suspended until you're more mature."

"Well, it hasn't happened again if that's what you mean. I know that I was wrong for experimenting with something like that, especially bringing it home. I'm sorry, ma. I know that I'm too young to be having sex anyway. I've decided to take some time and get to know myself better before having anymore sexual contact with anyone male or female."

"Malique, I'm so proud of you. You really are growing up," she said, reaching up to embrace him.

"Ma, is there anything I can do to make you feel better?"

"Baby, don't worry about me, I'm fine. Your father will talk to you soon, I promise. And you'll see that his moving out has nothing to do with your life."

"Okay, ma," he paused, then added, "Thanks for listening to me."

"Malique, please remember that I'm your mother, and I love you very much. I want you to live a long and happy life. Hopefully, someday you'll grow up and get married and have children of your own. Until that time comes, I want you to talk freely with me about anything. Is that understood, young man?"

"Yes ma'am. I understand, and I love you, too, ma. Thanks for being patient with me."

Malique bolted from the sofa and ran up the stairs to his room while Tina remained sitting, contemplating the predicament of her marriage and how she would ever work this out. *Right now, I don't see a happy way for this to end at all.*

Arriving early at the shop wearing her favorite bright orange sundress, Tina was hoping to finally finish the updating on her accounting books. As she sifted through the stack of mail that had accumulated on her desk over the last week, a brown envelope with a return address from the Internal Revenue Service caught her eye, and she tore it open first.

When Tina finished reading the letter, she slumped down into her high back office chair, stifling the urge to scream. Just as she was getting caught up with her backlogged paperwork, the IRS wanted to do a complete audit of her business covering the last three years of operations. *I just don't know how much more of this I can bear. I can't believe that the IRS wants to audit my hair salon. I mean we're doing well, but there are businesses out there that are much larger than mine and making a lot more money. How in the world did they single me out?*

Tina was on pins and needles waiting for Shenedra and Taneka to arrive at work. They would probably be even more shocked than she had been to receive this news. She didn't have to wait very long because less than an hour later, they were entering her office.

"Tina, don't worry about it. It'll be all right. You're caught up on all your records," Shenedra said, sounding optimistic after hearing the taxing news.

"I don't understand why they would audit your business, Tina, but I guess that's just the IRS for you. You just never know who they're going to bother next," Taneka stated, turning her head.

"Yeah, you're right about that. But I'm worried because I was so behind that I might have missed something rushing through all those documents."

"Look, we'll help you go back over everything again or you could hire my cousin, Racine, who is an accountant. She can come in and review the books for you just to make extra sure that you have everything in order for the auditors."

"That's a great idea. How soon can you call her for me because they're only giving me ten working days to have all the documents available to them?"

"I have her cellular phone number so I can call her right now to see how soon she can meet with you."

"Thanks, Shenedra. Girl, you always have my back."

"That's right, and don't you forget it," she teased. As they hurried out to the main working area, customers were already pouring in. Most of them had appointments and a few wanted to just walk-in and get something done, but Tina had stopped being able to accept walk-in customers a long time ago. While it pained her heart to turn someone away, she preferred to maintain the ability to provide quality services and not have overlapping client appointments.

It had been an extremely busy Saturday afternoon for Tina, and Shenedra's cousin had not returned her telephone call regarding helping them with the taxes. She had kept back to back appointments all day long without taking a break or eating, trying to keep her mind off of the upcoming audit. Before she realized what was happening, Tina starting feeling extremely light headed and nauseous, and collapsed to the floor right in front of Taneka's hair station. "Shenedra!" she screamed. "Girl, come here, Tina just fainted!"

"Oh, my goodness! Somebody call an ambulance and help me get her to the sofa over there in the corner," Shenedra and Taneka were trying to lift Tina while Tammy dialed 9-1-1. After they got Tina lifted onto the sofa, they splashed her face with cold water, trying to bring her back to life. Tina's eyes began fluttering as she incoherently babbled at them, trying to move her hands. Shenedra had instructed the patrons in the salon to stand back against the wall on the other side of the room as she propped open the front door for Tina to get some fresh air.

By the time the ambulance arrived, approximately ten minutes later, Tina was still in a semiconscious state of mind. The two paramedics, a female and a male, quickly made it to Tina's side. The female paramedic, Marla, immediately took her blood pressure while asking Shenedra questions regarding Tina's medical history. "Ma'am do you know whether or not she's a diabetic?" The male paramedic, Howard, stood by carefully monitoring their conversation.

"Yes, she is a diabetic, and she has high blood pressure!" Shenedra responded, sounding fearful.

"I see her blood pressure is extremely high. I'm going to check her blood glucose level, too," she said, pulling a glucose monitoring kit out of the black medical bag. She skillfully pricked Tina's right index finger, planted the blood on the strip, and waited five seconds for the results. Just as she had suspected, Tina's glucose level was forty-four, well below the normal range of ninety-to-one hundred thirty.

Addressing Shenedra, Marla asked, "Miss, do you know what type of medication she's taking?"

"No, I don't, but I know that she carries it in her purse. I'll go get her bag and be right back." Shenedra was back within a matter of seconds with both of Tina's prescriptions and handed them to Marla.

After propping Tina up on the sofa and giving her the prescription medication, Marla instructed her to drink a cup of orange juice. Slowly, Tina began to stop shaking as her eyes focused on the paramedic.

"Tina, can you hear me?" Marla was staring in Tina's flushed face.

"Ah, yes, I can hear you just fine," Tina replied, blinking her eyes.

"Well, you should be okay for now. Have you eaten at all today?"

"No. No, I don't think that I've had a bite of anything yet," she stated, trying to recall whether that was true or not.

"You were suffering from hypoglycemia. I'm sure you know about the consequences of not eating right when you're a diabetic. As you can see from the episode today, it can be very damaging to your health. I suggest you try to eat a healthy meal right now and rest yourself for the remainder of the day."

"Thank you very much. I feel better now, but I know that I need to eat something right away."

"I also suggest that you go see your primary physician tomorrow for a check-up, just to be sure that everything is fine," she said, packing her medical bag and standing straight up.

"Yes, I intend to do just that. Thank you, again," Tina replied, standing up. Everyone remaining in the shop gathered around her, releasing a sigh of relief as the paramedics loaded up their equipment and left.

Arriving at Dr. O'Hara's office early on Tuesday morning, Tina sported a black loose fitting pants suit on a rainy day. She had a frightening thought as she waited for the nurse to call her name. *Oh, Jesus, what if I'm pregnant? Please, Father, don't let me be pregnant now.*

"Tina Carlisle! Please come on back," Nurse Cathy called out.

Tina pushed herself up from the armchair, forcing herself to walk quickly on wobbling knees. She was more anxious than ever to get this examination over with now that she had these terrifying thoughts. She needed answers right away.

After the nurse weighed her in, she took Tina's blood pressure and glucose levels. Tina asked the nurse if they would also run a pregnancy test today.

Several minutes passed as she waited for her doctor to enter the room. "Tina, do you think there is some possibility that you might be pregnant?" Dr. O'Hara asked, smiling at her patient, checking her medical charts.

"I don't think so doctor. I just want to be sure after that fainting spell I had the other day and the nausea that I felt."

"Well, your blood pressure and glucose level looks fine today. However, I am sending you to the lab for additional blood work so that I can be sure that there aren't any additional health problems developing. Now you need to be more careful as far as your diet goes, and remember that you need to also get more exercise."

"Yes, doctor, I'm working on that."

"You can go down the hallway and turn right at the lab entrance to have your blood work completed. By the time you return, we should have the results of your pregnancy test."

"Thank you, doctor," Tina responded, taking the lab request form approving her blood work from Dr. O'Hara.

About twenty minutes later, Tina returned from the laboratory, stopped at the front desk, and requested to see Nurse Cathy regarding her test results. After several minutes had passed, Nurse Cathy came out to see a frightful looking Tina.

"Mrs. Carlisle, I have the results of your pregnancy test," she stated, holding the side door open for Tina.

"Thank you, Nurse Cathy," Tina replied, stepping through the doorway.

"The tests show that you are not pregnant, Mrs. Carlisle."

Tina took a long deep breath and let it out as slowly as she could before verbally responding. "Thank you, Nurse Cathy. Thank you so much."

A very relieved Tina headed out to her car, walking through the light rain, saying a silent prayer. Once she was inside of her Corvette and sitting behind the wheel, she placed her head down for a minute and took several deep breaths. As Tina looked at her weary face in the mirror, memories flashed through her mind about the conversation she and Marty had over five years ago regarding having another child. They had debated trying to produce another offspring, the daughter they both wanted. But after considering how busy their professional lives were, they decided to be content with the two boys they already had. Right now, Tina couldn't imagine having another child with any man besides Martin Carlisle and thanked God again that she was not pregnant from Debonair Jenkins. Wiping the tears from her eyes, she turned on the windshield wipers as soon as she started the car.

Realizing just how careless she'd been, Tina vowed that she would never be with Debonair again. She would fight the temptation with all the strength that she had.

On her way to the hair salon, Tina drove through McDonald's and ordered a sausage and egg biscuit with a small container of milk so that she could take her medicines. She had to start playing by the rules as far as her health was concerned. There were many serious consequences that she would have to face if she allowed these two medical problems to escalate out of control. Tina was more than cognizant of the fact that she didn't need to create any additional problems for herself. Her health was the one area that she could positively control on her own.

As she pulled into the parking lot for the *Braids and Locks Shop*, Tina remembered that she needed to start preparing for the upcoming trip to Fort Lauderdale. The National Conference for Hair Shop Owners was scheduled to begin in July, and she hadn't made any preparations. However, she was looking forward to getting out of Jacksonville for three days and spending some time completely alone with herself. She still needed to check with her parents today to make sure that the time-share duplex was available before making a hotel reservation. *That would make it the ultimate getaway,* she thought, opening the doors to her salon.

Shenedra followed Tina into her office, trailing the scent of food. Taking a seat in front of Tina on the other side of the desk, Shenedra watched her as she uncovered the food. "I'm glad to see that you decided to get you some breakfast this morning."

"Yeah, I think it's time that I take better care of myself, and that includes eating at least three balanced meals a day. I can't go all day again without eating. That episode the other afternoon scared the mess out of me. I don't ever want to go through that again. You know?"

"Hey, I know exactly what you mean. You scared everybody in the shop Saturday with that one, girl."

"I bet I did. I just hope I didn't frighten any of my good customers away."

"Nah, I don't think so. People understand that most of us have some health issues. I think it was a wake-up call for all of us to get checked for diabetes, though."

"Yes, that is a good idea, because most people ignore the warning signs until they get tested and find out they have it. And by that time, some people are already in need of insulin shots. I just hope that I don't ever get to that point. I just don't think that I could shoot myself in the arm or anywhere else with a needle every day. I mean it takes all my strength just to prick my little finger two or three times a day," she said, laughing at herself while holding out her pinky.

"I know that's right. I've already scheduled my physical for next week. So keep me in your prayers."

"Shenedra, you don't have anything to worry about. You don't have a history of diabetes or high blood pressure in your family."

"No, I don't, but that doesn't mean a thing from what I've read. If you have it in your family, you can be more prone to the disease, but that doesn't mean that you can't develop it over time as an adult."

"Yes, that is true now that I think about it. Let me know how your tests come out."

"Of course, I will. You finish your breakfast while I get back to the shop. Take your time, okay?"

"You know, your cousin, Racine, called me back today on my cell phone after I left the doctor's office. She said that she can come by this evening around 5:30 and examine the files with us."

"That's wonderful news. I told you that she would call you back as soon as she got a chance," Shenedra responded, rising from her seat.

"Shenedra, wait a minute. I have one more thing to tell you before you leave," Tina paused, studying her friend's face before continuing. "I've decided to file for divorce from Marty."

"Tina, please, I think that you're making a major mistake if you do that," Shenedra responded, sitting back down on the edge of the chair.

"Well, I don't see any reason to keep prolonging the issue. We're so far gone from one another now, I don't see any possible way for us to get back to where we where before this nightmare began."

"Why are you rushing for a divorce if Marty hasn't asked you for one? Obviously, the man still cares about you."

"I don't think that's the case, he hasn't filed for divorce because he's too hurt and ashamed of the fact that I cheated on him. So I've decided to let him off the hook and file first. I just can't live with the pain that I've cause him anymore."

"Maybe you should talk to him about this before you make that drastic move, Tina."

"I've already spoken to an attorney friend of mine and asked her to help me file the paperwork. If Marty doesn't contest the divorce, and I doubt that he will, it'll be a fast and easy settlement. According to the lawyer, he should be receiving the papers in the mail one day this week."

"Girl, are you sure about this? I think that you still have a chance of getting him back. You should at least wait another month or two and see what happens."

"Shenedra, please, Martin won't even have a decent conversation with me or our sons. I can't bear talking with him face to face because of the way he looks at me—like I'm a piece of gum stuck to the bottom of his shoe that he can't scrape off. There's no chance of us getting back together, and we both need to move on. I don't want to spend my life pining away for a man that's snubbing his nose at me."

"Tina, I love you, and I'll support you either way. It's your call."

"Thank you, Shenedra. I appreciate you being my best friend. You'll never know how much your friendship and support means to me."

"Well, that's what best friends are for, right?" Shenedra asked, reaching across the desk to hug Tina before leaving the office.

Chapter 19

"Hey, Marty, man where have you been lately?" Billy asked, welcoming Martin back to the Chauffeur's Bar and Lounge after three months of absence. Lifting his hand up to Marty, he grabbed his fingers and pulled him onto the barstool.

"Man, you won't believe what I've been going through the last few months," Marty began, "I'm telling you the truth."

"Well, let me order you a drink, and you can tell me all about it," Billy motioned for Lucius, the bartender, to come take his order.

"All right, fine. I'll have a club soda since you're buying."

"A club soda, wow, that's going to break me," Billy laughed, covering his mouth.

"Yeah, right, I—I, ah, quit drinking, and I've been attending AA meetings for almost three months."

"Well, what the hell are you doing in a bar?" Billy asked still laughing as Lucius approached them.

"Is that Marty Carlisle sitting beside you, Billy?" Lucius asked, bending down and squinting at his friend.

"It looks like him, but he claims that he's quit drinking, so I don't believe it's really him. What do you think, Lucius?"

Lucius had to laugh at that one before uttering a word. "Marty, is that true? You quit drinking man?"

"Man, I haven't had a drink since my first AA meeting. I just wanted to stop by to holler at you guys and let you all know how things turned out with my father."

"Oh, yeah, that's right. Your ol' man showed up here looking for you several times. What happened with that?"

"Well, we finally hooked up and basically, we spent a little time together, you know. Now we're on speaking terms and plan on getting to know one another better. He stayed here over a month, but he's back in North Carolina right now with his family. We plan on seeing each other again later this summer." Martin deliberately didn't mention anything about the episode with his brother. He wanted to move pass that and concentrate on building a stronger bond with his father.

"That's good news. I'm really glad to hear that," Billy chimed.

"I agree with you, that is good news, man. It's never too late for your family," Lucius added.

"Honestly, I feel like taking a drink because I did get some disappointing news today. You know, there's always some bad news around the corner as soon as you get some good news. I figured if I could come in here tonight and leave without taking a drink of alcohol, I'm cured," he gave a nervous laugh.

"What type of news did you get today, Marty? Has there been a death in your family or something?" Billy asked as Lucius looked on, anticipating his reply.

"No, it's nothing like that. But, ah, my wife had me served with divorce papers today after seventeen years of marriage."

"Man, get out of here. I didn't know you were separated from your wife."

"Yeah, we've been separated for awhile. We split up the first week of May. I guess she's ready to move on with her new young man since I'm getting old. You know I have a birthday coming up the same week as my divorce settlement."

"Nah, I didn't know about your birthday. But I don't believe that Tina is seeing a younger man, Marty, you're lying," Lucius looked shocked.

"Why are you surprised? I've told you fellas once that love don't last always. Women come and women go, it's what they do. Now I have to tell you though, my friend, I thought you had it all. I really thought that you and Tina would make it. Seventeen years is a hellava long time," Billy stated.

"Lucius, man, let me have a club soda with a slice of lime, please?" Marty asked. "I'm starting to get depressed over here."

"You really are being strong, Marty," Billy commented.

"Yeah, this is my test." Marty replied, stiffening his shoulders. "Man, what is all that noise over there in the corner? Looks like the sisters are celebrating something tonight." When Marty entered the bar tonight he noticed a group of six well-dressed black women appearing to be having a celebration of some sort. They kept the drinks coming to their table and stayed on the small dance floor laughing and cutting up with each other.

"I don't know what they're celebrating though, but they keep looking over here at us. I'm just playing it cool, pretending like I don't see them over there making that loud racket," Billy laughed with Marty.

Lucius returned with Marty's club soda, and asked the attractive female standing next to him wearing a black gold-studded tank top with a short flouncy skirt, if she wanted another drink. Leaning in towards Marty with her right elbow on the counter, she ordered a Seven and Seven as she ran her fingers through her long straight black hair, eyeing Marty in the process. "Hi, I'm Dorene Marshall," she said, extending her right hand to Marty, "How are you doing this evening?"

"Hello, I'm doing fine, and my name is Martin Carlisle," he replied, shaking her hand.

"Listen Martin, my friends and I are having a celebration over there. Would you like to join us?"

"Ah, no, not right now, but thanks for asking."

"Well, if you change your mind just come on over, all right?"

Martin just nodded his head as Lucius returned with her drink. She gave him one last look before turning to walk away. "Maybe I can buy you a drink later on. What are you drinking?"

"I'm just having a club soda tonight. I'm trying to quit drinking. I—I just came out to visit my friends."

"I see. I'm here with my friends celebrating my final divorce decree today."

"Really, how long were you married?" Marty inquired.

"Too long is all I care to say," Dorene smiled shrewdly at him. "What about you, Marty, are you a married man?" she asked, looking down at his left hand.

"Yes—I mean—no—I mean, I'm separated, but I received divorce papers in the mail today," Marty replied, shaking his head at his own confusion.

"Oh, so you're here celebrating, too."

"Not exactly," was all that he could manage to get out.

"I better get back to my party. My friends are watching us," she said, looking over Martin's shoulder. "Maybe we can talk a little later. We're almost ready to wrap up our celebration here."

"Yeah, sure, that sounds good," Marty stammered.

Dorene sashayed back to her table, knowing that Marty and Billy were eyeing her plump behind. She swayed extra sexy and smooth for them. Her big sable brown eyes had spotted Marty the second he entered the establishment wearing his long jacket Armani suit and expensive handmade dress shoes. Dorene knew quality when she saw it, especially if it was on a fine lonely looking brother like Martin.

"Marty, man, I don't know what it is, but you still got it," Billy laughed and slapped Marty on the shoulder as soon as Dorene glided away.

"Man, I don't know what you're talking about. That lady was just trying to be nice to me."

"Let me share a little secret with you, all right. Nothing cures a broken heart faster than a new woman, you know what I mean?"

"Yeah, I know what you mean, but I'm not ready for a new woman. I haven't divorced the first one yet."

"Please, you said yourself that she's already got a new man. And from what I can see tonight," he began, glancing at Dorene's table. "It's time for you to get a new woman. Man, I'm not telling you to marry the lady. Just let her ease you through the night."

"Billy, you're insane," Marty stated, downing the last of his club soda. "Look, I've got to get out of here," Marty slid off the barstool.

"Why are you leaving, its eleven o'clock on a Friday night," Billy stated, raising both hands, looking baffled.

"I've passed my test. I was able to come in here and down one non-alcoholic drink, but I'm not trying to press my luck, you know."

"Yeah, yeah, I understand. You take care, and I'll see you around."

"Good night, Billy. Lucius! I'll check you later!"

Both men waved good-bye to Marty as he turned, heading out the door. Walking towards his car at a steady pace, Marty heard someone calling his name as he reached for the door handle to his SUV.

"Martin! Martin! You mean you're leaving without me?" Dorene asked, approaching him with a smile.

"Lady, I don't know you, so why would I leave with you?"

"Well, I thought maybe you might want to get to know me better. I know that I would love to get to know you better. We do have something in common, you know."

"Really? And what might that be?" Marty asked, staring down at her.

"I've just gotten divorced, and you're about to get divorced. I say we get together and console each other. I mean—we're too grown adults, you can handle that can't you?"

Marty laughed nervously, stared into Dorene enticing eyes, and decided to throw caution to the wind. "What did you have in mind?"

"I just thought that maybe we could get a nice hotel room close by, have a cold drink, and see what else we have in common. I like the Embassy Suites, and there's one not too far from here on Baymeadows Road. Do you know where that is?"

"Yeah, I know where it is," Marty replied softly.

"Well, ah, why don't I do this? I'll go check in at the Embassy, and if you should decide to join me, just stop at the front desk and ask for Dorene Marshall's room number," she cooed, walking away from Marty.

He watched Dorene walk away, slide into her Volvo S-80 silver four-door sedan, back up quickly, and then drive away before entering his vehicle. Marty was amazed at her brazenness to say the least. He had never had a female to approach him so boldly and without any reservations. Even though Tina was the only woman that he'd ever been with, he was a very experienced lover from years of a loving marriage. So Marty started his BMW, turned on the radio, and listened to the entire classic song that was playing by Al Green. *I know what you mean, brother. I'm so tired of being alone, too.* After shifting the gears, he slowly drove off in the same direction in which Dorene had driven.

Even after arriving at the hotel, Marty remained in his vehicle, contemplating whether or not to join a woman in her suite whom he had just met at the bar tonight. Knowing that this wasn't his style, Marty wasn't sure if he wanted this because he was attracted to the dark eyed mysterious lady, or if he just wanted to get back at Tina for being unfaithful to him and filing for divorce. At any rate, he knew that if he made this move with her tonight, there would be no going back to his marriage. With that in mind, Marty exited his vehicle, strolled pass the huge tropical atrium to the front desk, and casually asked for Dorene Marshall's suite. Minutes later, he was standing outside her hotel door raising his hand to knock.

"Come on in, it's open," Dorene stated, after hearing a light tap at the door.

Marty turned the door handle and slowly entered the two-room suite, looking around for Dorene. She was sitting to his left on the sofa with her legs crossed and her mini skirt raised high on her smooth thighs listening to the soft music of John Legend on the radio.

"I was hoping that you would join me," she eyed him sexily, holding a glass of champagne.

"I—I just thought that we could talk for a minute, if you don't mind."

"We've got all night to talk," she stated, placing her glass on the coffee table, rising from the sofa and taking him by the hand. "Let's slow dance first."

She moved close to Martin, pressing her chest into his chest, resting her cheek against his cheek while humming with the music as she seductively moved to the enchanting beat. Marty realized that he was dancing with temptation as he gently placed his hands around her lower waist. Resisting the urge to touch her firm protruding bottom, he willed his manhood not to rise.

Soon as the song ended, Dorene pulled him by the hand heading towards the sofa. Sliding down into the seat, she smiled up at him.

"Come sit with me," she said, patting the cushion beside her. "Would you like some champagne?"

"Ah, no, thank you," he replied, easing down into the cushiony taupe colored sofa.

"That's right, you're trying to quit drinking," she said deviously, pouring another glass for herself.

"Yeah, that's right," he replied, smiling at his evening companion.

She promptly swung her slim shapely legs around into Martin's lap, scooted up close to him, and whispered in his left ear, "What would you like to talk about, sweetheart?"

"I just want to know a little more about you, that's all. I mean, all I know so far it that you got divorced today."

"That's true. Well, let's see—I'm thirty-eight-years-old, I work as an administrator for a well-known insurance company, and I have an eighteen-year-old daughter who just graduated from William Raines High School. She has a full scholarship to Florida A&M University in Tallahassee to major in Business Administration."

"That's great, you must be very proud of her."

"Yes, I am extremely proud of my daughter, Joiree."

"Do you mind telling me why you got divorced?"

"No! I don't want to talk about that," she responded. "I want to concentrate on us right now. We have this beautiful suite and a bottle of champagne. Let's enjoy ourselves," she said, leaning in closer to his lips, taking control of the situation. Wrapping her arms around him, she pulled Martin nearer to her, consuming his lips with hers. She was tired of talking and ready for loving.

At first Martin was hesitant to return her kisses, but after a few seconds of feeling her fiery tongue salivating around his mouth, he zealously returned the fire. Her hands were busy removing his clothes while he lifted up her top and reached around to unsnap her lace trimmed push-up bra.

Sliding the bra straps down her shoulders, he slid his tongue over her palpitating chest until her breast nipples slipped right into his hot mouth. He tantalized one breast with his scorching tongue while gently palm rolling the other one before switching up. Dorene moaned in pleasure, stroking the thin hairs on the back of his neck.

Minutes later, Dorene had masterfully stripped Martin down to the waist, and she was naked except for the red thong panties that she wore. Feeling the pressure against his crotch area, Martin stood up, swept her into his arms, and carried her into the second room. She was clinging to his neck, biting and pulling his earlobe between her teeth as he slowly lowered her to the mattress.

Suddenly Martin stopped, "What's wrong?" Dorene asked, panicking from the weary expression on his face.

"I'm sorry, but I just can't do this," he replied softly, easing down on the bed beside her.

"Baby, come on, I know that you can do this," she cooed, touching his rigid body.

"Yeah, I guess I can, but I won't. You see, I just realized that you're not my wife and even though she did me wrong, I can't go through with this."

"But, baby, don't you want this? Don't you want me, Martin?"

"Yes, I do. I—I want you, but I can't make love with you—not like this. Not knowing that I'm still married."

"Oh, you make me sick!" she snarled at him. "Get the hell out of my room! You're a punk ass joke! Get out now!" she yelled, screaming and kicking at him. Martin fell to the floor trying to avoid one of her sharp kicks.

"I'm sorry," he mumbled, rising to his feet and backing out into the front room. He swiftly gathered up his clothes, put them on, and left without saying another word to Dorene, who was still pouting and cursing in the bedroom. All her plans were ruined. She was hoping to get Daddy Rich into the sack tonight and comfort him right on through his devastating divorce so that she could eventually be the next Mrs. Martin Carlisle. She recognized who he was the moment he waltzed into the bar looking all good and solitary wearing his expensive suit, Brazilian shoes, and custom made jewelry. She thought that her ship had finally come in since her recent divorce had left her almost destitute.

Damn! I maxed out my credit card paying for this room on top of all my other bills, trying to impress Daddy Rich. Oh, well, let me finish this bottle of champagne, she thought, pouring the remainder of the liquid into her tall flute glass. After digesting a few long swigs of the bitter juice, her sordid mind began to wander. *Now I can enjoy the rest of the night by myself. He must really love his wife. Well, I feel sorry for his weak behind because some married women just don't know how good they have it*, she rationalized, slipping into a drunken haze.

Feeling tyrannized over the way he treated Dorene, Martin suddenly realized that he was pulling into his own driveway at 12:15 in the morning. *How in the world did I end up here? Man, my mind must be playing tricks on me.* He sat there in the BMW staring at the outside of his house, looking for some sign of life. Martin stayed there in his SUV for another fifteen minutes before he started the engine again and cruised back down the driveway.

About twenty minutes later, Martin pulled up at Michael's house in Meadow Bay. Since it was almost one in the morning he hoped that he wouldn't disturb them by coming in this late even though he had a key to their place. After leaving his vehicle, walking up to the front door and sliding the key in the lock, he slipped off his leather shoes, and stepped lightly to the kitchen. To his surprise, Michael was stretched out in his cloth recliner in the den watching the end of the movie, *Love Jones*, starring Nia Long and Larenz Tate. When Michael sat up in his recliner and clicked off the television set, he saw Martin standing in the doorway. "Hey, Marty, I see you made it in. Where did you go tonight, man?"

"Mike, believe me, you don't want to know." Marty entered the den and sat down on the end of the sectional sofa.

Michael stood, stretching his long body while eyeing his friend. "Man, that was a good movie I just saw," he said, sitting back down in his chair.

"I saw it a long time ago, but I don't really remember it. I don't recall it being one of my favorite movies, you know," Marty stated, propping his feet up on the ottoman.

"Well, I've seen it at least four or five times, and I like it better every time I do. It's a love story about this young couple that keeps breaking up and getting back together until they finally get it right in the end."

"Well, I guess everybody can't have a happy ending in love."

"I have to disagree with you on that one, man. You remember this time last year, don't you? Alese and I were separated, and I didn't think that I had a chance of ever getting her back. Then you came to my rescue and saved my marriage."

"Mike, man, I didn't save your marriage. You and Alese were going to get back together whether I intervened or not."

"If that's what you want to think, then so be it. But tell me now, what's going on between you and Tina? Are you two ready to get back together?"

"Ah, man, that's an overdone turkey, if you're asking me. Tina had me served with divorce papers today."

"Marty, have you talked to her yet? Did you try to call her?"

"No, there was no reason for that. She spoke to me loud and clear when I received those divorce papers from her attorney," Marty replied, throwing his hands up and then dropping them on his thighs.

"Man, she's just trying to get your attention. I'm telling you, she still loves you as much as you love her."

"Well, she certainly has a funny way of showing her love, wouldn't you say?"

"Sometimes people don't know how to express the love that they feel in their hearts, so they end up doing things that are hurtful to those they really love. But I'm a strong believer in what the Bible says about love."

"Oh, yeah. And what is it that the Bible says about love, my friend?"

"You know in First Corinthians, it reads that love bears all things, believes all things, hopes all things, and endures all things. Love never fails. You see, I believe that couples who don't stay married are just not really and truly in love with each other. Now they might think that what they feel is love, but in reality it's not because according to God's own words, love never fails. Marty, just think about what you've gone through with your father and your brother in the last few months. Man, love brought your father back to you and love will make you two a family again."

"Mike, I appreciate what you're saying, and I know that you're trying to make me feel better. But I have come to the conclusion that love just don't last always. Man, nothing lasts forever."

"All right, we can debate this back and forth all night long, but I'm going to bed now. You know, I don't want to preach to you. I'm asking you to search your soul like you never have before. Marty, think about what really matters in this world to you and don't let nothing come between you and that. That's all I'm saying tonight."

"I hear you, Mike, now take your tired self on to bed."

"Oh, and one more thing, if you're going to sit up for awhile, I want you to read two Bible verses for me."

"I thought you said that you weren't going to preach. Didn't you just say that?"

"Marty, I'm not preaching, I'm just asking you to read something in the Bible for a friend tonight," he stated firmly, handing Marty the Bible with the pages earmarked and the passages highlighted for him to read. "Now thank you and good night," Michael stood and walked out the room.

Martin immediately went back to surfing channels on the television. Minutes passed before he noticed the open Bible on the table where Michael had left it. Reluctantly Marty picked up the book and started reading the two chapters that his friend had marked by Ephesians 5:25:26:

> *Husbands, love your wives, just as Christ also loved the church and gave Himself for her, that He might sanctify and cleanse her with the washing of water by the word.*

Martin read the Scriptures several times before closing the Bible. He didn't understand the meaning behind the passages and being too tired to concentrate, he fell asleep on the sofa. Dreaming about the love that he used to have, Martin woke up with tears in his eyes.

Realizing that he was still wearing his suit clothes, he turned off the television, went to the guest room, and undressed before climbing into bed. He lay between the covers pondering his life, tossing and turning for several more hours as sleep evaded him. Finally, Martin got out of bed and got down on his knees to pray, something he hadn't done in months. When Martin finished asking the Lord for guidance, peace, and wisdom, he lay back down and pulled the sheet over his head. Within a matter of minutes, he fell into a sound sleep.

Chapter 20

Since she'd endured a long boring day at the National Shop Owners Conference in a Donna Karan fuchsia pants suit with matching high heeled sandals, Tina was ready for a relaxing weekend on the beach in the gray wood frame, two-bedroom, time-share her parents owned in Fort Lauderdale. After submitting all the proper documents for the tax audit, Racine Compton, her newly hired accountant, had assured Tina that there was nothing to worry about. It appeared that she had been randomly selected for an audit and not because of any improprieties on her part. So after two weeks of scuffling through three years worth of paperwork, everything had been turned in on time and already cleared with the IRS. And Ms. Compton had even installed the latest accounting software on Tina's brand new Dell slim line notebook computer.

Tina was happy to be out of town this weekend, especially considering the fact that Martin had received the divorce papers by now. She was surprised that Martin had not called to curse her out for sending him legal documents without talking to him first, but she naturally assumed that he must be in agreement with the divorce proceeding as planned. She wanted to be far away from Jacksonville when he got those papers in his hand. This was just the type of serene place that she needed to be to celebrate her new start in life.

Pulling up to the beachside parking area in her green Ford Taurus rental car, Tina turned off the engine and sat there quietly for several minutes with her head resting back against the seat. It was a bright sunshiny day in Fort Lauderdale, the temperature was almost ninety-nine degrees in the shade, and Tina was savoring the scene. Enjoying the sound of the ocean, hearing the music blasting from boom boxes, and the sight of parents and children playing around on the beach, she realized that she had not been to the duplex in years. Justifiably it had been one of their favorite vacation spots when Martin and she wanted to get away someplace really romantic. They thought that there was no place in the whole wide world more romantic and sensual than this spot on the beach, where the reddish sun set on the waves of the beautiful indigo colored water.

Tina could still vividly remember one particularly bright day they had spent together on this beach where she was dancing to the funky sounds on the portable radio they carried everywhere with them back then. They had just returned from a late lunch and decided to take a stroll on the beach before the sun set. Lip synching the words along with Natalie Cole singing, "Our Love," Tina danced with gladness as the short black halter dress that she was wearing with a wide swing tail moved with her swaying body to the blaring beat. She'd taken off her new black high heel strap sandals and danced for Marty in the sand while he stood there in a trance watching her with his arms folded. His beige short sleeve shirt was unbuttoned, showing off his tight chest, over a pair of loose fitting jeans. Dancing her way over to the shore edges, Tina dipped her toes into the cool evening water, threw her head back, and laughed along with her husband. Marty ran over and scooped her up into his firm embrace, twirling around and around until they both fell to the ground in dizziness. It had been a magical day that she would never forget. Tina could still hear the laughter, the words to the song, and the music playing in her ears from that day. When Natalie hit the high notes toward the end of the tune, Martin swept her up into his arms again, spinning them around until they fell into the warm sand feeling crazy dizzy in love.

Sometimes they would take an old blanket, a bottle of wine, cheese and crackers, and lay out on the white sand until way after the midnight hour. Eventually, they would stumble barefooted carrying their shoes into the duplex's master bedroom holding on to each other and giggling like they were at ComicView on BET. Then they would make sweet amorous love to each other for hours until the morning sun crept through their window pane before drifting off into a deep intoxicated sleep for most of the day.

Finally, Tina lifted up her head, breathed in, and then slowly breathed out. She opened up the car door, reached over and grabbed the small bag of groceries off the front seat, and headed to her side of the duplex. As Tina neared the left side of the building, she began to feel strange, almost as if someone was watching her back. She stopped and then glanced over her shoulder to the left and to the right before proceeding. Then she saw them, two dozen gorgeous peach-colored long stem roses were in two opened boxes on the doorstep with a note attached. *These are so beautiful! Who would be sending me roses down here? Only a few people even know that I'm here. I bet the note is from Marty! Oh, God, let me read the note!* Tina juggled the key in the door and then kicked it on open. She threw her purse and the bag of groceries into the green armchair by the door before she came back and snatched up the two boxes of flowers. Her heart was pounding ferociously as she made it back inside, closed the door, and took a seat on the green floral rattan sofa. She inhaled deeply and pulled the note out of the envelope. *To the one that holds my heart. I love you.*

As soon as she read the last word on the note, the ringing doorbell interrupted her trance. Without even stopping to think for a second, she ran to the door and swung it wide open. Low and behold, Debonair Jenkins was standing there with his locks flowing in the wind, dressed in gold pants with a tropical printed red, white and gold summer shirt, showing her almost every tooth in his mouth.

Tina almost fainted; she was so smitten from his breathtaking appearance. "Debonair, what are you doing here?"

"I came to make sure that you got the flowers that I sent you. Aren't they beautiful, my lady?" he stated, entering the room, his eyes never veering from Tina.

"Yes—yes they are. How did—how did you know that I was here?" she asked, closing the door behind him.

"A little birdie told me that you were out of town, and I remembered that day I was at the shop getting my hair done, you mentioned something about a conference down here in July. So I just pulled out all my resources and tracked you down right here."

"What made you think that I wanted to see you?"

"Look, Tina, I've missed you. I've missed the scent of you. I've missed the taste of you. Don't tell me that you haven't missed me, too," he moved closer to her.

"This is wrong, Debonair. This is so wrong."

"Baby, if loving you is wrong then I won't ever be right again, I mean it. It's just that simple."

"Can't you see that there is nothing simple about our relationship? I have a husband and two children to think of, Debonair."

"Is that why you're filing for divorce from Martin?"

"How did you know about that?" Tina asked, eyeing his smirking face and then shaking it off. "Never mind, I guess you have your resources. I'm divorcing Martin because my relationship with you has destroyed our marriage."

"I'm sorry, but I feel that you and I were meant to be together."

"Is that right?"

"That's right. I know everything that's been going on in your life. And I know that you've been just as miserable as I have."

"I thought I told you not to bother me anymore?"

"No, actually, the last thing you told me was not to call you anymore, and I haven't done that. When I realized that you were down here alone, I couldn't stand the thought of you being here on the beach by yourself, especially knowing that I'm head over heels in love with you," he stated, moving even closer to her jittery body, taking her hand into his.

"Wha—what did you say?"

"I said what I've said before, I love you and I want to be with you right now and always. I just want to be with you, Tina. Can I please just stay here with you tonight, my lady?" he asked, enticing her with his penetrating eyes.

"I don't think that's a good idea. I really don't," she stated, stepping back from him. But he stepped closer to her, stretched his arms around her waist, drawing her nearer to his manly, appealing lips.

Favoring the idea of being wanted and needed by a much younger and attractive man, Tina relaxed her tense muscles against his sturdy chest. Debonair seized the moment as he gathered her up into his arms and carried her to the master bedroom as she buried her face in his smooth neck.

Laying her gently onto the bed, he lingered closely to her face, admiring the slight dimples in her rosy cheeks while smoothing her naturally wavy golden brown hair between his fingers. Tina had decided weeks ago to give her hair a break from the braids and showcase her natural hair for the summer.

"Umh, I love your hair like this, I really do," he moaned in her ear. "It's so soft and beautiful. I love the way it feels in my hands, baby."

"Thank you, I was truly tired of braids and extensions in my head."

"You should wear your hair like this all the time. It makes you look sexier."

"Yeah, right, I bet it does."

"I mean it, Tina. You look much sexier with your hair down like this. I'm telling you that I love it."

"What else do you love about me?" she asked.

"Let me see," he began, lowering his back against the bed comforter, "I love the way you smell, too. You always smell so incredibly fresh, like you just stepped out of the shower or a bubble bath. And I love the scent that you're wearing now. What's the name of that?" he asked, nuzzling his nose against her scented neck.

"Ah, the name of the scent I'm wearing right now is Pleasures."

"Pleasures. Well, that's a very appropriate name because it's giving me lots of pleasure smelling it on your soft skin, baby." After a pause, his lips curved upward as he stated, "Hey, I've got a terrific idea. Let's undress each other and take a long warm shower together. I want to feel your soaking wet body against mine," he said, rising from the bed, pulling Tina by the hand into the bathroom.

They took their time undressing each other; constantly kissing every part of the other's body as it was slowly revealed to the other. "Oh, how I love your body," Debonair moaned. "It's so perfect. I don't want you to lose a pound anywhere, do you hear me?"

"Yes, I hear you."

"I want you to be totally uninhibited with me tonight, all right. I want you to live whatever fantasy you've ever had as I do anything and everything that you want me to do."

"Are you sure about that? I might have a wild fantasy for you."

"I'm not worried about it. Now that I have you completely naked, let's go take that shower together."

Debonair stepped into the shower first, holding Tina by the hand as he let the lukewarm water flow over his face and body. Tina slowly moved around in front of him so that the water was spraying against her front section as he caressed her from behind. He took the bar of soap and lathered up her entire body as he meticulously washed her from head to toe and then she returned the sensuous favor.

After they rinsed all the suds from their bodies, they towel dried each other, frolicking back to the full sized bed. Tina fell backwards against the silky comforter, laughing while Debonair covered her body with kisses going downward all the way to her freshly painted French pedicured toes which he proficiently licked and massaged with his moist heated tongue. Placing a partial foot in his mouth, he heartily feasted on all five of her thin toes at once. Slowing moving his lips up and down, he didn't stop until all ten of them had been thoroughly moistened.

By this time, Tina was more than ready for him as he ascended upward. Gently pulling himself upon the bed, clutching both her hands, Debonair wasn't able to resist flicking his hot tongue in and out of her navel several times. With each taste of her body, he felt Tina's stomach contracting as she began gasping for breath, rapidly pulling more air into her dry lungs.

Seconds later, they were eye-to-eye, hip-to-hip, and lip-to-lip. "Are you ready for me, baby?" he teased, hovering over her panting mouth.

"Oh, yes, I'm ready," she moaned.

They moved and grooved together all through the night. After they were completely satisfied and unable to perform any further,

Debonair made a proposal. "Tina, baby, are you asleep?" he asked, tapping her shoulder lightly.

"I'm not asleep, but I'm not exactly awake either," she grumbled.

"Turn over and look at me, please. I want to ask you something."

Tina turned towards him and looked past him at the digital clock on the nightstand. "Debonair, we've been up all night long, what it is that you have to ask me at 5:15 in the morning?" she asked, turning on the lamp.

"I want to ask you to marry me." Tina was too surprised to speak, staring at him in amazement as he continued. "Wait a minute— wait just a minute, now I know what you're going to say. I know exactly what you're going to say, but listen to me, please. I'm crazy about you, and I want to marry you as soon as your divorce becomes final. And just to show you how serious I am—I've already bought you an engagement ring," he stated, rising from the bed and retrieving a small gold case from his pants pocket before easing back under the covers butt naked.

Debonair slowly opened the ring box as Tina propped up in the bed, still staring at him. The two-carat marquise shaped diamond engagement ring pushed her doubts away as it twinkled by the lamp light.

"Okay, I know this is a lot, and you don't have to answer me right now, okay. Just wear the ring while you think about it," he said, placing it on her bare left hand. Tina hadn't worn her wedding rings since filing for divorce from Martin.

Gently kissing her on the forehead, Debonair reached up, turning off the bedside lamp. He pulled the comforter up snuggly around them as he held Tina in a warm embrace.

Relaxing in his arms, Tina wondered what she'd gotten herself into. She'd never intended for things to go this far with the younger man. What would her children think of her marrying Debonair Jenkins?

Chapter 21

Waking up to a glorious Saturday morning sunrise, Martin realized that this was the weekend that Tina had the conference in Fort Lauderdale. *That's why the house was so dark last night. The boys must be with their grandparents.* Marty rolled over in bed, picked up the telephone, and dialed the number to his in-laws' residence.

"Good morning, Sloan residence," Delilah Sloan answered.

"Good morning, Mrs. Sloan. This is Martin. How are you?"

"Martin, I know who you are, and I'm doing fine."

"Yes, ma'am, are my sons out there?"

"Yes, they are, but they're both still in bed right now."

"I see, have you all made any plans for today?"

"No, we haven't. My husband had to go into the hospital to see a patient early this morning, so I'm just going to fix them breakfast after I get up and get dressed. Why don't you come on out here and join us, Martin? That would be great."

"Ah, are you sure about that, Mrs. Sloan?"

"Yes, I'm positive. I would love to see you, Martin. Give me about an hour, and we'll be ready for grits and gravy."

"Well, that sounds good to me. I'll be there, all right."

"Okay, Martin. Bye, sweetheart," Mrs. Sloan hung up the phone, and jumped out of her bed. She needed to have a good heart to heart with her son-in-law before it was too late. Her motherly intuitions told her that time was running out on her daughter's marriage; she needed to do something fast.

Delilah didn't waste any time getting Malique and Jordan up for the big breakfast she was planning on preparing for them. When she told the boys that their father was on his way to see them, they leaped out of bed with joy and hurried to the bathroom to wash up. Jordan was especially happy because he had missed his father taking him to sporting events, playing video games, and watching movies together. Malique was just happy to know that his father wasn't still mad at him. After having a brief conversation with Martin weeks ago, he realized that his father wasn't angry with him anymore. Even though his mother had tried explaining to him that he wasn't the reason that Martin moved out, Malique still felt guilty as if he had somehow contributed to the downfall of their marriage.

Arriving a little over an hour later, Martin's mother-in-law met him at the door with a genuine smile and her hair pulled back into her usual bun. Delilah was casually dressed as she was on most weekends, wearing a purple soft knit pant suit and her favorite pair of Oriental styled purple house slippers. Martin looked like he was ready to go to a baseball game wearing a Dodger's T-shirt with blue jeans, a baseball cap, and his Nike athletic shoes. "Hello, Mrs. Sloan," Martin smiled, greeting her with a kiss on the cheek.

"Hi, Martin, I'm glad you made it out okay. Give me a hug."

"Yes, ma'am," he said, obeying her as he stretched out his arms to embrace Delilah.

"Daddy! Daddy!" Jordan shouted, running towards his father. Malique dragged behind him with a sheepish grin on his face.

"Hello, son, how are you doing?"

"Daddy, I missed you. Daddy, I really missed you," Jordan complained, wrapping his arms around Martin's waist.

"I missed you to, but guess what? We're going to spend the whole day together, if you like."

"Ah, man, that would be great! Is Malique coming with us, too, daddy?"

"Of course he's coming with us. We're having an all men's meeting day. How does that sound, Malique?" Martin asked, reaching out to embrace his oldest son.

"That depends on what we're doing," he responded.

"You all can come on in the kitchen. Breakfast is almost ready," Delilah interrupted.

"It really smells good in here, Mrs. Sloan. I could smell your biscuits cooking from a mile away," Martin said, laughing as he followed her into the kitchen.

"Well, I knew my homemade biscuits would get you out here this morning," she responded, smiling back at her son-in-law.

"Yes ma'am. That would get me up early everyday of the week."

Delilah set the table for four people with the biscuits, ham, eggs, grits, and gravy in the center of the table. All of the fellas' mouths were watering just from the smell of the smoking hot food. Being anxious to get started eating, they gladly helped her bring the condiments to the table. Martin sat to the head of the table in Dr. Sloan's absence and said grace for them as they all held hands. Martin decided to start the conversation as he smoothed butter across his first biscuit.

"So have you guys thought about what we're going to do today?"

"I want to go the video arcade, daddy," Jordan said.

"No way, Jordan. How about we go see a movie, daddy?" Malique asked.

"Who wants to sit in the dark watching a boring movie?" Jordan rebuffed.

"Hey, you guys, I have the perfect solution. We'll go to the video arcade for an hour, and then we'll go see a movie."

"That works for me," Jordan replied, smiling up at his father.

"Sure, dad, I guess I can suffer through the video arcade for one hour," Malique retorted.

After the boys finished breakfast and headed upstairs to get changed for the day ahead of them, Martin helped Delilah clear the breakfast table. "Marty, would you like a hot cup of coffee? Have a seat at the counter, and I'll get us some coffee," she said, not waiting for him to reply.

"Yes, ma'am, coffee sounds fine."

Delilah poured them two strong black cups of coffee and then added plenty of cream and sugar to both their containers. She was stirring her coffee slowly as she spoke to Martin. "I'm really glad that you came out here today to visit with us. I've wanted to talk to you about my daughter, but I didn't know how to approach the subject with you. Now I'm really worried about Tina."

"Mrs. Sloan, I don't know if we should be talking about this, you know. Tina and I are separated, and she's already filed for divorce."

"I know that. I also know that she's making a grave mistake. I know for a fact that she still loves you, Marty. That young man that she's seeing means absolutely nothing to her. She's simply acting out of loneliness," she noticed Marty squirming in his seat. "Now think about this—just hear me out. You two hadn't been close for months when she started up with this fellow. It was simply an act of loneliness."

"I don't know what you expect me to do. She's the one that filed for divorce, and I'm certainly not going to oppose her on it. I know this is hard for you to handle, Mrs. Sloan, but Tina has made her decision, and we both have to live with it. Besides, so much has happened now that I don't see any way for us to ever live together as a couple again."

"All right, but I tell you, some people have survived much worse than this. I've been married a long time, and I've seen a lot of people divorce for less than this. Then on the other hand, I've also seen some couples that went through much worse than what you're experiencing now and somehow stayed together. Just remember that nothing is impossible, and there's no sin too great to be forgiven," Mrs. Sloan stated, taking a long sip of her beverage.

"Look, I admit that I still have some feelings for Tina. You don't live with a person for seventeen years and just stop loving them overnight. I know that I was wrong for lying to my wife and pulling away from her the way that I did. But I didn't tell her to turn to another man for comfort."

"I know you didn't, baby. You have to understand that women see things differently from men. We need to know that we're wanted and loved all the time. When you turned your back on her, she felt alone and frustrated. I'm not trying to justify her actions; I'm just trying to put myself in her shoes. You need to understand how she was feeling."

"Well, Mrs. Sloan, I don't believe that if you were in her shoes that you would have done what she did."

"No, I would never do that, but Tina and I are two different people. I love my daughter, and I love you for loving her all these years because I know how spoiled she is. Her father has placed her on a high pedestal for her entire life. She wants whatever she wants right now. I begged her to be patient and communicate her feelings to you, but it didn't do any good, and I'm truly sorry, Marty."

"It's not your fault. I don't blame you for any of this, all right? You're still my kids' grandmother, and we'll always be family."

"Thank you, Marty. I just hope that you find it in your heart to someday forgive my selfish daughter for her actions. I believe that she's probably already regretting her decision."

"Hey, daddy! We're ready to go!" Jordan was running down the stairs with Malique stepping behind him.

"Okay, you guys," Marty said, standing up and walking towards his sons. "Give your grandmother a hug good-bye so that we can go."

Both boys quickly hugged their grandmother and headed towards the front entrance. Delilah trailed behind them, wishing that her conversation with Marty had gone better. Hugging Martin last, she watched the boys walk out to the vehicle. Clutching his shirt from the back, Mrs. Sloan whispered in Marty's ear, "Think about what I said, son. I love you."

Marty had a wonderful time spending the day with his two sons. He could tell that they had missed him almost as much as he had missed being with them. They were a very close family before his nightmares drove him to drinking and spending all his time at the office. *How could I have been so blind and foolish? I had the whole world in the palm of my hand, and I traded it all away for nothing. I had a love that I could feel, and I lost it,* he thought, observing his sons eating across the table from him at the Barnhill's Family Restaurant later that evening. Nothing could replace the fun-filled day they had shared together making each other laugh while strengthening their male bond. His boys really needed their father, and Marty knew that from personal experience, nothing could take the place of a loving man in a male child's life. He had vowed never to abandon his family the way that his father had deserted them, and this was his first time seeing their children in weeks. Marty dropped his head in shame, feeling like a terrible parent. *No matter what happens between Tina and me, I promise to love and support my sons from now on.*

After Marty took Malique and Jordan back out to their grandparents' home for the night, he placed a call to Ezekiel Harrison around 9:30 p.m. on his way back to Michael's house. His father answered the telephone on the third ring, sounding drowsy. "Hey, Ezekiel, did I wake you up?"

"Who is this?" he asked, sounding excited. "Is this Martin?"

"Yes, it's me. I was just calling to see how you were doing."

"Oh, son, I'm so happy to hear from you. I'm doing great. How is your family?"

"They're all doing well," Marty replied, not telling his father about his marital problems. "The boys and I just spent the whole day together."

"Really?" he questioned. "That's great. You know, son, I'm really proud of you. I wish that I could have been the type of father to you that you're being to your kids. Life is so short, I just wish that I could go back in time and try harder to be a good father."

"I—I'm really glad to hear you say that—to know that you have some regrets about leaving us. I don't understand but—I forgive you, and I want you to be a part of my life from here on out," Marty waited several seconds for Ezekiel to respond before he heard the choking sound of tears coming through the telephone.

"Son, I'm sorry. I apologize for hurting you, Walter, and your mother. I love you, and we'll be together again soon because all we have is each other. I won't desert you this time, I promise."

"I'm just looking forward to seeing you again soon because like you said, life is short."

Chapter 22

Sitting in the front pew of Noah's Ark Missionary Baptist Church at the early morning service, Martin sported a mocha striped suit, listening to the adult men's choir which included Michael Wayne. They were singing one of his mother's favorite gospel songs, "What a Blessedness," as he rocked to the music with the congregation. Martin could still hear Cora Lee's voice in his ears as he was transported back to a more innocent time in his life.

He couldn't pass on the opportunity of accompanying his best friend to church today and watching him sing in the choir this morning. Michael's wife and daughter had been gone all week to Kansas visiting with family so he asked Marty to ride with him to service. Alese's Aunt Lucy had taken ill and was suddenly hospitalized in Wichita. Being that Aunt Lucy was one of the only few surviving relatives that she had, Alese didn't hesitant to get on an airplane, even though she was almost eight months pregnant.

Standing proud in the new handmade black and white trimmed choir robe over his black suit, Michael looked down at his friend's smiling face from the choir stand. Marty appeared to be enjoying the service thus far, as evidenced from his clapping and singing along with the choir. Michael was glad to see a small smile on Marty's face. He had been praying consistently for his best friend's heart and marriage to be repaired. Yes, Tina had wronged him dearly, but he knew beyond a shadow of a doubt that Marty still loved Tina as much as she loved him. They had a long road to recovery. Hopefully, a little gospel preaching and a little holy singing would make that journey a bit easier to bear.

Knowing that Marty needed some spiritual guidance, Michael had spent a whole week hinting around for Martin to accompany him to the church today. Finally, last night, he straight out asked Marty to attend the early morning service for their annual men's day celebration they held on the third Sunday in July. Thinking that he would have to beg his friend to attend church, he was surprise when Marty agreed to go the first time that he was asked. *Maybe he's starting to come around. Maybe he's ready to try Jesus,* Michael thought, smiling inwardly.

Since the congregation had grown in size over the last year, Michael was delighted that Pastor Wright added another service and an assistant pastor to help with her duties. She was glowing in her purple gold trimmed robe as she came to the podium with her Bible in one hand and waving with the other. "Church, it is a glorious day that the Lord has made. What a mighty God we serve, angels bow before Him; heaven and earth adore Him, what a mighty God we serve! Hallelujah! I just thank the Lord for being here today to introduce a truly inspirational man of God. At this time I would like to introduce to some and present to others, the reigning pastor of Faith Hill Missionary Baptist Church out of Gainesville, Florida, Reverend Alfred Hodges," Karema went to her seat as Reverend Hodges stood and walked briskly to the podium. Being a big and tall man, he had to raise the microphone up a couple of inches to accommodate his size.

"Good morning, church. I'm very happy to be here, and I don't plan on holding you all too long today. I have a special message for someone sitting out there in the congregation right now. You see, I prayed before coming out here this morning, and the Lord has already told me to speak a word of love and encouragement to somebody that's coming into His house today that hasn't worshipped in a long time. They're coming in with a heavy laden heart," the pastor spoke slowly as he carefully enunciated each emotionally filled word. "You see, the devil is attacking us on every corner. He's attacking God's people that are in loving relationships whether they're married or not. But we have to especially pray for the married couples because they have been joined together in a holy union. We have more couples getting divorced today than we've ever had in the history of mankind. We have got to do something to save these marriages," he stated, turning pages in his Bible.

"My message for today will come from the book of Proverbs 10:12 which reads:

Hatred stirs up strife, but love covers all sins.

"We have to remember, church, that love covers all sin. Now you might ask me, pastor, what about lying? Love covers all sin. Pastor, what about adultery? Love covers all sin. Pastor, what about stealing? Love covers all sin," he stated, pausing for a couple of seconds.

"I want you to imagine for me, if you will, a house that has fallen into a state of total despair. I mean the paint is chipping, the roof is leaking, the plumbing is rusty, and even the lawn is untidy. Obviously, this building has survived a lot of storms over the years and suffered from neglect. Now my question to you is this, should the old run-down building be demolished?" The pastor paused here, looking down at the congregation before he continued his sermon. "If the foundation is strong and the structure is solid, the house can probably be restored. Does the condition of that house remind anyone here today of their marriage? Over the years, severe thunderstorms, trials and tribulations, may have taken a toll on your marriage, so what do you do?" he asked, looking out over the quiet congregation.

"I'm reminded right here of a couple that came to me for marital counseling awhile back. And I'm sure that they won't mind me sharing this. They had been married for fourteen years and the wife told me, she said: "Pastor, the only thing that I have in common with my husband is that we're married to each other," he paused, listening to members of the congregation laugh, encouraging him to keep on preaching. "Now even if your marriage has reached this point, do not be dismayed. Just like that dilapidated house, your marriage can be rebuilt! Nobody is perfect I tell you!

"People get divorced everyday over the simplest of things. He snores too loud, she's gained too much weight, he can't hold a job, she won't iron my shirts, and the list goes on and on—I know that some of you have more serious issues that you're dealing with in your relationships, but if you have love in your life, you can look beyond the faults of others. Now I'm not telling you to let anyone mistreat you because God don't want His people to be mistreated or held up in unrighteous relationships. He wants His disciples to love each other and flourish together in holy matrimony."

Reverend Hodges continued his speech on the state of marriages today and how love covers all sin. Martin followed each Bible passage that was presented as the pastor went through several verses pertaining to love, relationships, and marriage. Towards the end of the sermon, the guest speaker introduced his wife and family to the congregation, informing everyone that they had been married for twenty-one years and produced three children together.

"We've been separated three times during our union. Yes, we allowed Satan to get in the middle of our marriage and pull us apart when we showed weakness in our faith. But how many of you know that what God has joined together," members of the church joined in with him to complete the statement after a brief pause, "Let no man put asunder. Amen," he concluded with pride, returning to his seat as Pastor Wright shook his hand before sitting down.

Prior to church being dismissed, the men's choir graced the congregation with one final selection. Martin stood, watching his friend with pride as they sang, "Oh, Happy Day," as their closing song. Everyone was standing and singing along with the men, clapping and swaying to the upbeat music.

Immediately after church dismissal, Michael introduced Martin to several members of the congregation that hugged them or shook their hands as they inquired about Alese and Bianca. "Thank you for your concern," Michael told them. "They should be back in time for church next Sunday," he politely responded.

"Man, this has got to be the hottest July that I have ever seen in my life. It's hot enough out here to fry an egg on the hood of your car," Marty joked, squinting his eyes in the bright sunlight, removing his suit coat as they walked outside towards the car.

"You're not kidding about that," Michael laughed, removing his black suit jacket as he approached his vehicle.

Riding home together in Michael's Nissan Murano, Marty was looking out the side window. "So what did you do, man, put in a request to have Reverend Hodges preach to me today?"

Michael laughed at the thought. He could not have asked for a better sermon to be directed at his friend. "No, I didn't do that. Besides, I just met the man today myself. But sometimes God will send us exactly what we need."

"Yeah, well, there's one thing Reverend Hodges didn't talk about."

"What's that?"

"Marriage is a two way street. It takes two people to make a marriage work."

"Marty, sometimes in marriage we have to play the percentages game, don't you know that? Sometimes marriage is fifty/fifty, and that's the perfect match, but sometimes its sixty/forty or eighty/twenty, you know. Sometimes it can be even more one-sided than that."

"Yeah, I know," was all Marty could manage to say.

"Listen, why don't we go home, change clothes, and then go pick up the boys for a day in the sun and brotherly fellowship?" Michael asked, glancing over at Marty in the passenger's seat. "You guys left me out of the loop the last time you had an all male bonding day."

"All right, all right. Let me call over there and see what they have planned for today," Marty replied, pulling his cellular phone from his front pants pocket and dialing his home number.

"Hello," Jordan answered the phone.

"Hi, Jordan. What's going on, son?"

"Daddy! I'm glad you called. I forgot to tell you about my baseball game today at the city park."

"What time is the game, Jordan?"

"It starts at 4:00 p.m., daddy, but I have to be there by three o'clock. Can you make it?"

"Of course I can make it. Uncle Mike and I will be over to pick you and Malique up around 12:00 p.m. so we can have lunch together before the game. How does that sound?"

"That sounds perfect! I'll let Malique know so he'll be ready, too."

Martin clicked off his cellular phone and turned towards Michael, "Okay, buddy, we have just enough time to change clothes and pick the boys up for lunch."

"Marty, I've been meaning to ask you something and don't get upset about this. Are you still attending those AA meetings?"

"Yeah, I'm still going. I don't think that I really need them, but I appreciate the support that I get from those people. When my nightmares stopped, I no longer had the desire to drink so it's been pretty easy for me to stay on the wagon."

"Good, good, I'm just glad to hear that. I could tell that you hadn't been drinking, but I thought that maybe you had stopped attending the meetings. I was also scared that after you separated from Tina, you would have a hard time staying sober."

"No, I'm still going to the meetings. I'm really glad that I started them before Tina and I separated though or I might not have made it. I still meet with my sponsor once a week, too. He's a young black attorney that's been through a lot worse than I have, believe it or not."

"Really? What's his story?"

"Ah, man, his wife left him over two years ago for a rich older white man that she met at work and took his ten-year-old daughter with her to live in Miami. He was so devastated from his loss that he started hitting the bottle so bad he lost his law practice, home, and everything he owned."

"You're telling me that a sister left a brother, who's an attorney, for an older white man? I don't get that."

"I did say that he was rich, didn't I? Color does not matter when that old family money is involved, you know what I mean?"

"Yeah. What's happening with him now?"

"Now he's cleaned himself up, started a new practice, bought a smaller house, and got a new girlfriend. He's thinking about joining the ministry, and he's always inviting me to attend Bible study with him at the church he attends."

"That's not a bad idea since I can never get you to attend with me."

"I don't remember you asking me to Bible study, Mike."

"Man, stop teasing me. I've asked you to attend with me every Wednesday since you moved in with us."

"Oh, I forgot about that, but I'll come with you this Wednesday night if you want me to."

"That's a deal, Marty, and I plan on holding you to it. I definitely intend on holding you to that, my friend."

"No problem," Marty replied. In fact, he was actually looking forward to it.

Almost an hour later, Michael and Martin had both changed into short pants and short sleeved polo shirts with earth toned sandals as they turned into Jacksonville Beach Estates. Turning onto the long driveway leading up to the Tudor styled house, Jordan was already outside on the front lawn dressed in his summer league baseball uniform wearing a leather glove and tossing a ball in the air. "Heah, little man, throw me the ball!" Marty yelled, getting out of the car.

Jordan threw the ball directly at his father with all his strength. Marty had to stretch his arm up and jump to catch the ball before it went over his head. By the time he landed on his feet with the hard ball clutched in his grip, Jordan had made it to him and wrapped his arms around his waist in a loving hug. "I miss you, daddy!" he said.

"I miss you, too. I really miss both of you guys," Marty stated, returning Jordan's hug and looking up to see Malique in the front doorway.

"Well, what about me? Uncle Mike deserves some love today," Michael teased, stretching out his arms.

"Hi, Uncle Mike," Jordan said shyly, hugging his adopted uncle and pulling him out into the yard to play catch.

Martin walked towards Malique and spoke to him as he entered the house. "Hi, dad, I need to run upstairs for a minute, and I'll be right down."

"Sure, I'll be waiting for you in the den."

Upon entering the family room, Marty hesitated for a second when he saw Tina walking in his direction. She was looking good in that yellow sundress with a green floral design in it. He was taken aback with her smiling face and warm honey glowing eyes as she spoke to him.

"Hi, Martin. The boys were looking forward to seeing you today. Thanks for coming to get them."

"Well, they are my sons, Tina. I want to spend as much time with them as I can now that I'm putting my life in order."

"I just wanted to let you know that I appreciate you doing things with them and being there for them."

"I see you're holding up fine," Marty traced the length of her body with longing in his brown eyes. Covering his mouth with his right hand, he faked a cough. "Look, Tina, I just want to tell you that I'm glad that we can work out a divorce settlement on our own without involving the high priced attorneys in our business."

"Marty, I think that you're being more than fair and generous considering what I've put you through during these last few months," she stated, holding up her hands while clasping them together in front of him.

Suddenly Marty's heart dropped to his stomach and flipped over several times before returning to its rightful place. He noticed the diamond ring sparkling on her left hand. Staring at her ring finger in amazement, he spoke, "I see you aren't wasting any time moving on, Tina. Is that an engagement ring?"

"Oh, no, of course, not—it's just a present from a friend—that's all," she stuttered.

"Well, I see. You must have a really good friend to give you a diamond that size. Excuse me," Marty said, leaving the room. He had to get out of there before his anger rose to the surface again.

"Marty, wait!" she called after him.

Martin stopped and turned towards her, aggravation showing through the lines on his forehead. "What is it, Tina?"

She rushed towards Marty with widened eyes, "I just want you to know that what we had was real to me. I never stopped loving you, I got caught up into something that consumed me like a drug, and I was too weak to fight it."

"Dad, I'm ready now!" Malique shouted, shuffling down the stairs, "Are you ready to go, dad?" Malique asked, approaching his parents.

"Yes, I'm ready," Marty replied, backing away from Tina. "Let's go."

Chapter 23

Tina knew that she had hurt Martin to the core once she saw his facial expression change the second he laid his eyes on her new ring. The only reason she had put it on today was to get a reaction out of Marty, but that wasn't quite the reaction that she was expecting to get. She didn't know what to really expect Marty to do after realizing that she was donning an engagement ring. She hadn't told her two closest friends or her parents that Debonair had asked her to marry him as soon as her divorce from Martin was finalized.

Tina still hadn't given him an answer to his proposal nor had she been wearing the ring. She informed Debonair that she needed some time to herself to think about his request. Although she had spoken to him over the telephone several times in the last two weeks, she hadn't laid eyes on him since their rendezvous in Fort Lauderdale at the beach house.

Lying back in her brown leather chaise, Tina began to think about how her life had drastically changed over the course of one year. Last year at this time, her friend, Alese, was separated from her husband while Martin and she were perfectly happy together. They had sworn that they would never let the same thing happen to their marriage. Now their marriage was about to end because of her selfishness. *What am I going to do? There's no way in the world for me to make this right so I might as well marry Debonair. At least I won't have to live the rest of my life alone because I'm certainly not getting any younger. I'd better not pass on this opportunity to get married again while I have it. I mean he's not as wealthy as Martin, and we'll have to move into a much smaller house, but I think that we can be happy together.*

The loud ringing of the telephone interrupted Tina's thoughts. She finally picked it up after the third ring.

"Hi, Tina, this is Alese Wayne."

"Hello, Alese, I'm surprised to hear from you. I thought that you were in Kansas with your family."

"Yes, I am. I'm visiting with my sick aunt. How have you been?"

"I've been better. How is your aunt?"

"She's all right. She's out of the hospital, and I'll be headed back home tomorrow. I need to get back real soon before I drop this baby right here."

"How is the pregnancy coming? Are you all right?"

"Yes, I'm fine. I'm not due for almost another month."

"That's good. I'm happy for you. Maybe we can get together and talk when you return."

"Well, actually I have a few minutes now if you really want to talk, Tina."

"I've got nothing but time since Martin and Michael are gone with the boys."

"Yes, I knew they were out with the boys, and I just felt like I needed to call you today because you have been heavy on my mind. You know, we haven't seen each other a lot this year, and I haven't heard from you since that night at the party although I've called you several times."

"Yes, I know, but I just haven't been in the mood to talk with anyone that was at the party. I mean it was the most embarrassing night of my life."

"I can understand how it was. Tina, what I can't understand is what's happening between you and Martin. You're the last person that I expected to see going through this."

"Alese, I don't know what to say. I was just sitting here in my den thinking the same thing. I feel like such a hypocrite after what I said to you last year about Michael's infidelity. I had no right to judge your husband."

"It's all right, Tina. Sometimes people don't want to know what their spouse is doing, but it's best to have things out in the open. Once the vows have been broken, everyone needs to know what's going on."

"You're right, that's why I've decided to let Martin know that I'm going to marry Debonair as soon as we're divorced in September. I hadn't told anyone that he asked me to marry him, and he's already given me an engagement ring that I'm wearing today. Marty saw it when he came over to pick up the boys. I told him it was just a present from a friend, but I'm sure he knew that it was more than that."

"Don't you think that's kind of sudden? I mean you haven't given you and Marty a chance to work out your relationship. These things take time, Tina, and you can't give up hope just like that. I know good and well that you're not in love with Debonair."

"I think that I love him. Why else would I cheat on my husband and lie to him the way that I did if I wasn't in love with this other man?"

"People do things for different reasons. I'm telling you that what you're feeling right now is not love, its lust, plain and simple lust. Jumping from one relationship directly into another is not going to solve the problem, you need time to heal. You and Marty have been married for seventeen years, you can't recuperate from that dissolution in just a few months and be in love with another man already. Tina, think about what you're doing."

"I hear what you're saying, but I don't want to be alone. And if Martin does not want to be with me, I'm not passing on the opportunity to be with someone who does."

"Martin wants to be with you, Tina. He just doesn't know how to do that right now. You have to allow him the time that he needs to heal. Trust me, he'll find his way back to you."

"And what if he never finds his way back to me? What if he's found his was to another woman? I don't think he's sitting around waiting for us to get back together."

"Maybe not but you created this drama. Now you're putting all the pressure on him to carry the marriage. You have to accept responsibility for your part in this breakup and wait him out. Believe me, time heals all wounds. It's just an issue of time."

"I can't do that. I think that I've severed all ties with Martin. He's hurting so bad right now that there's no way for him to ever see beyond his pain. You know how black men are. They cannot handle their women cheating on them. Oh, its' all right for them to have multiple affairs, but they're never going to forgive us for doing the same things, and you know I'm telling the truth."

"Tina, the truth is that Marty loves you, and he just needs time to realize that. But, of course, he's not going to take you back if you're still seeing this other man and wearing a ring that he's given you."

"I appreciate your advice, I really do, but it's my decision to make. I don't believe Martin is ever going to forgive me, and I know that I can be happy with Debonair. He's really a wonderful person. I hope that you can get to know him eventually for yourself and you'll see what I'm talking about."

"I'm sure that he's a good person, I'm just not sure that he's good for you, Tina. You know last year I was ready to divorce Michael after learning about him and Lisa Bradford. Now where would I be if I had rushed to divorce him like I'd thought of doing? I didn't think that I would be able to forgive him either, then things worked out for us in a relatively short period of time."

"I know it did, and I'm so inspired by your renewed relationship with Michael, but I know Martin. Men are not as forgiving as women.

Martin turned his back on his own brother and father for twenty years and, quite frankly, I'm not willing to wait that long for him to forgive me. Now please just try to be happy for me, Alese."

"I want you to be happy, Tina. I just don't feel in my heart that you're going to find happiness with Debonair, but it's your life and I can't live it for you. Just know that you can call me anytime. I really want you to think about attending church with me when I return and at least attend one counseling session with Pastor Wright before getting married again. You know, marriage is not to be taken lightly."

"I'll think about it. I'll seriously think about it. I know that you're trying to help, and I really like Pastor Wright."

"Well, I'm sure that you'll find her very approachable. She's a really open-minded person and she's not going to judge you or talk down to you in any way. I really think that she'll be able to aide you in making a rational decision for yourself."

"Thanks, Alese, I'm glad that you called me today. I'll see you when you get back to Jacksonville. It's about time for you to have another salon visit anyway."

"Yes, that's true. I'm tired of twisting my own hair. So I'll be praying for you and looking forward to seeing you when I return. I'm going to let the pastor know that she can be expecting a visit from you. I'll also be willing to go with you if you'd like me to."

"Oh, would you, Alese? I'd like that very much."

"It's the least that I can do after the way you and Martin saved our marriage last year. Friends have to look out for one another, especially in times like these. Bye, Tina."

Realizing that it was past time for her to talk with Debonair and inform him regarding her recent decision, Tina picked up her Versace purse, checked to make sure that she had the key to his place, and left her house. It was time to find out if their relationship was based on lust, as Alese had mentioned, or love. She had never used the key that he had given her to his apartment. Thinking that it would be nice to make a surprise visit to see if he meant all the sweet things that he had said to her, Tina headed to her Corvette.

Having a life with a younger man that was totally into her, sounded like a dream come true to the soon-to-be-divorcee. Debonair was caring and sensitive, he actively listened to her, he did whatever she asked him to do and when they were in bed, he was like play dough in her hands, willing to please, tease, and satisfy her every desire. What more could a girl ask for, especially since he was begging to marry her on top of that?

He hadn't given her any reason to distrust him; therefore, she had no doubts involving her relationship with Debonair. He made her feel completely fulfilled whenever they were together—as if she was the center of his universe. She wanted to be with him twenty-four hours a day, seven days a week so that all of her problems would drift away while relaxing across his waterbed. When she was with him, all of her cares of the world seemed to flow downstream where, hopefully, they would stay forever.

Tina arrived at Debonair's apartment with a glowing smile on her face. Checking the front parking area for his automobile, she wanted to know if he was home. Sure enough, his white Volkswagen Passat was parked directly in front of the unit where he lived. Tina squinted from the sun as she looked up to the second floor for any sign of movement around his door. He had a small balcony where he would sometimes stand on a beautiful day like today, just to observe people passing by.

A few minutes later, she was turning the key to enter his living room. Everything looked in order, but Tina noticed the faint smell of smoke throughout the apartment and proceeded to investigate. Knowing that Debonair wasn't a smoker, she walked briskly to the kitchen to check the oven and the stove top for burning particles. Everything there was fine, so without calling his name, she walked down the hall to the bathroom door that was closed, and then looked to the left through an opened bedroom door. Just as she was about to knock at the bathroom door, Debonair walked out with a funny looking cigarette in his mouth. "Debonair! What is going on up in here? I didn't know you smoke!"

"Baby, baby, calm down. It's just a little herb, you know. Don't tell me that you've never smoked a marijuana cigarette."

"I didn't say that I've never smoked reefer. What I said was that I didn't know that you smoked that stuff."

"I just smoke it every now and then to ease my nerves. You haven't returned my telephone calls lately, and I just needed a toke to help me relax. See, I'm putting it out right now," he said, returning to the bathroom. After taking another short drag on the cigarette, he flushed the bud down the toilet bowl. "Here, let me spray a little bit of air freshener and everything will be fine." He grabbed the potpourri air freshener from the counter and started spraying the tiny bathroom.

"I haven't smoked weed in over twenty years. How long have you been smoking?" Tina asked, sounding disappointed with him.

"I told you I smoke on and off. I mainly smoke when I'm lonely or upset about something. It's been several months since I've touched the stuff. This is my first time smoking anything since I started seeing you. Baby, I mean it."

"I just don't like it, Debonair. I didn't know you were into drugs at all."

"Hey, I'm not into drugs. Everybody smokes reefer sometime. It's really no big deal."

"Well, it could be a big deal to me. If you smoke that stuff you might dibble and dabble in some of the stronger drugs, and I'm not into that scene."

"I'm not into that scene either. I don't do any of the hard stuff; this is the extent of my drug use except for alcoholic beverages. Now just relax and tell me why you're here. I'm glad to see that you finally used that key I gave you," he lowered his voice, moving nearer to her.

"Martin came and got the boys for the afternoon. So I decided to pay you a surprise visit to discuss our relationship."

"Well now, that would be my favorite topic, my lady. May I taste your lips before we get started?" he asked, pulling her into his arms, covering her mouth with his in search of her moist tongue. After slowly releasing her from his kiss, he took her by the hand and turned to the right, "Come on into my bedroom, and let's talk about us."

"No, no, let's go into the living room and have a seat on the sofa. This impromptu visit is not about to end up in the bedroom. I need to know that we have more than a sexual relationship, Debonair," she declared, releasing his hand, marching past him towards the main area.

"Baby, how could you question the validity of our union?" he asked, walking behind her, raising his hands as he spoke. "I've had a lot of women in my past, and I've never asked any of them to marry me, Tina. And you know why? Because they weren't real women; they weren't like you. I need a woman in my life that's confident, ambitious, beautiful, and sexy. Someone that can inspire me to reach greater heights, and that's you," he said, sitting on the sofa beside Tina. He moved in closer and placed his arm around her shoulder. "Now tell me how you feel about me."

"I—I care for you very much. I enjoy the time that we spend together. In fact, I find myself wanting to be with you all the time. I feel safe when you hold me in your arms."

"Okay, does that mean that you love me or not?"

"That's a difficult question to answer given the delicate situation that I'm dealing with right now. I just know that I want to love you the way that you love me, and I also want to marry you when the time is right."

"You see, that's what I wanted to hear," he pulled her even closer to him, entwining his right hand fingers with hers. "I intend to make you a very happy woman. I plan on going back to school to get my bachelor's degree and one day having my own business, maybe a coffee shop or something."

"Oh, yeah? Is that what you really want, Debonair?"

"I think so. I don't want to be working at the Insomnia Coffee House for the rest of my life. Seeing you with your own business also makes me want to have mine."

"Well, it's definitely possible for you to do that. You can major in business management or marketing, like I did. You already have on-the-job training for managing a coffee shop. So it's up to you what you decide to do with your life. I'll support you in whatever you want to do."

"I knew you would, and I appreciate that very much. That's what I mean when I said that I wanted a real woman. You see, a real woman believes in her man and supports him through all kinds of weather. You know what I mean?"

"Yes, I know what you mean," she said softly, cupping his face in her hands, peering into his darkening eyes.

"Do you have a court date set yet? I want us to be married the day after your divorce is finalized."

"Yes, we have a court date set for Friday, September third, at 9:00 a.m., but I don't think that we need to marry the day after, that would be too soon. You know, I have to consider my children. What would they think if I got married that soon after divorcing their father?"

"I guess you're right about that. It'll take the boys sometime to adjust to the divorce as well as your relationship with me. I hope that in time, they'll accept me as a part of their lives, too. I'm just so anxious to be your husband that I don't know what to do. I can hardly wait for us to start our lives together."

"You'll be my husband soon enough. Besides, I have to find another place for the boys and me to live. I won't be able to afford staying in the house after the divorce is finalized. Martin and I have already decided to sell the house and split the profits. I can use that money to buy us a smaller house while you're going to school."

"You're a smart woman. I forgot to put that on my list of the things that I love about you, Tina. A smart woman is a valuable asset to any man."

"You better know it," she replied, smiling inside and out.

"Baby, I want you to wait right here while I go get something for you, all right?" Debonair asked, rising from his seat, heading towards the bedroom.

"All right, I'll be right here when you return," Tina replied, removing her shoes and propping her feet up on the coffee table.

Seconds later, Debonair returned with a gold gift bag in his hand. "Here's a little something that I bought for you today. I was hoping that you would drop by sooner than later," he stated, handing the bag to Tina.

"What is this? You didn't have to buy me a present."

"I know, but it's just something that I wanted you to have."

Tina pulled out the contents of the bag and smiled with delight as she looked up at Debonair. "This is great. What made you buy me this?"

"Well, you always smell so delicious, and I know how you love perfume. So, while I was at the mall today, I went by the fragrance counter and asked for the sexiest perfume they had. The sales lady told me that this was one of their best selling products. Besides, I like the name, Beautiful, because it applies to you."

"Now see, you're just trying to seduce me into your bed because I told you that I didn't come over here for that."

"No, no, you got it all wrong," he replied innocently. "I didn't plan this. I was going to give this to you whenever I saw you again. You just happened to drop by here today unannounced and I remembered to give it to you."

"Well, thank you, this is so sweet of you. You're one of the sweetest men that I've ever met. Thank you for being so thoughtful."

"My lady, the pleasure is all mine. I plan to give you the sun, moon, and stars if you let me," he stated, laughing with her.

"I'm looking forward to it."

"Me, too," Debonair replied in a low husky voice as he leaned in, planting a moist light kiss on her lips. Tina licked his flavor from her lips, tasting the essence of him. Realizing that she was only seconds away from being completely seduced again, she rose from the sofa and slowly walked towards the front door.

"Why are you leaving so soon? You know that you're more than welcome to stay with me for as long as you like," he stated, rising from the sofa and following behind Tina.

"I know, but I think that it's best if I leave right now." Tina opened the door and took one last look at Debonair before she left. If she didn't leave this very second, she wouldn't be able to go. If she looked into those magnetizing eyes one more time, she might be tempted to sleep with him again. So she fled through the doorway without taking a backwards glance.

Rushing back to her home in search of solitude, Tina's mouth dropped open when she pulled into the driveway, stopping beside her father's black Lexus. Feeling that this was not a good sign, she reluctantly eased out of her low riding car, and proceeded to the front door.

"Hi, Mom! Granddad is waiting for you in the den. He said that he wants to talk to you." Jordan relayed her father's message then ran upstairs.

Dreading the confrontation with Malachi, Tina lowered her head as she neared the entrance to the family room. Regardless of how he felt about Martin, Tina knew that her father loved her and would be disappointed with her actions. To him, she was a perfect wife and daughter. *Now that I've committed the ultimate act of betrayal, I wonder what he'll think about me.*

Tina entered the den and her eyes drifted to the stiff male figure awaiting her arrival. Malachi was sitting in the recliner where Martin normally sat when they watched television together. The room was completely silent. Malachi eyes seemed to be staring into space. Slowly he turned to face his daughter who was standing over him. "Hi, daddy, it's good to see you." Tina said to her rising father.

"Hello, baby girl, I've been so worried about you. Ever since your mother told me about the separation, I've been meaning to speak with you," he stated warmly, embracing Tina's small frame.

"Yeah, I knew that mom had told you that we were separated. What else did she tell you?"

"I believe she told me all the details surrounding your separation especially the part about you being involved with someone else. Now that's what I find so hard to believe. Is it true Tina?"

Lowering her eyes to the floor, Tina whispered almost as if she was speaking to herself, "Yes, daddy, it's true. I never meant for any of this to happen but Martin and I were having problems, and I just sort of met someone else," she stated, finally raising her eyes to meet her father's angry stare.

"Let's have a seat," Malachi said, leading his daughter to the sofa. Sitting down beside Tina, he placed his right arm over her shoulder while holding her right hand. "Listen to me carefully," he began. "I know that I've never been fair to Martin. I didn't think that he was good enough for you, sweetheart. But he has proven to be a decent husband and a wonderful father. Those two boys are crazy about him."

"Yes, they are," Tina interjected, sniffling back tears.

"The one thing that I've grown to admire about Martin is that he's a man of integrity. I know that he loves you with all his heart. I don't believe that anyone could ever love you as much as he does, and I couldn't ask for more than that."

"But, daddy, Martin's gone. He left me on my birthday, the same night that he found out about my affair," Tina cried, dripping tears down from both of her rosy cheeks.

"I know, baby, I know. I'm sorry that I've been wrong about Martin all these years. But it is important that you two try to reconcile right now before it's too late. I'm telling you, you need to get your husband home as soon as possible."

"It's already too late, daddy. Martin and I have both moved on. We're getting a divorce."

"That's ridiculous. I just want to give you one piece of advice sweetheart. Don't lose a good man. Don't be foolish and misjudge him like your father did."

"I don't know how things are going to turn out. I do know that a part of me will always love Martin no matter what happens between us."

Malachi pulled Tina into his arms again and held her heaving body against his chest for several minutes. He waited patiently while she cried her heart out to him.

"Daddy, please don't hate me for what I've done," she stated, wiping the tears away with her fingertips. Tina still avoided her father's eyes by looking downward.

"You know that I could never hate you, baby girl," Malachi placed a finger under her chin and tilted Tina's head upward until her eyes met his. "I only want what's best for you and my grandsons. I don't see anything good that would come from you divorcing Martin at this point."

"I just don't know what else to do. He hates me so much right now."

"He doesn't hate you, Tina. The man's pride is simply hurt, and I can't blame him for moving out. However, divorce is another topic all together."

"I understand what you're saying. I just don't know how to get through to him anymore."

"I'm sorry for what you're going through, sweetheart, but divorce is not the answer," he replied, checking his watch. "Well, I need to get going. Your mother is waiting for me to have dinner with her," Malachi stated, placing a tender kiss on his daughter's forehead. "Just remember what I said and keep trying. If Martin is half the man that I've discovered him to be, he'll want to keep you."

"Thanks, daddy, I'm so happy that you came out to see me. I'm sorry for disappointing you."

"That's not what matters right now. You have to forgive yourself and humble yourself to your husband. I know that the two of you can overcome this setback if you just communicate your feelings to each other." Tina nodded, acknowledging her father words as she escorted him to the front door.

Minutes later, Tina stepped out the back door, heading down to the beachfront barefooted with the hem of her yellow sundress blowing in the wind. Listening to the waves gushing rapidly through the water, Tina's feet sunk into the warm white sand with each step that she took. Reminiscing about days gone by, she thought of the countless evenings that she and Marty had spent walking this beach holding hands, talking to each other as the sun set around them. When they first moved in this house, they loved running along the shoreline every spare minute that they had. Now it felt lonely being out there with only her thoughts of a love that she was certain would never be again.

Tina closed her eyes against the sunshine. Feeling the heat of the setting sun on her face, she fondly remembered Martin's touch, his voice, his smell, everything that made him the man that she'd first fallen in love with. *I wonder if I can ever truly love Debonair as much as I once loved my husband. Only time will tell,* she thought, heading homeward. *Only time will tell.*

Chapter 24

A hot August summer day in Florida is absolute misery unless you're sitting inside somewhere with a cold drink and a well tuned air conditioner. Today, Martin was sitting at the kitchenette wearing a pair of lightweight shorts and a white undershirt while reading the daily newspaper with a cold can of clear soda sitting on the table within his reach. Michael was already gone to work and had dropped Bianca off at preschool. Alese was still in bed trying to take it easy because she was due to have their baby boy any day now.

Feeling that he needed a personal holiday to recuperate from the past several months, Martin stayed home to reflect on his life and where he wanted to go from here. Last night he had been reminded of his past when another dream crept into his sub-consciousness sometime during the night. Only this time the dream wasn't about Ezekiel and Cora Lee like it normally was, but his Aunt Rhoda. She was searching for him, going door to door in the project building where they used to live calling out his name.

He remembered his aunt as a medium build, dark skinned woman with even darker round bulging eyes, and long thick hair. She was a single parent that lived in the same project building as them with her two children. Aunt Rhoda and his mother used to work at the same nursing home, but they usually worked different shifts. Right in the middle of his reminiscing, Martin had a spectacular idea. He jumped from his seat and ran to find a telephone directory to look up the number to the nursing home where she was once employed. Knowing that his aunt might have left this position any number of years ago, he still searched for the number to Edgewood Nursing Home. "Hi, this is Martin Carlisle; I'm looking for a relative that used to work at your facility. I'm not sure if she's still employed or not but her name is Rhoda Ingrams."

"I'm sorry, but I don't know of anyone currently working here by that name, sir. You might want to speak with someone in the personnel department if you're positive that she was employed here before. Would you like for me to transfer you to that extension?"

"Yes, thank you, that would be great."

After holding the line for several seconds, another voice came on the line. "May I help you?" she asked.

"Yes ma'am, I'm looking for a relative of mine that worked there about twenty years ago. Her name is Rhoda Ingrams. Do you have any records on her?"

"Hold on a minute, let me access the computer and see what I can find out." Martin picked up a pen and paper and started doodling while holding the telephone to his ear, waiting for an answer. About two or three minutes later, he heard the voice again, "Sir, I show that a Rhoda Ingrams was employed here up until about two years ago when she officially retired. However, that's all of the information that I'm allowed to give out."

"Yes ma'am, I understand. Thank you for your time." Martin hung up the telephone thinking that Aunt Rhoda couldn't be too difficult to find if she was still working two years ago. After searching the telephone directory in vain for her listing, Martin decided to take a drive. He didn't think that it was possible that she would still be living in the same housing projects after all this time, but he figured that was a good place to start his search for the aunt that had once been very kind and loving towards him.

It was time to return to his roots and confront his past head on. He'd lived a lie for more than seventeen years and now he was ready to face the truth that he'd kept hidden from his family and closest friend for all that time. His father had returned to find him and now it was his turn to search for the other missing pieces in his life.

Martin quickly threw on a pair of baggy jeans and a blue pullover shirt. Then he headed straight to the Dogwood Park public housing area where he had spent his entire childhood on the south side of town.

Not much had changed in the vicinity. The units were just as rundown as they had been thirty years ago if not more. You could tell that the government had made some attempts to keep the facility in livable conditions, but they were in dire need of extensive renovations.

Driving around the projects for almost ten minutes, Martin was trying to remember the location of his aunt's apartment. *Maybe someone can tell me where she lives now. Aunt Rhonda is such a lively character, somebody probably remembers her and can tell me where she moved to.*

It was almost noontime and in the heat of the day. Martin was sweating just from the few minutes that it had taken him to get out of his car and walk up to the front door of the one-story building. He wasn't sure if he had the correct unit, but he would try this one first. After knocking at the door and waiting a few moments, he heard a weak, elderly sounding voice respond, "Just a minute, I'm coming."

An older lady wearing a tattered housecoat, bent over holding a cane in one hand with long thin gray hair, answered the door. Her fingers were wrinkled and bent from arthritis, but she maintained a constant grip on the cane. "May I help you, young fella?" she asked, looking up at him. "Oh, my God up in heaven! Lord Jesus, its Cora Lee's baby boy!"

"Yes ma'am, Aunt Rhoda. It's me, Martin."

"Boy, I know your name," she reached around his neck and hugged him affectionately while Marty returned the tight embrace. He could feel the bones in her body through her plaid housecoat as she continued clinging to his neck and praising Jesus for being so good to her. "Child, come on in this house and have a seat over here with me. I've been thinking about you a lot lately. I knew that you were going to show up sooner or later," she stated proudly, smiling as broadly as she possibly could with her deteriorating false teeth.

Martin entered the apartment holding Aunt Rhoda's hand as she motioned with a nod of her head for him to have a seat on the worn down sofa. Turning herself around, she held on to the arm of the couch with one hand and eased down into the seat while clenching her cane in the other hand. Martin took a seat beside her but turned so that he could look directly into her face. "Aunt Rhoda, how are you doing?"

"Well, I'm doing okay. You know, I got this arthritis in my hands and knees really bad. The doctors want me to have an operation, but I told them that I'm too old for them to be cutting on me. How are you, Martin? Do you have a family?"

"Yes, I've been married for seventeen years, and I have two handsome sons. My son, Malique, is fifteen, and Jordan is eleven-years-old. However, my wife and I are separated right now and planning to get a divorce."

"Baby, I'm so sorry to hear that. You know, I hate to hear about people getting divorced. I was never fortunate enough to get married myself, but I sure hate to see married couples split up. Are you sure you all can't work it out after seventeen years together?" she stared at Marty as her tired face became more wrinkled than it was before out of concern for him.

"No ma'am, I don't think so," he replied, shaking his head, "but that's not why I came to see you. I came to see you because I thought that it was time for me to get in touch with my family again. I also have some rather sad news to share with you."

"Well, I knew that something bad had happened the second I recognized you at the front door. I figured it had to be something mighty powerful to bring you back to these parts."

"Ah, yes, it is. I hate to tell you this auntie, but my brother, Walter, is dead. He was shot the last day of March, and then remained in a comatose state for three weeks before he passed away. I would have come to see you sooner, but I've had so much going on in my personal life that I haven't communicated very much with anyone. Besides, I had no idea that you would be still living in the same place. I thought that I was going to have to hire a private investigator or somebody to find you," Martin stated, looking around the small room.

"I'm sorry to hear about Walter, baby. I knew once he started using those drugs that he'd come to a bad end someday. I blame that Ezekiel Harrison for ruining that boy's life. He was never the same after his daddy left you all the way he did."

"I know, auntie, but Ezekiel was here when Walter died."

"What—you mean Ezekiel Harrison has been here in Jacksonville?"

"Yes, he was here. He got to see Walter one time before he was shot. You know, Walter and I never had a chance to really make up; we went our separate ways and just never made it back to each other. Ezekiel and I were there with him everyday while he was hospitalized though. My father and I are not the best of friends, but we're at least talking with each other now and trying to have a relationship."

"Well, good, I'm glad to hear that. No matter how I feel about him, he's still your father and family is family, no matter what. It only takes a drop of love to heal the deepest wound."

"Speaking of family, auntie, where are your two children. Are they still living here?"

"No, child, neither one of my children lives here. Ethan lives in Pensacola and he's got some type of job on the naval base out there. Susan and her husband, Victor Swane, live down in St. Petersburg. She's married to a Baptist minister, and they have two children together. Let me show you a picture of my grandkids," she said, struggling to get up.

"No, auntie, you stay in your seat. Just tell me where they are, and I'll get them for you, all right?"

"Baby, look on the shelf over there above that television set, and bring that black box to me," she was looking in that direction and pointing at the old shoe box sitting in the middle of the shelf. Martin looked up, spotted the item, and then walked over to the shelf. Reaching up, he retrieved the box, then turned around and stepped back toward Aunt Rhoda.

"Here you go," Martin was handing her the dusty box.

"Thank you, sweetie," Aunt Rhoda took the shoe box from him and placed it in her lap. Right on top of the stack were several recent photographs of two beautiful girls with very long hair that looked to be teenagers. Auntie picked up a handful of pictures and passed them over to Marty. "These are my two granddaughters. The oldest one is Tameria, and she's sixteen-years-old. The youngest girl is, Natasha, and she's almost fourteen-years-old," she said proudly.

"They're both good looking girls. This is amazing, our kids are almost the same ages, and they don't even know each other."

"That's true, but it's never too late to get to know your people. I can understand you leaving and not wanting to come back here, Martin. I'm just glad that you decided to come and visit an old woman today. I have something in the bottom of this box that I've been meaning to give you," Aunt Rhoda was digging down in the box, searching for a special trinket. "I meant to give you this before you left home, but you never did come by to say good-bye to me. Well, I've saved it for you. I figured you'd be back someday."

Martin sat in silence, trying to concentrate on what his auntie was talking about. He deeply regretted not coming by to see her on the last day that he ever spent in the projects. Thinking that it would be better to leave without making an emotional scene, he opted to exit quietly and not tell anyone exactly when he was leaving. Finally, Aunt Rhoda pulled out a gold antique looking locket on a faded gold tone chain, and handed it to her nephew. "This belonged to your mother. She was wearing it the day that she was killed in that automobile accident. I retrieved it from her things when I went down to identify the body. I was waiting until after the funeral to give it to you, but I never saw you again."

"Did this really belong to my mother?" he asked, taking the necklace into his hands.

"Yes, it did. You don't remember her wearing that necklace? She rarely took that thing off after Ezekiel left you all. Lord, she really loved that man. She loved him so strong that I just down right felt sorry for her. I could never forgive him for leaving my sister like that."

Martin opened the locket and his mouth at the same time as his widened eyes rested on a picture of Cora Lee wearing a pink suit and a matching flat top hat with a wide brim. On the other side of the locket was a picture of Ezekiel Harrison dressed in a blue suit with his hair slicked to the side, and a long cigarette dangling from his mouth. They both looked to be very young, maybe in their early twenties. "Aunt Rhoda, you've had these pictures all this time?"

"Yes, I had it. I've been saving it for you. I started to give it to Walter with him being the oldest and all, but I knew that he'd never keep it safe like you would. He would have sold it for whatever he could get a long time ago."

"Thank you, auntie; you'll never know how much it means for me to have this. I'm serious. I will keep this with me until the day that I die."

"I'm just so happy to see you, baby. You really look well. I know a little bit about you."

"What do you mean by that?"

"Well, I know that you're a big time business man and you changed your last name. Umm huh, Walter used to come around here a long time ago talking about how rich you were and everything. He sure was proud of you."

"Aunt Rhoda, how are you making it? I mean how are you surviving here?"

"I get my little retirement from the nursing home. You know I worked there for thirty-five years, and I get a social security check. It's enough for me to get by on from month to month. The rent is not that much so the majority of my money is spent on buying my medicine. Even with Medicare and Medicaid, I still have to come out of my pocket every time that I go to the doctor and to the drug store."

"How do you eat everyday? I know that you're not able to cook for yourself and get around in the kitchen like you used to do," Martin was looking at his aunt's hands; they were crooked and wrinkled from years of arthritis pain.

"Those people from the *Meals on Wheels* come by here once a day and bring me a hot lunch. The rest of the time I just snack on whatever I can find around here to eat. When I need to go somewhere, I call Dial-a-Ride, and they send that little bus to come pick me up."

Martin looked around at the worn-out furniture in the apartment. The cloth sofa was sunken in the middle, and had several rips on it. One of the legs on the coffee table was broken and was being held up by a piece of a yardstick. The end tables were both leaning, the television set was barely showing a picture, and the padding was coming out of the seat of the dining room chairs. Deep in his heart, Martin felt that he could not allow his mother's closest living relative to continue living like this. He had to do something to help the only aunt that he'd ever known.

"Aunt Rhoda, I tell you what. I want you to be ready at eight o'clock in the morning. I'm coming to pick you up, and then we're going to go find you an apartment, duplex, house, or whatever you want, but

I'm taking you out of here." Martin stood and looked down at her frail body with tears in his eyes.

"Baby, I don't want you wasting no hard earned money on me. I've lived here this long, I might as well die here."

"No, I can't let that happen. Now I need you to be ready at eight o'clock in the morning, and I'll be back over here to pick you up. I mean it."

"All right, Martin," she spoke slowly. "I'll be ready. God bless you, baby. Your mother would be so proud of you, God rest her soul."

Lying in bed later on that night on a stack of pillows with both hands propped behind his head, legs crossed at the ankles, and wearing only gray silk pajama bottoms, Martin couldn't get his auntie out of his mind. He wondered how she could have lived that way for so long and never approached him for money. She told him herself that she knew he was wealthy. So why hadn't she asked him for help? Even Walter being the drug addicted bum that he was, had never asked Martin for anything. And Ezekiel had proven that he hadn't sought him out for financial purposes either. Yet, he had turned his back on all of them thinking that they didn't love him at all and would only want money from him if he shared any part of his life with them. What a foolish man he had been.

At that very second, Martin realized that he had to think of a way to get his own family back together. But how could he possibly do that? That was the million-dollar question. They would be in divorce court in less than a month and Tina was already engaged to marry another man. Yes, his wife would soon be another man's wife if he didn't take some type of action. It didn't matter whose fault it was, there had to be someway to get through the pain that was stabbing him directly in the heart at this moment. *But how, God, how?*

Clutching the gold locket in his hand that Aunt Rhoda had given him earlier in the day, Martin remembered a statement that she had made. "Family is family, no matter what. It only takes a drop of love to heal the deepest wound."

Just as Martin eyes had become very heavy and he was about to drift off into sleepyland, he heard a commotion going on in the hallway. Springing from his bed, Marty opened the bedroom door to see Michael trudging towards him carrying an overnight bag while assisting his pregnant wife through the doorway. She was holding Michael by the arm with both hands for support wearing a white housecoat over her loose fitting pink nightgown.

"Hey, Marty, I was about to wake you up," Michael stated, looking Marty in the face. "Alese is in labor, we're heading to the hospital. We need you to stay here with Bianca, and I'll call you later. We got to go right now," Michael explained, hearing his wife scream in pain again.

"All right, man, I'll be right here. Don't worry about a thing, okay? You just take care of your wife and the new addition to your family." Martin secured the front door behind them, and then stood at the open window watching Mike help his wife into the passenger's side of his car. Martin stood there long after they drove off before leisurely returning to the guest bedroom thinking again about what his aunt and the preacher had said. *Family is family no matter what. One drop of love heals the deepest wound. Love covers all sins.*

He also remembered the Bible verse that Michael had left for him to read one night and finally realized what his friend had been trying to say. Husbands should love their wives just as Christ loved the church and us, we are one. *What would Jesus do?* Martin asked himself.

Chapter 25   D-Day

"All rise! Court is now in session! The Honorable Judge Marjorie Coffman is presiding!" The bailiff shouted as the Judge entered the courtroom and took her seat wearing a black robe with a white collar framing her pecan brown face. She had her salt and pepper hair in loose curls that were barely touching her shoulders.

Tina stood on the left side of the judge behind a podium as Martin stood to the judge's right. Both of them wore gloomy looks on their faces, not daring to look at each other. Tina looked down at the St. John's navy pants suit and navy pumps that she was wearing; Martin looked straight ahead as he crossed his arms in front of him wearing a tailor made tan suit.

They both watched the judge as she entered and took her seat in a high back black leather armchair. Judge Coffman picked up a folder with their court papers and scanned the contents before she looked up over her reading glasses and spoke in a moderate tone.

"Good morning. I have before me on this third day of September, a petition for divorce for Antina Carlisle versus Martin Carlisle. Mrs. Carlisle, would you please tell the court why you are here seeking a divorce from Mr. Carlisle after seventeen years of marriage? I would like for you to start from the beginning of your relationship, tell me how you two originally met, and what has led you to divorce court," the judge stated, staring directly at Tina. Then she turned to Martin and said, "Mr. Carlisle, I'm going to ask that you please remain quiet while your wife is speaking and when she's finished, I will hear from you." She looked at Martin for confirmation that he understood what she was saying. After Martin nodded his head, the Judge turned back to look at Tina.

"Well, your honor, Martin and I met almost twenty years ago while we were both college juniors at Jacksonville State University in the Business Department. Anyway, we had several classes together, and one day I was in the business department's library doing research for a term paper. I noticed that Martin was there sitting at a cubicle studying a business finance book for one of the classes we were taking. So I sat down next to him for a few minutes and pretended to be studying. When I went to stand up, I dropped a book, and Martin picked it up for me. That's when we started talking, and I invited him to join me for a cup of coffee at the student union and he said yes. We went to the coffee shop and ended up staying there until it closed that night. We made plans to meet after class the next day, and we just started dating from there."

"I see, and what was it that first attracted you to him?" the judge asked, still watching Tina's expressions.

"Ah, he was very intelligent and really nice looking. He was always neatly dressed, and he was very respectful to me whenever we were together. He had this broad enticing smile and a twinkle in his eyes whenever he saw me," Tina smiled at the judge as she continued reminiscing. "I thought that he had the smoothest brown skin that I had ever seen on a man, and I just liked that he was clean-shaven and carried himself like a gentleman. He was also very out-spoken and talkative, just like me. I was an only child and at the time, I thought that he was an only child, too, and we had that in common."

"What do you mean by 'at the time,' you thought that he was an only child, too?"

"Your honor, I found out after seventeen years of marriage that my husband had been lying to me about his father being dead and him being an only child," Tina briefly glared in Martin's direction.

"I see. Well, we'll get to that later when I hear from Mr. Carlisle."

"Yes ma'am."

"Now how long did you say that the two of you dated?" the judge asked, raising her arched eyebrows.

"We dated for almost two years, your honor, before he proposed to me at the coffee shop were we met each other almost every day. He asked me to marry him about a week before we both graduated from JSU. We got married about a year or so later at my parents' house. We had the most romantic wedding that you could imagine outside on the lawn of my parents' property right at sunset. The sun was a beautiful radiating red and yellow color as we exchanged our vows holding each other's hands in front of several hundred guests."

"Okay, that was a good start. Now tell me what happened during the course of the marriage after this romantic wedding was behind you."

"We were happy at first. As a matter of fact, we were very happy for a long time. Martin started a business with his best friend; we had two handsome sons together; I opened my own hair salon; we bought a beautiful house and fancy cars; we traveled when we wanted, and just had quite a wonderful life together. I mean we had our arguments and problems, but we were happy to be with each other."

"My goodness, that sounds fabulous. I can't wait to hear what went wrong here," the Judge interjected, sounding quite curious.

"Well, almost a year ago things started to change. Martin started drinking heavily and working late almost every night of the week. We weren't making love because he had become impotent due to the excessive drinking and stress from overworking. I couldn't get him to open up and talk to me about anything. I suggested that we talk with a marriage counselor, but he didn't want to hear that. I even went so far as to make an appointment with a male relationship counselor, hoping that would entice him to attend at least one session. But he still didn't want to do that. He never tried to get any help for his impotence, so then I eventually met someone else that I started seeing."

"You mean you started having an affair with another man?"

"Yes ma'am, I did," Tina replied pitifully, dropping her head. "And then I found out that Martin had lied to me about his past. His father is still alive, and he had a brother living right here in Jacksonville. So I felt like I didn't know this man at all."

"I see, and how long have you been involved with this other man?"

"I've been seeing him for almost six months now," Tina replied in a low voice.

"So you started seeing the other man before you found out that your husband had lied to you about his past, is that correct?"

"Yes, I did. But we were having serious problems in the bedroom by that time. I tried everything to get him to see a doctor and to get help for his drinking, but he wouldn't listen to me," Tina was almost in tears. "I didn't set out to have an affair with anyone. I was just very weak and in desperate need of attention. At that time, Martin and I were barely speaking without getting into an argument where he would leave the house and use that as an excuse to continue his drinking." Tina was sobbing now.

"Okay, thank you Mrs. Carlisle," the Judge responded, turning to look at Martin. "Mr. Carlisle, thank you for remaining quiet while your wife spoke. Now I'm ready to hear from you."

"Where would you like for me to start, your honor?" Martin asked, clearing his throat.

"I want you to start from the beginning just like she did and tell me if you agree with everything that she has said."

"Basically, we met in college just like she said and things pretty much progressed from there the way that she explained it to you."

"Okay, then tell me what first attracted you to your wife."

"Your honor, in one sentence, she was beautiful. I mean—that's all I can say."

"So you just fell in love with her because she was good looking? You didn't look at the person at all?"

"Yes ma'am, I did look at the person. I knew that she was different from any woman that I had ever met in my life. She treated me kindly, your honor, and we immediately became good friends. After we started dating, I found out that she was an incredible person inside and out with ambitions just like me. We had a lot of fun together; Tina could make me laugh no matter what I was going through. We talked a great deal about our dreams. We both wanted to own our own businesses someday, we were both business majors, we both wanted children and a big house, so we definitely had a few things in common."

"All right, Mr. Carlisle. Tell me why your relationship has changed in the last year."

"Judge, my father abandoned our family when I was about nine-years-old. My mother was killed in a car accident shortly after my eighteenth birthday. My older brother turned to the street life, and we parted ways. My other family members and I never really got along so I changed my last name and cut off any contact with them. They thought that I was being uppity because I wanted a better life for myself than any of us had at that time. So rather than deal with their negativity, I just stopped communicating with them after my mother died," he gulped before continuing.

"Then when I met Tina, I knew that I could have the life and the family that I'd always dreamed of having. You know, I had a chance to be a better man than my father had been. My immediate family with Tina was my whole life and world combined. When our two sons were born, I was the happiest man on earth. I shed tears of joy and thanked God for giving me the opportunity to be a decent father. So our life was great, and we had everything we ever wanted. Then about two months before I heard that my father was in town, I started having nightmares about him and my deceased mother. Then when I heard from my father after all those years and found out that he wanted to see me and meet with my family, I couldn't handle that. I didn't know how to tell my wife that I had lied to her for all those years. So I increased my working hours and started drinking even more to fight the pain that I was dealing with, your honor."

"Excuse me, Mr. Carlisle, but I have to ask Mrs. Carlisle a question before you continue," she stated, turning towards Tina. "Mrs. Carlisle, I'm very curious about something. You mean to tell me that you'd been with your husband for almost twenty years and you had never met any of his family?"

"No, I hadn't, your honor. He told me that he didn't have any surviving family, and I believed him. I never had any reason to doubt his words. Martin said that his mother didn't have any family here that he knew of, and he'd never met his father's family up in North Carolina."

"All right, then. I guess that sounds logical. Now back to you, Mr. Carlisle. I sympathize with you regarding your family background. But I can't understand why you didn't talk to your wife or seek help from someone else. I mean seventeen years is a long time to live with a lie, and there are all kinds of medical and psychological doctors that could help you with your sexual problem."

"I understand what you're saying," Martin replied, nodding his head in agreement. "You know, I was just too proud to admit that I had a problem, especially one of a sexual nature. It's hard for a man to admit to having a problem with anything. So trying to seek help for a sexual dysfunction was out of the question for me. I thought that with time and my own determination things would work out, but the deeper I got into the bottle, the harder it was to recognize what the problem was. I just kept pushing my wife farther and farther away from me because I couldn't handle hurting her anymore than I already had. Then later on, I found out that she had been sleeping around with someone else and that hurt me to the bone like I was burning in hell."

"Please tell me how you found out that your wife was having an affair, Mr. Carlisle."

Martin shook his head, hung his arms at his sides, took a deep breath, and slowly exhaled before speaking again. "Well, we were having a party for my wife's forty-first birthday at our house. We had about a hundred people gathered there in the great room. I went into our bedroom to get something—I can't remember what it was, I think that it was a new digital camera or maybe her birthday present. But, anyway, I heard voices outside in the front yard. I went to the window, pulled the curtain back and looked outside, and that's when I saw Tina embracing and kissing this other man."

"Oh, my word!" exclaimed Judge Coffman, slapping her hand against the podium. "I'm almost afraid to ask, but what was your reaction to that?" she asked, sitting up straight in her chair.

"I lost it, your honor. I totally lost it, but thank God, nobody got seriously hurt." Martin omitted telling the judge that he had tried to strangle his wife. And since Tina was embarrassed regarding the whole situation, she didn't provide the judge with any additional information.

"Yes, Mrs. Carlisle, you and your friend were very lucky," she turned towards Tina and then redirected her attention to Martin. "So how long have you all been separated now?"

"We've been living apart now for over four months. But I've finally gotten myself together," Martin stated with pride. "I've been living with my best friend and his family."

"I understand. And where are you today as far as your drinking and other problem?" the judge inquired.

"I'm a recovering alcoholic, your honor. I've been in treatment for the last five months, and I've been sober during that entire time. I've resolved my issues with my father and my brother. And my sexual problem has corrected itself since I stopped drinking and working so many hours every day. In addition to that, I've started going to church; I've gotten saved; and I have turned my life around."

"Well, I certainly commend you on that, Mr. Carlisle. I love to see people that can turn their lives around, especially when they accept a religion, regardless of what it is. So tell me, are you in agreement with this divorce?" she asked, tilting her chin upward and eyeing him suspiciously.

Martin squared his shoulders, stared the judge directly in the eyes and took his time before answering her question. He had thought long and hard about this for the past couple of months. Even though he felt that Tina was wrong for turning to another man, he knew that he still loved her. And he honestly believed that she still loved him, but he was about to find out for sure as he answered the judges question. "No, your honor, I am not in agreement with this divorce." He slightly turned his body to face Tina as he swiftly raised his tone of voice. "In fact, the only reason I'm here today is to ask my wife to please give us another chance."

Tina's heart dropped down to her stomach and bounced around a few times very quickly before flying to her knees. Her eyes lightened a couple of shades and enlarged tremendously as her face became distorted from pain and embarrassment. She stood in place on wobbly knees, staring at Martin and shaking her head from side to side in disbelief. She hadn't suspected that when she walked in the divorce courtroom today that Martin would want to remain married to her. Yes, she still loved him, but how could they possibly get around this, especially when she was wearing the engagement ring that another man had given her.

The judge was waiting patiently while Tina and Martin stared at each other as if they were communicating without actually speaking to one another. Her eyes darted back and forth between the two of them yearning to see who would be the first to speak. Several seconds passed before she decided that it was time for her intervention. "Mrs. Carlisle, I believe your husband is waiting for a response."

"Your honor, I love Martin with all my heart. I just don't see a way for us to get back to where we were before all this took place," she responded with tears streaming down her face.

"I'm not asking you to go back to where we were, Tina. I want to move forward from where we are right now. You see, none of this matters to me," he said, raising both hands in the air and waving them. "Nothing really matters except how we feel at this moment. We have a family, and I won't walk away from my family the way that my father walked away from us. There is one thing that I have learned from this whole ordeal, and that is that family should always stick together no matter what happens. We made a vow to love each other until death do us part. As long as there is breath in my body, I want to be married to you."

"Bailiff, would you bring Mrs. Carlisle some tissue please?" Judge Coffman requested, glancing over at the bailiff as he politely followed her directions. Tina was heaving and shaking to the point that the judge could even feel her pain.

"Martin," Tina said, gasping for breath, and wiping her tears away, "Martin—I don't see how or why you can accept me back as your wife."

"Mr. and Mrs. Carlisle, I'm going to call for a fifteen minute recess, and I would like to meet with you all in my chambers please," the judge humbly stated.

"Okay, your honor," they replied almost in unison.

Judge Coffman struck her gavel against the dark hardwood and shouted, "Court will now recess and resume in fifteen minutes! Bailiff, please show Mr. and Mrs. Carlisle the way to my chambers," she sternly requested, rising from her seat to exit the courtroom.

"Yes, your honor," responded the bailiff as he walked towards Tina and Martin. He motioned with his hands for them to follow him as he turned.

Martin didn't waste any time rushing over to Tina's side of the courtroom. He placed his chiseled arms around her heaving shoulders as he escorted her to the judge's chambers. Tina closed her eyes and leaned her head against his firm chest. She was so close to Martin that she could feel and hear his heart beating rapidly as they slowly proceeded out of the somber filled courtroom together. Neither spoke a word as they gracefully followed the bailiff through a maze of people, rooms and offices before reaching Judge Coffman's chambers. Her tastefully decorated office looked just like the judge: dark, warm, and inviting with a few colors added here and there.

Once they were both comfortably seated in front of the judge's dark wooden desk, they eased back in their seats and waited for her to speak. Tina had dried her eyes, but she was still lightly sniffling as she solemnly sat there with wet tissues in her hands. All of her make-up had disappeared, and her sore eyes were now blood shot. She had no idea what the judge was going to say or why she wanted to see them in her private office. All Tina could think about at this second was that Martin, the man she had pledged to love for the rest of her life, still loved her and wanted to be with her for the rest of his life. She had no indication that he cared for her at all or that she was even still in love with him prior to his admission in court earlier. He had barely spoken to her at all in the last four months and now here he was, declaring his love and commitment to her. Tina didn't know what to make of him at this point.

Judge Coffman sat behind her freshly polished oversized mahogany desk and clasped her hands together on the desktop. She appeared to be in deep thought as she stared at the space on the wall over their heads. She wanted to carefully choose the words that would provide the right message to the wayward couple sitting across from her. Slowly, she began speaking directly to Tina.

"Mrs. Carlisle, I have been a judge in divorce court for over twelve years, and I have never seen a man that wanted to stay with his wife after this type of catastrophe in a marriage. Now I believe that you're a good woman, and you have a good man. You have to make a decision today that's going to affect you for the rest of your life. I don't mind sharing this with you: I have been married and divorced twice, and I have two beautiful grown children to show for it. So I'm speaking to you from experience. Both my husbands habitually cheated on me and one even abused me. Ninety percent of the cases that I see in this courtroom are for those same reasons. So I know what I'm talking about," she paused, lightly tapping her desk but kept her dilated pupils on Tina.

"You have a husband that has supported you and been by your side for over seventeen years. I would advise you to give careful consideration to your marriage at this time. I know your boyfriend is probably encouraging you to seek a divorce and telling you all the things that he's going to do for you, but this man has proven himself to you through his deeds and words. Now I know he lied to you about his background, and I'm not trying to excuse that. But you need to weigh all of the good against all of the bad, you need to weigh the years against the tears and come up with an answer," she stated sternly. Then she stopped as another thought occurred to her. "By the way, how old is your boyfriend?"

"He's thirty-years-old," Tina answered softly.

"See, that's just what I figured. A young man will promise you anything and quite frankly, you're old enough to know better. Now I don't normally interfere with couples when they come into my courtroom, but I had to take an exception with this case and try to impart some wisdom on the two of you. My grandmother used to tell me that going through a marriage was comparable to driving down a dangerous highway. You keep your eyes open and pray that the other driver never crosses the line. Because once he or she crosses that line, you're both in trouble. So right this minute, Mrs. Carlisle, your marriage is in serious trouble, and it can go either way," she stated firmly. "Now I've said all that I have to say. I think it's time for you two to talk to each other." Judge Coffman sat back in her plush chair, crossing her arms as she waited for one of them to speak.

Martin reached out and took his wife's trembling hands into his, gazing directly into her sorrowful eyes. Watching the tears roll down her swollen cheeks, he gently squeezed her small hands. Trying to control his emotions so that he could speak coherently, he took several deep breaths. Feeling like he had a golf ball in his throat, he swallowed hard and licked his full lips. "Baby, I know you love me. You wouldn't be sitting here in tears if you didn't love me. Now I've been told that love don't last always, but I don't believe that. I can't believe that, Tina. We do have a love that can last forever. I just need for you to give us another chance. Please, I need you to give us one more chance, that's all I'll ever ask of you," Martin paused for a second, lowered his voice to a soft loving whisper, leaned in close to his wife's voluptuous lips, and made a polite request, "Say you love me."

"I love you, Martin," she whispered back to him without hesitating. "You know I do. We have a love that will last always," she said, batting her long curly eyelashes and smiling up at her doting husband. Tina hugged Martin with all her strength as she carefully slid off the diamond ring that she was wearing behind his back. Palming the two-carat ring, she glanced over at Judge Coffman, winked at her, and mouthed, "Thank you."

Tina and Marty made it home from court around noontime. Tina pulled into the driveway first; Marty was right on her heels as they both bolted for the front door. They were overly excited after proclaiming their undying love for each other in court and could not wait to consummate their new lease on marriage. By the time they made it to their spacious bedroom, they were both completely naked as their bodies melted together on the plush green carpet. One's tongue searched for the other as if they were devouring the greatest dessert that either of them had ever tasted.

Tina raised her thighs high as Marty placed his muscular body on top of hers. Seconds later, they were making heated love, enjoying the sex they'd missed over the last four months. Taking both of her small hands into his, Marty gradually raised them high above her head as he continued stroking the love of his life. Tina was so excited that she never wanted this single act of love making to end as she kept searching for his hot flickering tongue. Knowing that it would be impossible to prolong their orgasms much longer, Tina closed her eyes and concentrated on the sensations that she was experiencing.

Locking her strong legs around Marty's waist, she tightly squeezed her inner thigh muscles. A few more moments passed before Marty and Tina screamed out in unadulterated pleasure. Their appreciative moans of passion were the only sounds that could be heard throughout the corridors of their home as they exploded simultaneously. Lying with their bodies entwined on the Berber carpet, they finally recuperated enough to ease themselves up, pull back the covers, and climb into their king sized love nest.

As they lay together in bed, still caressing and fondling each other in the middle of the afternoon, Marty felt the urge to sing to Tina. Even though he couldn't carry a tune in a bucket, he decided to serenade his lady love with a song from her favorite artist, Maxwell. Marty popped in a homemade CD as the melody, "Fortunate," began to play. Martin gyrated his bare torso to the slow beat of the smooth flowing music. Pretending to be holding a microphone, he sung and danced his way around to her side of the bed and knelt down on his knees as the song was ending. "Tina, I love you. I love you more than I love my own self. If I had to choose between you living and me living, it would be an easy choice to make because I would die for you, baby."

"Martin, sweetheart, that is the most beautiful thing that anyone has ever said to me. I love you, too."

Marty jumped up as her next favorite song, "Lifetime," came on. He slow danced his way back to the other side of the bed as Tina threw herself back against the warm satin sheets, laughing heartily at him. Lying down beside her, Marty playfully pulled the cover over their heads. Tina rolled over on top of her man, gently lowered her breasts down on his muscular chest, and covered his entire face with tender kisses as she worked her moist lips in a counterclockwise motion. She and Martin loved each other for the remainder of the afternoon as

Maxwell sang in the background. The last song Tina remembered as she drifted off into sweet sleep was, "Until the Cops Come Knocking."

By the time the boys came home from school, Tina and Martin had finally drug themselves apart long enough to get cleaned up. They wanted their sons to see them together as soon as they made it home from school.

Jordan came bursting into the den and stopped cold at the sight of his parents embracing where they stood in front of the sofa. "Hi, mom and dad, what's going on? Weren't you guys supposed to get divorced today?" he asked, looking confused.

"Well, guess what, baby? We decided not to get divorced. So what do you think about that?" Tina asked.

Jordan didn't verbally respond. He fled to his mother's waist and wrapped his arms around her as tight as he could. Then he turned and hugged his dad, too. They all fell back on the sofa together with Jordan in the middle.

"Hello, is anybody home?" That was Malique making his way into the family room, looking around suspiciously.

"Hi, son, you look surprised to see your old man sitting here. Are you all right?"

"Yes dad, I'm fine, but I am surprised to see you here. Didn't you guys go to divorce court today?"

"Yeah, but you know a funny thing happened after we got there. You see, we decided not to get divorced."

"That's great, dad! Does this mean that you're moving back in with us?" Malique couldn't control his joy.

"It certainly does, baby." Tina quickly interjected with a wide smile.

"So what happened? Dad, you have to tell me what happened!"

"Yeah, I want to know, too!" Jordan exclaimed.

Martin directed Malique to join them beside him on the end of the sofa. He put one arm around Jordan and the other arm around Malique as he spoke softly but in a deep voice.

"The bottom line is that your mother and I love each other very much, and we're a family. We're always going to be a family because that's what families do, they stay together and continue loving each other no matter what. Now some things are going to change around here, all right. For one thing we're going to all start praying together every day and going to church together every Sunday. And we'll have our own Bible study right here at the house at least once a week. We have to put God first in our lives and, hopefully, we won't ever have to go through anything like this again. We'll still have problems here and there, but with God in our lives, we'll be able to make it without as much pain and suffering. Now I think it's time for us to all bow our heads and thank the Master for bringing us back together as a family today."

Chapter 26

The next morning, which just happened to be Martin's forty-first birthday, he and Tina were preparing for a special praise and worship service at Noah's Ark Missionary Baptist Church. Once a month they had this type of meeting on a Saturday morning usually after a baptism. Since it had become so popular with the congregation, they decided to do this on the first Saturday of each month whether they had a baptism or not. Today, they had even decided to have a church family picnic after service on the lawn and Martin, along with his sons, was in charge of the grilling. Martin was looking forward to seeing his best friend's family especially his healthy new Godson, Donnelly, who was born weighing almost seven pounds with a curly head of black hair.

    Martin pulled out his favorite green chef's apron to put on over his long jeans and white T-shirt after service. Now that he was ready, Martin stopped to admire the brilliant color of the casual turquoise two-piece skirt suit that Tina had on with the pretty embroidery around the neckline and the hemline. He couldn't resist the urge to reach out and pull her scented body into his longing arms as he said, "You know, the sermon for today is going to be about faith, hope, and love. We just might be able to testify, baby, what do you think?"

    "I think that I need to ask you something before we leave for church today."

    "Go ahead, baby, ask me anything."

    "How did you find it in your heart to forgive me?"

    "Tina, the Bible says to let him that is without sin cast the first stone. I can't stone you without stoning myself first because sin is sin. I lied to you for seventeen years, and you were dishonest with me for six months. You do the math, baby."

    "Thank you, Martin, for loving me. I promise you that nothing will ever come between us. No one will ever be able to lead me into temptation again. I'm turning my life over to God just like you have. Thank you for praying with me last night."

    "You're welcome. I plan to pray with you every night for the rest of our lives together. So you better get used to it."

"Oh, I'm looking forward to that as well as loving you for the rest of our days on earth."

"That's good because my love for you will last through any temptation, Tina, and there's absolutely nothing that you can do about it."

"The only thing that I plan on doing is returning your love and showing you how much I love you, birthday boy. Now let's go make sure that your sons are up and getting ready for service this morning. You know, we're supposed to be there at ten o'clock, and I want to be on time."

"What are you getting me for my birthday?" he asked, trying to read her face.

"I'm not telling you a thing. It's a surprise," Tina smiled, turning away from him.

Walking to the edge of the staircase, she called out for Jordan and Malique to come downstairs at once. Minutes later, they were both tumbling down the staircase fully dressed and ready to go. As Martin was holding Tina's hand and leading the way to the exit, he heard someone outside tapping at the front door. He looked at Tina with burrowed eyebrows, wondering who their unexpected company could be at this time of the morning. Tina just shrugged her shoulders, indicating that she had no idea who it was. Martin proceeded to cautiously open the door and they all gasped in shock after seeing the visitor standing on the other side.

"Ezekiel!" they all shouted together.

"Happy birthday, son!" he replied, stretching his arms out to embrace the family. Martin was overwhelmed with his father's surprise visit. As he returned Ezekiel's hug, Marty thought that the only person missing from this gathering right now was Aunt Rhoda. So after loading everyone into his five-passenger sports utility vehicle, he dropped them off at the church picnic grounds and headed to the newly decorated condominium he'd bought for his aunt only ten minutes away from their home.

"Hi, Aunt Rhoda, this is Martin. Today is my birthday and I'm on my way to pick you up," he piped into the cell phone receiver.

"Well, happy birthday, baby. How are you doing this morning?"

"I'm great. Listen, I just dropped my family off at a church picnic, and I thought that this would be a perfect time for all of us to get together. I want you to get dressed and I'll be there in about fifteen minutes, all right?"

"I'm already up. I just need to get changed into something presentable. I'll be waiting on you, bye."

Martin clicked off the cell phone remembering how happy his aunt had been when they first saw the newly built three-bedroom complex. She fell in love with the place immediately. Aunt Rhoda refused to look at any of the other places on the list that Marty had from the realtor.

"This is the most beautiful place that I've ever seen in my life," she stated, staring up at the nine-foot cathedral ceiling in the center of the great room. "But what am I going to do with all this space?" she asked, wrinkling her brows at Martin.

"I'm going to hire you a live in nurse to help you out, Aunt Rhoda. And you'll still have a spare room for when your grandchildren come to visit. What do you think about that?"

"Baby, I think that's wonderful! I'm looking forward to living here. But you better promise to come and visit me often."

"Definitely, that will not be a problem," Marty replied, smiling from ear to ear. He was overjoyed to see his aunt so happy with the place he'd picked for her to live.

Martin's mind returned to the present day as he pulled into the driveway at the condominium complex. After ringing the doorbell twice, Aunt Rhoda's nurse, Miss Bethany, answered wearing a navy striped dress along with a polite smile, ushering him into the hallway.

"Hi, Martin, your aunt is ready. She's waiting for you in the living room," she stated, leading him into the open area. He stepped into the room, staring at his aunt sitting patiently beneath the Palladian ceiling fan silently spinning above her. Aunt Rhoda's smiling face beamed up at Martin as she stretched her right hand out to greet him.

Five minutes later, they were on their way to the church picnic ground. Marty smiled over at his aunt's happy face in her bright yellow printed dress with a matching pillbox hat. She was clutching her black purse in her lap, staring out the window like this was her first time taking a trip outside in months. When they arrived at the picnic area, Marty's family ran over to greet Aunt Rhoda, including Ezekiel.

Stopping dead in her tracks, Rhoda stared down the man that had broken her sister's heart over thirty years ago. Right then and there she decided to let go of her resentment towards him whether he was a changed person or not. The only thing that mattered to her at this moment was that they were all together as a family again.

Stretching out her long arms to embrace Ezekiel, Rhoda smiled at him, and pulled his thin body close to hers. Patting his back, Rhoda let out a tiny laugh as she looked over at Marty, and winked her right eye at him. All had been forgiven. It was time to move forward as a unit because she had learned after many years of hatred and heartache that family was the most important thing in her life. Being with Martin and his family on this special day was all that mattered to Aunt Rhoda.

Chapter 27

Tina had mixed feelings about the telephone call that she was about to make. On one hand, she was happy that her marriage issues had been resolved, but now she also needed to resolve her relationship with Debonair Jenkins, and that would not be an easy task knowing his personality. He'd always been very determined where she was concerned; it would be difficult convincing him that she was rededicated to her husband after the intimacy they'd shared. Still, Tina picked up the telephone receiver and dialed the number to his home. She knew he was expecting a call from her and quite frankly, Tina was surprised that he hadn't called her yesterday especially since he knew what time she was supposed to be in divorce court. Thankfully, he'd honored his word not to show up at the divorce proceedings.

"Hello, I'm so glad to finally hear from you," Debonair answered, picking up on the second ring. "I started to call you last night but decided to give you some time to yourself. I figured that you would want some time alone with you sons to explain everything to them. How did it go yesterday?"

"That's why I'm calling. I need to see you as soon as possible."

"All right, is everything okay?"

"Yes, everything is fine. I just need to speak with you in person if you don't mind."

"Of course I don't mind, my lady. I can't wait for us to be together again. How soon can you get here?"

"I'll be there in about thirty minutes."

"I'll be waiting," he replied, curving his sensual lips upward, anticipating her arrival. Debonair noticed something in Tina's voice that he hadn't heard before, but he quickly dismissed it with thoughts of them becoming husband and wife. He would make everything all right once she was there in his loving arms. *Oh, Tina, you just need some good loving, my lady,* he thought, rushing to straighten up his one-bedroom apartment.

Debonair answered the doorbell on the first ring without checking the peephole to see who it was. His heart had already told him that it was Tina ringing his bell. Opening the door filled with the anticipation of seeing his lady love, Debonair took a step back in shock as Tina, dressed in a V-neck blue dress, walked through the doorway with a man about his height following behind her.

"Hi, Tina, I didn't know that you were bringing someone with you," Debonair stated, staring at the stranger. Closing the door behind them, he placed his hands into his khaki pants pockets.

"Martin this is Debonair. Debonair this is my husband, Martin," Tina stated, directing a hand at Debonair and then towards Martin. Neither man spoke to the other, they simply nodded heads at each other.

"What's he doing here? Didn't you two get divorced yesterday?" Debonair asked, moving his eyes between the two visitors.

"Actually we didn't, that's why we're here. I came to tell you that it's over between us. Martin and I are back together again."

Debonair stared at Martin in disbelief, easing his lips into a sly grin. "So you brought him here to face me?" Debonair asked.

"That's right," Martin quickly interjected. "I'm here to make sure that you get the message loud and clear that my wife is through with you. Now whatever it is that you thought you had with her is over."

"Tina, baby, please. I know that this is not what you want. You can't be serious about going back to him," Debonair pleaded with Tina, taking a step in her direction.

Martin swiftly moved in front of Debonair, blocking his view of Tina. "Step back and stay away from my wife," Martin demanded, raising a hand to Debonair's chest, using a stern voice, he stared directed into the jilted man's eyes. "I didn't come here to fight with you because the battle is already won. I've got my wife back and that's all that matters to me. Now we're leaving here in peace. I hope that this is the only time that we will ever have to meet. Do you understand me?" he asked. Martin did not flinch a single muscle as he spoke to his wife's ex-lover.

"I get the message," Debonair replied, backing up from Martin. "If this is what she wants..."

"It's exactly what I want," Tina stated boldly, stepping out to stand beside her husband. Reaching into her blue handbag, she removed the emerald bracelet, the bottle of Beautiful perfume, and the diamond engagement ring that Debonair had given her and placed them gently in the palm of his left hand. Then, taking Martin by the hand, she opened the front door with her other hand, and lead her husband outside without looking back at the man she'd been engaged to marry.

Martin and Tina rode all the way home in complete silence. Both of their minds where too busy thanking God for bringing them through this difficult situation. This was a test that they were proud to have passed together. From this day forward, they would be one again.

Later that evening while Martin was out taking a walk with their sons, Tina did a three-way telephone call with her two friends, Shenedra and Taneka. They had been waiting to hear about the confrontation with Debonair ever since Tina had informed them of her marriage reconciliation last night.

"Hi, Tina, I've been waiting all day to hear from you. How did the meeting go with Debonair and Martin?" Shenedra asked, getting straight to the point.

"It went well considering everything that could have happened," Tina replied.

"Was Martin able to maintain his cool or were punches thrown?" Taneka asked.

"Marty was very cool and direct with him. He didn't go there to start a fight. He just wanted to make sure that Debonair understood that things were over between us. I was very proud of the way he handled himself."

"Well, all right, I'm proud of him, too," Shenedra said, smiling to herself.

"I'm just glad this whole episode is finally closed in my life. Thank you both for praying me through this. Believe me, I felt all of your prayers," Tina said, silently thanking God for such true friends. "And if I ever come close to making another foolish mistake like this, I want both of you to slap me as many times as necessary."

"It'll be my pleasure," Shenedra said, laughing at her best friend.

"Just remember that you asked for it," Taneka added, laughing along with both of them.

"Seriously, though," Tina began, changing the tone of her voice. "I'm one lucky woman. Martin could have divorced me and moved on to a more deserving person. But he decided to stay with me and honor our marriage vows. I'll never make this selfish mistake again, I promise both of you that."

"I hear you, Tina," Shenedra stated, empathizing with her friend. "I can see that you're much stronger and determined now. I'm sure that you and Marty will be together forever."

"That's all that I'm praying for." Tina said, shortly before ending their three-way conversation.

Epilogue

"Happy Anniversary, baby, you sure smell good. What is the name of that?" Marty asked, nuzzling Tina's neck with both arms wrapped around her waist from behind. Over a month had passed since their reconciliation day in divorce court.

"It's called Paradise, sweetheart," she replied, placing her hands on top of his.

"Well, Paradise is very nice. I like living in Paradise," he rapped the words to the once popular song recorded by rapper LL Cool J.

"I do, too. This is so incredible," Tina stated, looking out over the tantalizing blue sea water from the top deck of the Carnival luxury cruise ship. From the private balcony outside their extra large Penthouse Suite, they had a fantastic view of the ocean and each destination on their seven-day cruise. Tina relaxed in his arms wearing a periwinkle strapless bathing suit while Marty sported his black and white Speedo swimming trunks. They were both wearing dark Matrix Reloaded styled sunglasses to protect their eyes from the sun glaring off the waves rippling through the ocean. Thinking that this was the happiest that they'd ever been together, Marty stared at Tina with a warm look of love in his half closed eyes, admiring the refurbished locket that he'd given her before leaving on the cruise. Martin had taken the tarnished locket which once belonged to his mother, gotten it cleaned up, and placed on a thin gold chain for his wife's anniversary present. Tina was so touched by his sincere gesture that she had shed a few tears.

"I'm glad that you didn't throw away those tickets for this cruise to the Bahamas that I gave you for your birthday. I would really be upset with you if we had missed all of this," Marty said, waving his right hand in the air.

"No, I didn't throw them away, but I had forgotten about them until you were moving your things back in. It was a wonderful idea to use them for an anniversary cruise since the tickets were good for a whole year from the date of purchase."

"Yeah, that was a good idea, and I have a few more good ideas that I plan to tell you about later on tonight. I'm going to make you scream my name over and over again before I'm through with you little girl," he whispered teasingly into her left ear.

Tina rested her head back against his and moaned from the thought of Marty making good on his promises since he definitely had his groove back. "Sure Big Daddy, you love to make promises," she teased. "But, ah, we don't have to wait until tonight to make love."

"Is that an invitation for me to take you inside and ravish you right now? Because, you know, I don't make any promises that I can't keep. I've got some lost time that I intend to make up for while we're on this cruise liner."

"All right, then, I'm looking forward to making up that time with you, Big Daddy. But you know what? I could stay here like this forever in your arms and on this cruise."

"Sweetheart, you're welcome to stay in my arms forever, but even a rich fella like me can't afford to stay on this ship forever," he laughed at his joke

"Marty, you are so crazy. You know what I mean."

"I think that you mean you love me, right?"

"That's exactly what I mean, sweetheart."

Just as Tina said that, one of her favorite Maxwell songs, "Ascension (Don't Ever Wonder)," came over the sound system. Turning around to face Marty, they held each other by the hips, moving to the sultry music. Singing the words to each other, they danced their way back inside the cozy cabin until they reached the queen sized bed. Tumbling to the bed, they laughed together as the heavy kissing caused their passion to escalate to the next level. Thankful that they were no longer dancing with temptation, Martin and Tina were excited to be making love with each other between the heated sheets.

They spent the remainder of the seven-day cruise together locked away in their love haven. Savoring the taste of each other, they ate very little food offered from the extravagant menu. Even the most delectable dishes served aboard the ship were unable to satisfy their starving appetites. They talked openly, evaluating their marital relationship, and agreed to be more adventurous with each other in the bedroom beginning with oral stimulation, something Marty would never have approved of in the past. Now he was willing to please his wife in every way she desired. And in return, he appreciated the immeasurable oral pleasure that she was giving him.

Tina's life had finally returned to normal. She had the kind loving and affectionate man that she had originally married. He freely shared his every emotion and thought process with her, but most importantly, they were attending church together again as a family. It had been a painful heartbreaking spiritual journey for all of them. With a lot of love, patience, prayer, and understanding, they were able to make it through the storm. Now it was time for real joy and sunshine to consume their reborn lives.

"Hey, what's on your mind? Your body's here with me, but your mind seems to be somewhere else," Martin stated, propped up on his right elbow in the bed, staring into his wife's pure honey eyes.

"I was just thinking about how lucky we are to be together right now," Tina replied.

Leaning over and planting a soft kiss on her moist lips, Marty responded, "Baby, it's not luck. It's love."

The thief does not come except to steal, and to destroy.
I have come that they may have life,
And that they may have it more abundantly.

John 10:10

The end

Acknowledgements

First, giving honor to God, I thank Him for His continued guidance.

Secondly, I would like to thank everyone who bought my first novel and helped to spread the word about it. I hope that you enjoyed reading this one even more.

Thanks to my husband, Wilbert, for his unconditional love and understanding.

I thank my daughter, Amani, for always being herself.

Thanks to all my family and friends for their continued support. I appreciate all of the encouragement that you all have dispersed over the last two years.

Thanks to my editor and major supporter, Jessica Wallace, for her honest feedback and critiques.

I also thank my friends, Patrice Price and Yvonne Powell, for their proofreading help. I really appreciate you both.

In addition, I thank all the book clubs, bookstores, colleges, on-line magazines, sororities, and universities that support my work.

Reading Group Questions

1. Was Tina justified in cheating on her husband after his refusal to seek medical or psychological assistance? Why or why not?

2. Even though Tina was starved for affection, how could she have avoided becoming involved with a younger lover?

3. Since she felt guilty after her first act of betrayal, should Tina have terminated her association with Debonair at that point? Why didn't she?

4. What would have happened if Tina had confessed to Martin after her first romantic encounter with Debonair?

5. Do you agree with the way that Tina and Martin handled the situation with Malique, their teenage son, regarding his sexual misconduct?

6. Why was Debonair so attracted to Tina? Do you believe that he was really in love with her? If so, why?

7. Did Tina file for divorce too quickly after Martin left or should she have tried harder to win him back?

8. Why did Martin wait until the eleventh hour to tell Tina how he really felt about her?

9. Will Debonair try interfering in their marriage again? Would Tina be tempted into sleeping with him?

10. Can Tina and Martin truly be happy together after coming so close to divorcing? Why or why not?

11. Would you like to see them have another child together?

12. What is the moral of this story?

About the Author

Barbara Joe-Williams was born and raised in Rosston, Arkansas. She currently resides in Tallahassee, Florida, with her husband and young daughter. She is a full-time writer and independent publisher.

She spent four years in the U. S. Navy prior to attending college. Barbara is a graduate of Tallahassee Community College and Florida A & M University. She is also a former school teacher, guidance counselor, and reading assistant. She has enjoyed reading romance novels all of her adult life.

Barbara has already completed the third installment in this four-part series to be released in November 2006. You may also check out the website for additional ordering information for these books:

Forgive Us This Day, ISBN 0975285106
November 2004, $13.95

One Sister's Guide to Self-Publishing, ISBN 0975285114
July 2005, $14.00

Website address: **www.Barbarajoewilliams.com**

FREE shipping available on all orders!

Coming November 2006 ...

Falling for Lies

Is Pastor Karema Wright falling for Deacon Pye or is she simply falling for his lies?

Pastor Karema Wright has been in charge of Noah's Ark Missionary Baptist Church in Jacksonville, Florida, for the last seven years. The small church has flourished in membership to the point that she's added an early morning service to the program. The love of her life, **Deacon Mitchell Pye**, is a local building contractor who has convinced her to design a million dollar facility to accommodate the growing congregation.

After ten years of praying for Mr. Right, Karema Wright believes that her prayers have finally been answered when she falls in love with Deacon Pye, the most eligible bachelor in the church, and he proposes marriage to her after dating for less than a year. Will she finally have it all, a new church, a new home, and a new husband?

Only time will tell if she can survive the financial burden of constructing her dream chapel, deal with futile gossip, learn the meaning of true love, and remain a sanctified woman. **Falling for Lies** is a testimony that all women want, need, and seek true love, yet it shows that no woman is exempt from falling in love with the wrong man.

|Chapter 1|

"All right, gentlemen, unless someone has something else to add, this will conclude our Deacon Board's business meeting for this evening on the first Tuesday of December. I'd like to thank our newest member of the board, Deacon Mitchell Pye, for joining us here at Noah's Ark Missionary Baptist Church. After six months of dedicated membership and an impressive letter of recommendation from his previous pastor in Mobile, Alabama, it is clear that we are very fortunate to have him as a member of our small family. We're not the largest church in Jacksonville, but we have some of the most devoted members that you'll find anywhere in Florida," Pastor Karema Wright said, wearing a smile. Glancing down at her forest green suit, she checked her gold band Citizen's watch for the exact time that they were closing the meeting.

"Thank you, Pastor Wright. I feel blessed and honored to serve with such an established board of deacons under your directorship. I look forward to being a part of this distinguished congregation for many years to come. I want you all to know that as a single man, I'm available to each of you at any time. Please don't hesitate to call upon me in your time of need." Deacon Pye made eye contact with each of the other five members sitting at the round table. Resting his eyes on Pastor Wright, they stayed with her for several seconds before he looked away. In those few moments, Karema felt that his words might have been directed more to her than they were to the older men at the meeting. All evening she'd felt his eyes on her, following her every movement, and listening intently to her every word. Now as she looked away from the gaze of his deep set brown eyes, she noticed the moisture on her palms. Vigorously rubbing her hands together, she tried to retain her composure by sitting up straight in her chair, but the pounding of her heart and head was getting in the way.

Seconds later, Karema could still feel Mitchell's presence throughout her being as if he was right under her skin, touching every single thread in her nervous body. Telling herself to calm down, she tried harder to concentrate on closing the meeting.

Each of the elders took turns shaking Deacon Pye's hand as they walked out of the boardroom in single file. Finally, Karema was the last one to leave. Mitchell took her extended hand, pulling her in closer for a warm embrace which he gently held until he felt her starting to pull away. Being reluctant to let her go, he held on to her upper arms as he spoke. "Pastor Wright, if you don't mind, I'd be happy to walk with you to your car. I know that the parking lot is lit, but it's still pretty dark out there," he smiled, expressing concern for her.

"That's fine, Deacon Pye, I'll be ready to leave in two minutes. Let me put these papers in my office, make sure everything is locked up, and I'll be right out," she replied, turning away from his embrace.

When Karema made it out to the front steps, Mitchell was there waiting for her just like he'd promised. She was grateful that she'd taken a few seconds to stop by the ladies room and freshen up before meeting him in the cool night air. As they made it to Karema's mineral green Toyota Camry parked at the front of the church, Mitchell took her keys and unlocked the car door for her. Holding the door open for the pastor like a true gentlemen, he handed the keys back to her, making sure that his hand lightly grazed hers. Sensing the pastor's nervousness, he took her left hand into his, stroking it gently with his right hand as he spoke softly, "Pastor Wright, I admire you as the leader of this church, and I am a saved man. However, as a single man, I would like to be your escort for the Christmas Extravaganza next week. That is, unless you have a better offer."

"Well, Deacon Pye, I don't know if that would be appropriate or not."

"Why wouldn't it be?" he asked, cutting off the apprehensive statement he'd already anticipated would follow. "I mean—we're two saved and single people. We don't have anything to hide, so why can't we go to the ball together? Even a pastor should have an escort for social events, especially those sponsored by her own church," he added, flashing a smile for good measure.

"You know, you're right. There's no reason why we can't go to the gala together. Why don't you call me tomorrow and we'll work out the details." Karema returned his broad smile and flashed her own pearly whites. Her life would be changed forever after this night.

Deacon Pye made it his business to call her the next afternoon. They chatted for several minutes that day and the day after that and the day after that until the night of the Christmas Extravaganza. They had truly enjoyed each other's company the entire evening. Engrossed in a stimulating conversation over dinner, they only had eyes for each other. With both of them wearing navy blue outfits, they looked like the perfect pair. Karema wore a long evening gown with a long sheer jacket covering the top, and Mitchell wore a navy suit with satin trim on the jacket collar. They couldn't have looked better together even if they had actually planned it.

The Christmas gala turned out perfectly. Every local choir that was invited to the program had shown up on time. Karema and Mitchell clapped together and happily sang the Christmas tunes as they smiled at each other from ear to ear. Feeling the holiday spirit until almost midnight, they were the last one's to leave the church.

When he walked Karema to the door of her condominium on Meridian Court after the gala, Mitchell made the fact known that he wanted to be more than a member of the adored congregation. Cupping her face in his masculine builder's hands, he whispered, "You're the most beautiful sanctified woman that I've ever seen. I respect you, and I want you to know that I have deep feelings for you inside my heart. I want you to be my Nubian Queen."

Karema didn't know how to respond to that. It felt like centuries since a man had held her that close to his face or spoken to her in such a romantic tone. Being a full-time pastor, she hadn't found much time for love or encountered anyone that she'd felt the least bit attracted to. Of course, she'd had her share of propositions, but until now, she was never interested. The trembling of her body gave away her true feelings, making it impossible to keep them hidden. Placing his arms around her shaky frame, Mitchell held Karema in his heated arms for almost a full minute before releasing her. As soon as he softened his grip on her body, she opened the door and quickly entered her home. Holding the door slightly ajar with jittery hands, she managed to say in an audible whisper, "Good night, Mitchell," before closing the door.

Deacon Pye returned the sentiment with a straight face and an inward smile. Knowing that he'd accomplished his goal for the evening, he strutted to his pearlescent white Cadillac Seville feeling proud of himself. Whether Pastor Karema Wright was ready for him or not, he was going to be the love of her sanctified life.

Printed in the United States
37276LVS00006B/133-204